DOUGLAS JAMES TROXELL

Trumptopia!

The United States of Walmart

Cover Artwork & Design by Ashley Siebels

First edition

ISBN: 9798604880227

This book was professionally typeset on Reedsy.
Find out more at reedsy.com

For America.

Hang in there, buddy.

I

America: 2026

Chapter I

Explosions were not usually part of my morning routine.

Usually, I woke to find my wife, Millicent, had eaten whatever I was planning to eat for breakfast. Then I checked my texts. I had two waiting for me—both from Millie.

Text #1: *Jonathan! Emergency! Out of instant coffee! Buy more!*

Text #2: *Sale on instant coffee at Walmart. Great Deal! Oh, and tampons. I need tampons! Buy the big box!*

I ate whatever was in the cabinets while I scanned the latest headlines on my phone.

Today's headlines for July 20, 2026:

"Trump Won't seek 4th Term!"

"Trade Talks with China Break Down!"

"Mass Casualties in Iran!"

"Grand Opening of Hyattsville's Mega-Walmart!"

The exclamation points encouraged me to be excited or concerned or outraged, but I had expended a lot of energy and emotion playing my latest mobile game addiction, *Candy Assassin 3: The Reckoning,* until 2 AM the night before so I met the morning's headlines with the appropriate indifference.

By the time I changed into my suit jacket and khakis, I was already running late. I jogged out into the driveway, scanning my texts, and said, "Unlock doors."

That's when my car exploded.

My ancient '97 Civic became a geyser of fire and metal in the driveway.

This was just more proof that no one ever listened to me, not even my phone. Saying, "Unlock doors," was supposed to trigger the iLock mechanism installed in my vehicle, not make the car explode.

Big difference.

I crashed onto the cement walkway next to the hydrangea bushes as flaming car parts rained down on the lawn. The only reason I wasn't instantly incinerated was because the explosion kind of … gave up. I don't know how else to explain it. The thundering boom was suddenly muted, and the ball of fire that was once my P.O.S. car remained in place as if someone had paused a movie. The wreckage hung in the air around me defying gravity and common sense.

I glanced around praying someone was nearby to confirm the miracle in my driveway. My neighbor, Maureen, drove by in her SUV, but her eyes were focused like laser beams into her lap. Either she was messing with her phone or she was having a riveting conversation with her lady bits. Either way, she was completely oblivious to the intriguing half-explosion that had knocked me on my ass. On her rear bumper was a weather-worn Trump '24 bumper sticker with the slogan: *Why Stop Now?*

No, the only eyes I found were those being reflected in the cracked rearview mirror hovering directly in front of me. I found a scarred version of Jonathan Savage (That's me, by the way) staring back. He looked confused and scared, too, but a comforting smile slowly crept onto the face in the mirror, assuring me I was fine. He understood.

Then someone hit the rewind brutton, and the twisted metal hovering in the air was sucked back into the ball of fire as if the Civic had changed its mind about the whole blowing up thing. The ball of fire flashed purple and then everything—the car frame, the parts, the ball of fire—blinked out of existence. They were gone.

The only evidence anything had even happened was a giant sinkhole of melted asphalt where the Civic had once been and a burning American flag hanging over the front porch, which I had forgotten to take down after the Fourth of July.

Not the best start to my day.

I considered calling the police but, really, it would be a waste of time. Budget cuts due to the Second Great Recession (The Re-Recession as many had dubbed it) had all but gutted Hyattsville's police department. It would take hours for anyone to show up, and when they did, there wouldn't be any evidence to support my claim—just like the last time. Besides, I had another Civic (a beat-up burgundy hatchback) parked on the street in front of the house.

The '94 Civic was the third vehicle I had lost in the past month under less-than-usual circumstances. The first incident involved my car melting into a puddle of liquid metal while I drove down the highway until it was just me, a frame, and four tires. Then there was the day my car had been crushed by some invisible force until it was the size of a tin can.

I had managed to escape both incidents with minor bumps and bruises and some pretty serious road rash on my ass. I certainly didn't have an explanation for any of these events, but I suspected my vehicles might be suicidal.

The first incident had really freaked me out, but now it was more of an inconvenience than anything else. I considered buying my next couple of Civics in a six-pack. The damn iLocks I installed cost more than the actual cars.

When I finally made it back to my feet, I thought there were stars floating in front of my eyes (like in the ancient cartoons with giant mallets and cats chasing mice), but the stars were just a swarm of stink bugs dive-bombing my head. Our house had been infested with the pungent pests ever since Millie and I first moved into our new home.

They were a constant annoyance and seemed to follow me wherever I went.

Thinking of Millie made me instinctively scramble to find my phone. I prayed for its safety. If *I* had been blown to bits, *that* I could have accepted, but if something happened to my phone, then I was in real trouble. Millie hated when I didn't have it on me, and if I made her upset, then my car exploding would only be the second worst part of my day.

Luckily, I found my phone (in its vintage James Bond cover) nestled among the flaming hydrangeas. I dusted it off and unlocked the backup Civic from the driveway. When it didn't explode, I got in, unzipped my pants, and drove off to work.

I had nearly climaxed when I hit the back end of a traffic jam near the site of the new Mega-Walmart. A gaggle of protesters stood in the intersection waving signboards and chanting and being generally disruptive. The whole thing seemed a bit disorganized. Most of the signs were denouncing the latest Walmart takeover, but there was also a smattering of signs opposing the war in Iran and the usual anti-Trump stuff.

"Protect Main Street!"

"Bring Home the Troops!"

"Down with Emperor Trump!"

The Hyattsville Wire had spent the last several months denouncing the purchase of The Mall at Prince Georges by the Walmart Corporation, but all the petitions and public outcry hadn't done anything to stop the commercial juggernaut from taking over. The Walmart absorbed all the other businesses in the commercial park. Only the Starbucks survived. People complained the Mega-Walmart would be bad for Hyattsville's already-struggling local businesses but, hey, that's progress!

As shopping malls across the country became a thing of the past, Walmart moved to replace them as the be-all and end-all of the physical retail world. Their rebranding cultivated an expanded online strategy to compete with Amazon and their in-store services such as cosmetology, eye care, and automotive expanded to include things like landscaping, HVAC, banking, and (unfortunately) catering services. Sam Walton's love child was growing out of control and not everyone seemed happy about it.

So, there I was sitting patiently in my Civic with my hand shoved down my khakis when some bulldog-cheeked kid in a knit cap and a chinstrap beard jumped onto the hood of my car.

"End the corporatacracy!" he screamed through the windshield.

One can imagine my surprise, quietly trying to service myself when a complete stranger *thumped* onto the hood of my vehicle. To be honest, I was more ashamed of being seen in a Civic than I was about the masturbation.

"I'm sorry," I yelled through the windshield. "I don't know what that is. Wouldn't it be more effective to use simpler words to get your point across?"

Chinstrap Beard seemed swayed and screamed, "Fuck Walmart!" through the windshield.

"Much better. That I understand."

The car ahead of me finally lurched through the intersection, but I was unable to continue due to my new bearded hood ornament.

"Trump's pro-corporate agenda is destroying small businesses! Walmart's consuming Main Street! If we don't do something, soon *everything* will be Walmart!"

I sympathized with the kid's cause, but what could I do about it? Walmart was threatening to make me unemployed, too, and I couldn't even save myself. I was just one person and an extremely unimportant person at that.

"Soon you won't have a job to go to, lad, unless it's at Walmart!" he continued. "How can you sit there on the sidelines when Trump and these corporate pigs are buying our country out from under us?" He pressed his beard against the windshield and stared down at my unzipped pants. "Hey! What are you doing in there?"

I quickly turned on the windshield wipers and lurched the Civic forward, sending the chubby-cheeked protester rolling onto the asphalt, before continuing on my merry way.

As I drove off, I could hear Chinstrap Beard screaming at the back of my car.

"Walmart's coming! Walmart's comin' for ya!"

Good for Walmart, I thought. At least one of us was coming.

Chapter II

That morning's explosion and the protest had me running way late for my catering gig—way later than my usual late. Millie and I ran a small catering business (although I did most of the running and she spent most of the money). We had tried to come up with the most recession-proof business we could think of, and eating seemed to be something people would want to do regardless of the state of Trump's roller coaster economy.

The gig was a fundraiser for Charles Beatty, a congressional hopeful from Maryland running on the platform of helping small business owners. And trust me, we needed help. Truth be told, Walmart's new catering division had my business on life support.

Ironically, the fundraiser was being held at the newly-christened Walmart Plaza Community Center.

The brunch was well underway by the time I marched back into the sweltering kitchen. Luckily, Julia, my number two, had things under control.

"God, boss, what the hell happened to you? Is Millie beating on you again?"

I still looked like hell from the car explosion/implosion incident, but, to be honest, I only looked slightly off from my usual. At least I had a reason for my shabby appearance for once. Julia, however, looked pristine. She had just cut her hair back to her shoulders, placing her collarbone on full display. It's tough to explain, but she had the sexiest collarbone I had ever seen on a woman. It whispered of the wonders that lay below.

"Car problems," I explained. "Where we at?"

"Salads."

"What do you need from me?

"Well, if you feel like actually earning your paycheck, whoever used this place last night left the trash for us—"

"On it."

Julia and I had developed this great rapport ever since she had come aboard as my number two, which was great because I was kind of a piss-poor leader. Check that. I was a *great* leader. I knew when to get out of the way and let more capable hands do the work since I was such a piss-poor leader. Seriously, though, it was nice to have someone I could count on, especially since Millie was usually MIA.

"Check this out," Julia said. She showed me her phone. It was a meme of Trump handcuffing himself to the Resolute Desk in the Oval Office. The caption read: *No, definitely not running for a 4th term!*

Trump had used the war in Iran and the escalating trade war with China as justification for remaining in office for a third term. Roosevelt had done it during World War II so there was a precedent. Of course, most people didn't place another Middle Eastern conflict and an argument about tariffs on the same level as an actual world war, but Trump had managed to pull it off by implementing his usual strategy of making loud noises and coming up with clever nicknames for those who opposed him. Since both wars were still ongoing (and still escalating), there was plenty of speculation he would try to run for his fourth term in 2028.

I laughed. "Maybe he means it this time. Didn't that twenty-four-year-old bimbo he married just have a baby? Maybe he wants to stay home and help out with the kid."

Julia rolled her eyes. "That sounds like a great reason to run for a fourth term. Did you hear what they named that thing? *Tiberius Winston Ivanhoe Trump.*"

"How does an eighty-year-old dude even get someone pregnant?"

She flashed her eyebrows. "Do you want me to draw you a diagram?"

"Trump for life!" one of our cooks yelled out. His name was Manny. He was decked out in a red cap that read: *Keep Keeping America Great!*

"Yeah! He built the wall! He saved us from illegal immigrants!" another cook, Metias, said.

"What are you two talking about?" I asked. "You're *both* illegal immigrants!"

"Exactly! Matias said. "And we don't want any *other* illegal immigrants comin' round and stealing our jobs! Trump's gotta keep 'em out!"

Julia told the cooks to get back to work, and then turned her attention back to me. She studied my face and frowned. "Jon, you gotta take better care of yourself. I worry about you."

She pressed the back of her hand to the side of my face, and her warmth melted into my cheek. Her hand lingered there a little too long, and I had to turn away to avoid her witnessing me turn into a cherry.

"I guess I'll … get that trash then."

"Sounds like a plan, boss man," she said. She leaned in close to whisper in my ear. "By the way, when you get a chance, check out the mustache at fourteen."

Julia and I had this running game where we attempted to spot the most awkward-looking individual at every job we worked. She was much better at it than me. She'd march back into the kitchen and say something like, "Check out Eyebrows at table seven," and, sure enough, I'd stroll out of the kitchen and there would be some old guy with two fuzzy caterpillars strapped to his forehead.

I turned toward the kitchen, praying the cooks hadn't witnessed the intimate exchange between me and Julia, but there was nothing to worry about. Most had their faces buried in their phones or their ears plugged with wireless earbuds. Two were even live-streaming their own first-person reality shows, which was the latest fad on social media sites like MeStream and Heliocentricity.

The alley outside the community center was full of dozens of homeless people. It was my fault they were there. I had fed them leftovers after a job in D.C. two months ago, and now they followed me from job to job. It wasn't difficult to do. All our jobs were posted on our social media pages so all they needed was access to the Internet and, hell, the homeless may not have had money to feed themselves, but they all had money for data plans.

The herds of homeless were everywhere in Hyattsville and everywhere else for that matter. No one seemed to care too much when it was just the illegals who couldn't find work with the new "America First" employment laws, but, lately, the herds of homeless had become much more diverse.

The Re-Recession had devoured thousands of jobs and there was no sign of any of them being regurgitated anytime soon with self-driving cargo trucks, Uscans at grocery stores, and self-serve fast-food kiosks becoming the norm. We had innovated ourselves into obscurity.

The destitute men and women in the alley threw dice (the national pastime of the down-and-out). Reese, the alpha of this particular pack of homeless, glanced up from the game and spotted me standing in the doorway holding the garbage bags I intended to toss.

"Hey! Richie Rich's here!" he said.

Reese and the rest of his troops put their dice game on hold and formed an assembly line between me and the dumpster. He grabbed the bags from me and the bags were tossed from person to person until they were finally deposited into the giant receptacle. It was all very organized for a group of people who smelled like catfish.

"You gonna hook us up 'ere Richie?"

He scratched his salt-and-pepper beard and flashed his bushy eyebrows.

I assured Reese and the rest I'd do what I could to make sure none of them went to sleep hungry that night. "And hey," I added, "the new Mega-Walmart just opened. Maybe they'll be looking to hire some people."

Reese made a sound like he had a chicken bone caught in his throat and spat onto the asphalt. "You jokin', right? Ain't nobody gonna work for no Walmart! We got our pride, man!"

For final emphasis, he adjusted the extension cord he used for a belt.

"What's wrong with Walmart? It's a job."

"You serious? Walmart the reason we here in da streets. I used to run ma own business makin' decorative lamps, and I had a family, and I done even speak propa English, and then Walmart come along and allasudden nobody want no dec-ro-tive lamps. No, now they wants cheap garbage lamps and that's 'xactly what Walmart gives 'em! Now nobody get no decorative lamps even if they wants one!"

I whipped out my phone and checked the time, hoping Reese's rant would wrap up shortly.

"But we be gettin' our revenge, oh yeah. We raidin' that store tonight," he continued. "We gonna rush in there and get us some cigarettes and beef jerky and rush da hell out. You wanna come, Richie Rich?"

"As fun as that sounds, I'll have to pass on the evening of theft."

"Theft! You wanna talk 'bout theft? Walmart be the one thievin'. That place puts hard workin' folks like you see in dis here alley out of a job and force 'em to work for the Walmart for next to nuttin' and wear some dumbass polo shirt. And thanks to Führer Trump's wall, we can't even leave if we wanna! We all trapped in dis 'ere hellhole with the Walmart!"

"Umm—" I said.

Reese placed his hand on my shoulder and I willed myself not to pull away. "It's OK, Richie. I'm gonna be OK." He opened his palm to reveal a pair of dice. "'Cause I'm about to hit it big! Here I come, baybay!"

When I returned from the alley, the kitchen was eerily silent. None of the cooks had their phones out anymore. All signs of joy and happiness had died. I was confused until I saw *her*. Millie—my wife, my better half, the 'ol ball and chain—marched through the kitchen on her lime green Crocs and, worst of all, she was marching straight toward *me*. I glanced around, searching for an escape route, but it was too late. All I could do was brace myself.

Millie was much better looking than me. She had blazing auburn hair that she hated if anyone called red and a svelte, firm body carved out of granite she earned through an obsessive dedication to crossfit training back in college. She was easily a 9.4 while I maxed out around 7.3 so I felt fortunate for marrying up the hotness scale. She hadn't aged a day since I met her five years earlier on an online dating site, and, when I say she hadn't aged, I mean, like, *at all*. It was as if she had been frozen in time as a hot 28 year old.

Unfortunately, all that hotness was usually buried beneath nine layers of sweatpants and hoodies. As soon as we got married, the tight tops and yoga pants disappeared, replaced with a messy sideways ponytail and oversized hoodies she bought by the dozen from Walmart. I realized it had been over a month since I had seen her naked. Lately, she had even started to get changed in the bathroom with the door locked … which was somewhat odd.

"What did I tell you about letting these idiots livestream from the kitchen?" she asked.

"My car almost killed me again."

"Are you *listening* to me? They need to be paying attention to what the hell they're doing. We're not paying them to livestream their bullshit lives here at work."

It seemed a bit hypocritical since she was staring at her phone while she told me all this, her ears plugged with wireless earbuds shaped like seashells (They had been on sale at Walmart). Lately, she had been obsessed with watching old sitcoms from the 90s on her phone, the kind with an obnoxious laugh track playing stale laughter after each and every corny joke.

"Millie, as long as they're working—"

"These mental midgets make enough mistakes as it is without any distractions! God, you're such a pussy sometimes. You're the boss, so be the goddamn boss!"

Laughter erupted from her phone.

And that's when I heard myself do what I had learned to do quite well in the past three years: surrender.

"You're right. I should know better. I don't know what I was thinking."

I had said it so many times at that point I should have made a recording of it to have handy for our next dispute.

You're right. I should know better. I don't know what I was thinking.

"What are you doing here, anyway?" I asked.

A guest appearance by Millie was a rare event. Most times, she claimed the gig conflicted with her reality television schedule (despite the fact all her shows were recorded and saved on our Stratus digital media library).

She smiled (which terrified me) and dragged me over to the industrial freezer by my tie. Then she shoved me inside. The frigid temperature bit into my skin immediately. I assumed this had something to do with the food so imagine my surprise when she ordered me to drop my pants.

"Excuse me?" I asked.

"Drop your pants."

"For what?"

"What the hell do you think?"

She pressed her marshmallowy body against mine and shoved her tongue down my throat. For some reason, I pictured a kid sticking his tongue to a flagpole. It sounds like a completely normal thing for a wife to do, but I would have been less shocked if she ripped her face off to reveal she was, in fact, some sort of octopus monster from outer space.

"I want you," she said.

"Why?"

"What do you mean? You're my husband, aren't you? Now drop 'em."

"You want to do it here? In the freezer?"

This was not normal behavior for my Millie. We had just surpassed the three-month mark without our genitals having crossed paths. The worst part was that, whether or not we were having sex, masturbation was not an acceptable alternative in Millie's book. Masturbation had become the equivalent of first-degree murder in my household.

Having sex with me was such a disgusting concept she didn't even want me to do it to myself. It got so bad I had taken to masturbating in odd places like the linen closet or the shed or in the car to avoid detection, but, somehow, Millie always knew—*always*. She'd sniff the air like a bloodhound and cross her arms over her chest and stare me down until even my penis felt ashamed.

"You've been *doing it* again, haven't you?" she'd accuse.

I learned not to even attempt to deny it because it only made matters worse. She'd lecture me on how selfish it was and how it was an insult to her (and her majestic vagina). When I tried to explain that the only reason I needed to do it at all was because we hadn't had sex in weeks, she dismissed me entirely.

"We'll have sex when you start to act more like the man I married," she said. "You're not a teenager, Jonathan Savage. You're thirty-six years old, and perhaps it's time you act like it."

The thing was that I was still the same horny guy she married three years earlier. The same could not be said for my lovely wife who said, "I do," on our wedding day and ever since spent most of her time saying, "I won't."

Needless to say, I was determined not to miss out on a rare opportunity for some naked interaction just because of sub-zero temperatures. Unfortunately, when I dropped my pants, my penis was not as determined as I was. The cold cut into my testicles like glass and attempted to chase my testicles inside my body. The constant laughter from Millie's earbuds didn't help either.

"Are you sure we can't do this somewhere more romantic like a janitor's closet or behind a dumpster?" I asked.

"No. Here. Now."

She leaned in close for a kiss but paused half an inch from my lips.

"Something's not right," she said. "Jonathan Milhous Savage, are you hiding something from me?"

And that was how it always started.

I froze my face in cement, and I swear to you I wore a look that said nothing more than *I'm cold as hell but still really, really want to have sex with you.* Millie studied my face like a detective interrogating a suspect on one of those cop dramas she was always watching. She furled her brow, wrinkled her lip, and tapped her finger on my chest.

I prayed, yes *prayed*, that just one time—*one time*—my wife wouldn't see my transgression etched onto my face and we could take off our clothes and jump on top of one another. But then her eyes grew wide and her mouth fell open, and I knew it was all over.

"You've had an *erection* today," she hissed, "You've been *doing it* again, haven't you?"

All this from nothing more than the expression on my face.

I could have tried to lie, but it was pointless. She was the Nostradamus of secret masturbation.

"And to think," she continued, "I almost felt bad erasing all your James Bond movies from the Stratus today."

I had uploaded every James Bond movie ever made onto our digital media library over the past few years. I was a huge Bond fanatic—had been ever since I was a kid. James Bond was debonair and daring, a true man of action. He was everything I wasn't.

"Why the hell would you get rid of my Bond collection?! That was nearly thirty movies!"

"I'm sorry, Jonathan, but I needed more room for my Kardashian collection."

The laugh track erupted into stale laughter on Millie's phone. I was under the impression my wife already owned every season of the reality series, but it turned out she needed the room for episodes of *The Kardashians: The Next Generation.*

Personally, I never got into the whole reality television renaissance, even after the country elected a reality television star as the leader of the free world. There's something about watching other people live their lives that just seemed kind of pathetic. I always figured that my time could be better spent living my own life rather than watching other people live theirs.

"Please, baby," I begged. "Can't we just get past this? I'm in a bad way here—and if you don't make a decision soon, I'm afraid my dick might turn black and fall off."

My balls were bluer than two drowned Smurfs, but it was unclear whether my condition was a result of the cold or enduring weeks of genital indifference. I leaned in close and kissed the spot where her shoulder connected with her neck. She accepted this and allowed me to follow up that initial kiss with a series of kisses that climbed up her neck and ended with the lower part of her ear in my mouth. It was quite a James Bond sort of moment, although I'm not sure Bond's preferred place for lovemaking would be an industrial freezer with his pants hanging around his ankles and his dick frozen to his leg.

I opened one eye to see how I was doing. Millie had her eyes closed and her head tilted back so she was into it. It was going to happen! The drought was finally going to end! A stink bug buzzed my ear and landed on the shelf next to Millie's shoulder. My hand shot out instinctively and smashed it against the shelf. Instead of the satisfying *smooshing* sound I expected, the bug's death was heralded by a more metallic *crunch*.

Millie's eyes snapped open. "What the hell was that?"

"Nothing. Just one of these stupid stinkbugs. Back to the kissing."

She pie-faced me out of the way and searched until she found the bug carcass. "What the hell did I tell you about killing these things? They're stink bugs. They stink!"

"I don't smell anything. And why the hell isn't that thing frozen?"

Her eyes quaked in their sockets. Then she slapped me in the chest. Then she hit me again, and again. "Why don't you ever listen to me! You are such a stupid Savage!"

She pushed past me and threw open the door to the freezer. The door struck the wall with such force it knocked several pots and pans off the overhead racks. The resulting ruckus caught the attention of every single person in the kitchen. They all turned in a single motion toward the freezer, where I still stood with my pants around my ankles and my penis shriveled like a dried-up worm. The last sound I heard before Millie disappeared was the dead laughter of the laugh track on her phone.

The freezer door swung back, and I caught sight of my reflection. I hoped for some sympathy from my other self, but even he looked ashamed.

Chapter III

The kitchen was usually my sanctuary until dessert and coffee were being served, but my very public humiliation drove me out early. My usual end-of-the-meal ritual included a visit to each table to ask how everything was. It was a good way to drum up business in case anyone wanted to use us for a future engagement. One should always be thinking about the future ….

Everything about the job was fairly routine. About a hundred local big shots sat around in $3000 suits and blubbered on about politics and helping the little man as they shoveled veal and lamb chops into their faces. Since everyone present was a Beatty backer, there was a lot of head-nodding and back-slapping and idiotic laughter. Like I said, everything was very routine.

Julia walked past and whispered, "Table fourteen."

Thankfully, Julia had been out on the floor when Millie left me cold and shriveled in the freezer. I didn't know why that was so important (she would obviously hear about it), but it seemed imperative that she hadn't actually witnessed my humiliation first-hand.

I had nearly forgotten her earlier comment about the mustachioed weirdo at table fourteen. As soon as I cast my eyes in that direction, it was obvious who she was referring to. At the table sat a pale mouse of a man with his dark hair parted to one side and a well-groomed handlebar mustache plastered onto his face by sweat. He wore a long wool suit with knee-high leather boots. He looked like he had come straight from a dinner theater production.

The other attendees at his table had moved their chairs into a tight crescent moon on the opposite side of the table. His salad, veal, and parfait sat in front of him, completely untouched. As far as I was concerned, the inward chuckle I experienced at Mustachio's expense constituted the only interaction he and I would ever have, but then our eyes met. There was something wild and unsettling lurking behind those eyes. I quickly averted my glance and buried my smile, but I could feel those eyes following me.

I turned my attention instead to the speaker's closing remarks as I circulated around the room, which was easy since most of the attendees were too busy checking texts to even notice I existed. Technology had replaced the cigarette as modern man's post-meal addiction.

The speaker was some Beatty flunky delivering the usual spiel about helping out small business owners and restoring balance to America's wealth distribution and blah blah blah. I could barely absorb any of it because I could feel Mustachio's wild eyes burning into my back.

When I couldn't delay it any longer, I dragged myself back to table fourteen. Mustachio was visibly sweating and seemed to be hyperventilating, his mouth hanging open as he exhaled great mouthfuls of air in quick, short bursts like a dog left in the car on a hot day, but those eyes continued to stare me down. Even under the scrutiny of those eyes, I went right into my normal routine hoping to make it back to the kitchen as quickly as possible and share a laugh with Julia.

I focused on the rest of the table. "How was everything today, gentlemen?"

"Fine," a man wearing a bad toupee answered from behind his phone, "considering—" He threw a sideways glance at Mustachio.

"Yes," a bald man agreed, "the *food* was fine."

Again, another sideways glance, this one more obvious, but Mustachio wouldn't have seen a neon sign with a giant arrow pointing at him. The intensity of his glare was enough to send me running for the hills and leave him for the old techno addicts to worry about.

"Glad to hear it, gentlemen. Enjoy the rest of your meal."

I didn't even bother to plug the catering business. I wanted to get as far away from Mustachio as possible.

But Mustachio had other plans.

He suddenly sprang to his feet, nearly toppling the table in the process, and screamed, "SIC SEMPER TYRANNIS!" From his overcoat, he pulled what looked like a soup can with a laser pen attached to it and pointed it at me—

But that's all that happened. He pointed the can at me and let the final word of his scream stretch out so it sounded more like "TYRANISSSSSSSSSSS!" The speaker stopped mid-sentence, and everyone peered out from behind their phones to see what the hell all the yelling was about. I was at least relieved to see that everyone in the fire hall appeared equally as confused.

"Umm … was there a problem with your meal, sir?" I asked.

Mustachio pounded the can with his fist. After a half dozen whacks, it emitted a high-pitched whine like a generator coming to life and then a blinding purple light erupted from the can. The purple light blasted through the ceiling, raining ceiling tiles, fiberglass, and metal onto everyone's head.

That's when I realized that this strange mustached man was trying to kill me. Everyone else seemed to realize this at the same time, too, because the room devolved into complete chaos, people falling over one another to get as far away from table fourteen as possible. Mustachio pointed the can at me again and sent a purple blast hurtling toward me that sailed over my right shoulder and turned the podium on the stage into firewood.

Leaving seemed like a good idea so that's what I did. I turned and raced toward the exit with purple light zipping past me and blowing holes in the wall. I squeezed through one of the larger holes and took off running down the long alley separating the community center from the building next to it. Reese and his homeless associates were long gone. The homeless seem to have a sixth sense for approaching storms, and they had up and left before getting caught in this one.

Unfortunately, I realized my mistake too late. The alley was at least thirty feet long with no cover except for a few garbage cans and dumpsters and offered nothing but a narrow straight away. Basically I had run into a shooting gallery.

Still, I decided to give it the 'ol college try. I figured if I was going to die, I might as well die running away like a coward. I was about ten feet from the end of the alley when a shot of purple overtook me and passed through a dumpster as easily as a boxer delivering an uppercut to a whipped cream punching bag.

A second shot struck the side of the building near the same dumpster, causing an explosion of bricks and mortar to rain down around me. A brick struck me on the top of the head and sent me rolling onto the asphalt behind a trash can.

My existence was nothing but swirling dust and the hard, indifferent asphalt beneath me. I rolled over and looked around, but the entire world refused to stay still. My hand reached to my ringing head and returned caked with blood. When the world finally decided to cooperate again, I saw that the explosion had pushed the dumpster out into the alley so that it blocked my exit ... not that it mattered.

Mustachio stood over me, jamming what looked like a purple paintball into the back of the soup can. He sighed loudly like this whole thing was a big inconvenience to him.

"Sic Semper Tyrannis," he said again with far less enthusiasm than his original outburst.

Then he pointed the soup can at my head.

I stared up at that soup can, but it wasn't fear I felt. I guess I was more annoyed than anything. I thought about how angry Millie was going to be once the Beatty people called and said they would not be hiring us for future events, and I felt relieved I wouldn't have to hear her tirade about how I had cost us another catering gig.

"Sic Semper Tyrannis," Mustachio repeated.

"Yes, yes, I heard you the first time," I said.

I could take getting plugged in the face with a purple laser shot out of a soup can, but I had no intention of being patient about it. Besides, Mustachio seemed to be milking the moment, enjoying it. He scratched his oily beard with his left hand, revealing three letters clumsily tattooed between his thumb and forefinger. Mustachio took a deep breath, exhaled, and thrust the can forward. It choked out a sound like a lawnmower dying, and his wild eyes went wide with panic. He pounded on the side of the can again.

That's when I decided the time for being patient was over. I dug around in my pockets hoping I had accidentally shoved a Taser or a grenade in my pants that morning. Unfortunately, the only thing in there was my phone, so that's what I chucked at Mustachio's head. It struck him just above the left eye, and the blow was enough to knock him off balance. He stumbled toward the brick wall, and the soup can suddenly erupted, exploding and burying my mustachioed attacker in brick and mortar.

I'm not even sure how I got there, but the next thing I knew I was in the parking lot sprinting toward my Civic. I didn't know how I was going to get inside the car since I had tossed my phone, but that problem became moot when the Civic transformed into what looked like a giant cheese curl and crumbled into orange dust that was picked up by the breeze and blown away.

"Goddamnit!" I said. "I am having one hell of a day!"

I detoured toward the catering van, expecting it, too, to transform from a typical motor vehicle into some sort of deathtrap. When it didn't, I jumped inside. Julia had a terrible habit of leaving the keys inside the van, but today her bad habit was my salvation. A few seconds later, I was behind the wheel of the van, dragging someone's picket fence behind me.

Chapter IV

Nothing seemed familiar on that drive home. The streets I had driven on hundreds of times all seemed like they belonged to a different world. When I finally stumbled upon my neighborhood, I parked the van in front of my neighbor's house since the sinkhole had swallowed most of the driveway. Millie's Escalade was parked in front of the house. I feared Mustachio had followed me, so I crept over to our place and snuck in the back door, silently praying for Millie's safety.

My senses were on high alert the second the door closed silently behind me because there was a strange voice coming from the living room. I prayed Millie was somewhere else—shopping or getting a massage or whatever the hell she did all day—but then I recognized her voice in the same vicinity as the stranger's. Our border terrier, Seymour, greeted me at the door, acting totally normal. That was a good sign.

I sent Seymour on his way and searched the kitchen for some sort of weapon. My two best options were to either arm myself with a butcher's knife or grab some liquid drain cleaner and try to convince whoever was in there to drink it.

I went with the knife.

Armed with a knife I had only used previously to hack ham, I crept closer to the wall separating the kitchen from the living room. I peered around the corner, expecting the worst. What I saw, however, was more confusing than anything else. Millie sat on the sofa (like usual) staring at our television (again, as usual), but the image that should have been on the television was instead projecting out into the living room like a 3D hologram only with more weight to it. It looked meaty. It was straight out of *Star Trek* or something. The image she was watching/interacting with was a shadowed figure who spoke in a robotic voice meant to disguise it.

"—out of nowhere?" Millie asked the hologram. "Don't we have any idea who he was working for?"

"The usual losers. Bad, bad people," the robot shadow answered. "Some anti-technite or historical preservationist nutjobs, but none of 'em have taken credit for the car boom-boom or the most recent … whatever. We gotta find the bastard before things become a total disaster."

Millie's fingers danced over the screen of her smartphone and then she shook her head.

"He must have lost his phone during the attack because the GPS tracker hasn't budged. Don't we have eyes on him?"

"We lost the feed in the explosion in the alley. Hold on a sec." The figure leaned forward and seemed to be wiping the air with a gold-stitched handkerchief. I realized he must be wiping down the camera on his end of the feed. "Better. The important thing now is getting that loser back on the grid and getting the show running."

"Are we even sure the dickless wonder is still alive?"

I assumed I was the subject of the conversation, and, if that was true, my wife had just referred to me as *the dickless wonder*, which was doubly insulting because, of all people, she should have known I was, in fact, the proud owner of a genuine penis.

"Police chatter didn't mention any deaths," the shadow said. "We're watching admissions at the local hospitals. Got my top guys on it. They're the best. Really, really fantastic what these guys can do. We'll find him."

"We better. People aren't going to watch reruns forever."

"We won't have to worry about that. After all this chaos, we'll have our highest numbers since honeymoon week. Really, really tremendous numbers. *Huge.* Plus, it gives us the chance to take care of some technical issues. Here. My tech guys—and these guys are terrific, by the way—just finished the new videosect models." He reached out and Millie took whatever he had in his hand. Yup. She took something from the hologram. It was freaky.

She placed whatever he had given her onto the end table. It was hard to make out at first, but then I finally saw what they were. A swarm of stink bugs rose up from the end table and hovered in a uniform formation.

"The tech guys tell me these new models are specifically linked to his DNA. Really amazing stuff," the shadow said. "You won't have to worry about them following you into the john anymore … which is too bad. You got a great ass. Just don't let the prick smash 'em again. They're very expensive. Cost us millions and millions. Give 'em a try."

Millie picked up her phone and a few seconds later one of the stink bugs broke formation and hovered over the television.

"Let's see what kind of picture quality we get with these things."

Her fingers danced across her phone's screen, and her image appeared on the television screen behind the hologram. She smiled at herself and ran a hand through her strawberry locks. Then she stopped. The smile plummeted off her face. On the screen, in the background, was a man's head peeking around the corner. The man's mouth hung open, and his eyes were wide. It took me a few seconds to realize the gaping mouth and wide eyes belonged to me.

Millie sprang from the couch and backpedaled toward the television. Her wild eyes moved from me to the stink bugs to the hologram. I dumped the knife on the floor and stepped around the corner, watching myself do the same thing on the television. The hologram shadow reached forward and instantly vanished from the room, leaving me alone with my wife. We stood staring at each other for a few seconds, neither of us speaking. Neither of us seemed to know what was supposed to happen next. In a lot of ways, it was similar to our honeymoon night.

I was the one who finally broke the silence. "Millie, what the hell is going on?"

It seemed a fair enough question.

In answer, Millie ripped the TV off the wall. It clattered to the floor and smashed against the brick fireplace. Then she grabbed her purse off the sofa and frantically rummaged through its contents.

"What are you doing? Who was that man you were talking to?"

Instead of answering, Millie whipped out her birth control container, opened it, pulled out a pill, and threw it at me. The room filled with a blinding light like ten thousand flashbulbs going off at once. The blast blinded me temporarily, dropping a curtain of light over the entire world. When I finally managed to blink my eyes back into focus, Millie was gone and the front door hung open.

I ran into the yard just in time to spot Millie's Escalade peel out and race down the street. Every instinct I had was screaming at me to slink back into the house and try to figure out what was going on, but, deep down, I knew the only person who had those answers had just taken off down the street—and I needed those answers.

I hopped into the van and raced like a madman through the streets for the second time that day. Lucky for me, spotting a giant Escalade wasn't all that difficult. It was the only time I was ever glad Millie had forced me to buy her the monstrosity. I plowed through stop signs and traffic lights without any hesitation. I figured after nearly being murdered by a mustachioed lunatic with a soup can and discovering my wife was secretly spying on me using insect cameras, a traffic ticket was the least of my concerns.

Millie weaved in and out of traffic with me trailing a couple hundred yards behind. The chase led to the outskirts of Hyattsville where there was nothing but a few scattered strip malls and office buildings, most of which had closed long ago after the expansion of the Walmart kingdom.

On the open roads, the Escalade pulled away and out of sight. I feared I had lost it for good. After everything I had experienced that day, I didn't think I could be surprised by anything, but I was wrong again. I spotted my lovely wife's vehicle parked in an isolated parking lot outside of ... *drum rooooooll* ... a dentist's office!

A wooden signboard outside the building welcomed me to Denham's Dental Practice. I parked next to the Escalade and cautiously approached the small brick building. The front door to the office was unlocked so I entered and found myself in a typical waiting room, complete with uncomfortable chairs, outdated magazines, and ancient toys from the 80s.

The only thing that seemed odd about the place was that there didn't appear to be anyone there. There was no one waiting in the uncomfortable chairs, no one at reception, and, most importantly, no Millie.

A sound like a high-powered vacuum rumbled to life in a room down the hallway from the receptionist area. I crept down the hallway and followed the sound to a door labeled: "Dr. Walton's Office." Again, the door was unlocked, so I entered.

I expected to find a room with a reclining chair and overhead light and a tiny sink and posters encouraging daily flossing. What I found, though, was anything but ordinary. The windowless room looked similar to the industrial freezer Millie had dragged me into earlier except much, much larger. The walls, ceiling, and floor were all made of stainless steel, and the temperature was so cold I could see my breath. Strangely enough, the only item in the room was a leaf blower.

Millie stood near the far wall, texting madly on her phone. She stood in front of an outline of a doorway cut into the wall, which seemed to be emitting the vacuum sound. The strangest thing, though, was that an aqua jelly blob the size of a basketball hung in the doorway, seemingly defying gravity. It pulsated and swirled and seemed to grow in size, reaching out and clinging to the door frame.

"C'mooooon!" Millie screeched to the blob, shaking her phone like a maraca.

I said her name. She whipped around and didn't look surprised to see me. Instead, the look on her face was one of total disdain, like I had walked in on her with another man and she was glad, glad to finally have the truth known.

"You just had to go and ruin everything, didn't you, you selfish prick?" she said. "You've ruined my career!"

"Your career? You don't even work!"

"You had everything I always dreamed of and you didn't deserve any of it." She shook her head in disgust. "Playing second fiddle to a pathetic spineless jellyfish like you. *I* should have been the star!"

Behind her, the jelly continued to fill the door frame, growing larger and thicker. Green lights lit up around the frame of the door, and the vacuum sound increased in intensity. She glanced behind her at the door frame as it completely filled with aqua jelly. Black stringy amoebas danced in the jelly, which continued to pulse, reaching out for her.

"What is happening?! Have you been lying to me this entire time? You're supposed to be my wife!"

"Consider this our divorce," she said.

She stepped into the jelly, which quickly engulfed her, and then she was gone. She completely disappeared.

The high-powered vacuum peaked and began to fade. The green lights around the door frame blinked to yellow. The aqua gelatin mold in the doorway stopped pulsing and settled back into the frame.

I approached the frame and stared into the aqua gelatin mold, but there was no sign of Millie or anything beyond the door frame. All the answers I needed had disappeared into that goop, leaving me with nothing but questions.

Had that been the end of it, I probably would have turned and drove back home, watched some television, and gone to bed. What else was there to do than return to my normal life, figure out how to divorce a spouse that had disappeared inside a Jell-O mold, and just chalk the day's happenings up to the single strangest day of my entire life?

But fate had other plans.

I turned to find Mustachio standing in the doorway, pointing his soup can directly at my face. There was a blast of purple, and I felt myself falling backward. Then the falling stopped.

I opened my eyes to find myself encased in the aqua gelatin. The jelly didn't seem to form around me as much as I seemed to have become part of it. There was no sense of motion. My body hung weightless in the center of the blob, which appeared to have expanded to encompass the entire room, except the room no longer existed.

Wherever I was smelled like the color yellow (if that makes any sense). There was a slight ringing sound that was faint at first but grew louder and louder until it was so ear-splitting that I thought my eardrums would burst. Then, as suddenly as it started, the sound stopped. I swam in silence. A pinprick of light shone through the aqua haze and, suddenly, I was falling again, but this time I fell toward the light.

II

America: 2076

Chapter I

When I reached the light, the aqua gelatin and the weightlessness were gone, and I lie sprawled on an old mattress covered in a brown membrane-like substance similar to the snotty stuff on French onion soup. The room I found myself in was totally white—floor, walls, ceiling—and contained a gateway similar to the one in the dentist's office. The letters FTTA were painted on the wall in swooping, red letters.

I wasn't alone in the room. A tall African-American man in a tan uniform stood over me, holding what looked like a leaf blower. His eyes were an otherworldly violet and appeared to have a glassy film over them. His nametag read *Wells*. He aimed the barrel of the machine at me, and I expected a purple laser to splatter my face against the wall, but, instead, the machine coughed out a hot jet of high-powered air. The high winds splattered the membrane gunk off me and against a nearby wall covered in crepe paper. The guy said something, but I couldn't quite make it out over the roar of the machine.

"I'm sorry. What did you say?" I asked.

The vacuum rush died, and the man looked out from behind the machine.

"I'm sorry. What did you say?" the man asked.

He appeared to be blind because he didn't look directly at me.

"I asked what you just said."

"Oh. I said welcome back to good 'ol 2076. How was your trip?"

Before I could answer, the machine roared back into action, and the rush of hot air nearly tore my lips off. Then the machine choked and sputtered until it died all together with a hollow *thunk*.

"Damnit," Wells said. *"Gonna need another blower on six."*

"What?"

"I'm not talking to you," he said, staring in my general direction. *"Gonna need another blower down here on six."* He smiled. "It will just be a minute."

"Did you say 2076 before? Like, as in, the year?"

"No, it's not *before* 2076. It's *exactly* 2076. Shame you didn't come back three weeks earlier. You could have caught the tricentennial celebration in the capital. There was a parade and fireworks … and some of them even worked! Of course, most of them didn't, and then there was a fire and a selection and a lot of people died. You know, the usual."

"What? Did you say people died?"

"You seem confused, sir. *Yes, now.* You're not intoxicated, are you? Because traveling through time under the influence of alcohol is against FTTA regulations. *Down on six.*"

"Six? What the hell are you talking about? Are you telling me I'm in the future?"

"No, you're in the present. You're right now. You're home."

A young woman in a matching tan uniform entered the room with another machine identical to the first. She, too, had glassy, violet eyes. She tried to hand the machine to Wells, missed, and then managed to get it into his hand. Then she left.

"Now, let's finish getting you cleaned up," he said.

"What is that thing anyway?"

His face scrunched up like he didn't understand the question. "It's a leaf blower, man."

He turned the machine toward me, but his aim was off so the nozzle aimed to the left of my head. He turned it on, but, instead of hot air, a burst of fire shot out the spout. I dodged out of the way and swatted at the embers burning the tips of my hair. Wells grumbled under his breath and tossed the leaf blower to the ground. It sparked and lit up like a small campfire.

"Oops. Sorry about that. *Defect in six,*" Wells said. *"Got a fire here."*

"I see that," I said.

The same young woman walked back into the room carrying two fire extinguishers. She set one on the ground, readied the other, and aimed the nozzle in the general direction of the fire. When nothing happened, she picked up the other extinguisher and took aim. This time, the nozzle vomited foam onto the fire, extinguishing the flames. The girl went to leave the room, crashed into the wall instead, bounced off, and then finally found the exit. She returned a few seconds later with a third leaf blower.

"Is that thing safe?"

Wells wrinkled his brow. "That voice. You sound familiar. Do I know you?"

"I doubt it. I don't even know where the hell I am!"

Wells kicked the leaf blower into action. Hot air flew from the nozzle instead of more flames. He did a thorough job of cleaning off the rest of the snot, and then invited me to join him at the counter on the far side of the room. I reluctantly agreed, still trying to figure out whether Mustachio had actually killed me and this was the check-in counter for Heaven.

"Hey," I said, "there's some guy trying to kill me who might follow me here, wherever *here* is. Can you turn that doorway thingie off?"

Wells glanced down into his empty left palm. "I don't see any more arrivals for today. Then again, I wasn't expecting you either, and here you are!"

I tried to emphasize how dangerous this weirdo was, but then I remembered Millie.

"Did a woman come through here?" I asked. "A woman—my *wife*—went through the doorway before me, but I don't see her here."

"Must have come in at another gate. I'm sure she'll meet you outside the terminal."

Wells circled around to the far side of the counter and jammed his finger into the palm of his left hand over and over again. There was nothing on the counter—no computer or sign-in book—except for what looked like a supermarket scanner.

"All righty," Wells said, finally looking up from his palm. "Now, I just need to scan your passport and we'll send you on your way. Can you hold up your iPalm for me, sir?"

I had no idea what he was talking about so I didn't do anything. I just said "Uh," and "Wha," until he repeated the instruction.

"Hold up your iPalm, sir. Please. My shift ended five minutes ago."

"Uh," I said. "Wha?"

"Hold up your hand, sir."

I raised my right hand, palm out, which merely elicited an eye roll from Wells.

"Your *other* hand, sir."

I raised my left hand, palm out, which I considered to be just as unremarkable as my right, but the reaction from Wells was anything but ordinary. He backed away from the desk until his back was against the wall and, even then, he continued to backpedal.

"Where's your iPalm? How can you be traveling without an iPalm? You must at least have a mobile!"

I assured him I had no idea what he was talking about.

"Your iPalm!"

He raised his left hand, palm out, and that's when I saw exactly what he was talking about. There, embedded in the dark skin of Wells's hand, and encompassing most of his palm, was a small computer screen. It literally looked like someone had sewn a smartphone screen into his hand, but instead of the screen looking like a solid object, it looked more fluid, like liquid. This time it was my turn to backpedal against the wall.

"Wait," he said. The violet in his eyes vanished, revealing a more typical brown, and he looked directly at me for the first time through squinted eyes. The fear suddenly washed off his face. "I knew I recognized that voice. You're *him*! From the show! It's *you*!" He started to chuckle like a moron and slapped his forehead with his non-computerized hand. "Of course, you don't have an iPalm. It's *you*!"

I slowly started to inch toward the exit, my back still pressed against the wall.

"*Yeah, you'll never believe who just passed through my gate,*" Wells said, staring directly at me. "*No. This time I'm serious. What show do you watch every night? That's right!*"

I lunged toward the door and darted out of the room. Wells called, "Hey!" after me, but I'd had enough of him and his liquid hand and violet eyes. I ran.

The room emptied out into a series of long hallways bathed in stale, white light. The hallways were lined with screens that projected 3D words into the air. *Thank you for traveling with the Federal Time Traveling Agency. Welcome home!* the words said.

I picked a hallway and ran until it emptied out into an area that resembled a baggage claim at an airport. The place was packed with people with violet eyes and liquid palms, but no one seemed to notice me as I sprinted past them. Many of them appeared to be staring directly at walls or the floor.

More voices yelled, "Hey!" and I had been yelled, "Hey!" at enough times in my life to know when I was being chased by security. The baggage claim area was located on a rotunda looking down on the lower level of the building, a long open space lined on both sides by storefronts.

It reminded me of every airport I had ever been in. Hundreds of people filled the area, but they were all dressed in similar clothing—lifeless tan and vomit green attire that looked like adult versions of school uniforms. The uniforms had an Asian vibe to them, like the tunics and loose-fitting pants people wore in old Kung Fu movies

More "Heys!" close behind drove me down the escalators and into the crowd, searching for some sign of salvation. But it didn't take long before the "Heys!" of the pursuing security agents were joined by a "Hey!" of recognition. I turned toward the voice, praying to be greeted by a familiar face, but the twenty-something female decked out in puke green responsible for the "Hey!" was a stranger.

"Hey!" she said. "It's him! It's him! It's *him!*"

Her fingers danced across her palm.

The eyes of every individual in the immediate area transformed from violet to more natural colors like brown and blue and green and looked up at me simultaneously as if these people were puppets suddenly yanked to life by a puppeteer.

More "Heys!" rang out. The entire crowd that I was hoping would be my camouflage, collectively turned its attention on me, failed to be a crowd of individual people and formed into a single collective beast, surging toward me. My name seemed to be whispered on various lips but that name grew louder and louder until it was a chant moving through the crowd.

"Sav-age! Sa-vage! Sa-vage! Sa-vage!"

The tan and green mass circled around me. Some pointed their palms toward me, projecting my face back at me from the fluid screens. I scanned the crowd for a familiar face, but, when I finally found one, it was the last face I wanted to see. There, standing at the top of the escalators, stood Mustachio. I stared up at that mustachioed face. He stared back at me. Our eyes met. Then the chase was on.

He made a clumsy leap off the balcony and landed on top of several members of the mob on the lower level. I took off in the opposite direction, pushing and shoving my way through the ring of humanity surrounding me. I tried to hug the exterior of the station where there seemed to be fewer people.

I passed a Walmart—and then a Walmart—and then a Walmart. And then I realized that *all* the stores were Walmart, even though they all appeared to be kiosks selling different food products and toiletries and knick-knacks—an entire row of Walmarts.

I bobbed and weaved and hurdled through the crowd and, with each step, I grew closer to the sunlight of the world outside. As I drew closer to the light, I speculated about what awaited me outside the building. If this was indeed the future, there could be anything out there.

Flying Cars … robots … hell, I could be in a cloud city and not even realize it.

But what awaited me outside the building had to be better than what was inside, especially with Mustachio lurking somewhere in the crowd.

The automatic doors opened and spit me outside into … the most unimpressive vision of the future one could imagine. The sky hung dark and gray over a city that looked suspiciously like the outskirts of Washington D.C., which is not what any city should aspire to be.

Torn and tattered America flags embroidered with the number 300 hung limply from the lampposts. Besides that, it all looked rather familiar. The rundown buildings were the same, the littered streets were the same, and the depressed people looked the same. The cars in the streets were not only earthbound but most looked like they were straight out of the 70s.

To say I was unimpressed would be an understatement.

A "Hey!" at my back drove me toward the street where a row of cars sat idle. When I reached the street, a car that looked eerily similar to a 1974 Pinto screeched to a halt directly in front of me, and a young woman stuck her head out the driver's side window.

"Get in, Savage!" she yelled.

I turned back toward the building where the vomit-colored mass emptied out of the building, oozing toward me, and I knew, somewhere in that mass, was a mustachioed man with a deadly soup can.

I did the only thing I could: I got in.

As soon as I threw myself into the passenger seat, the young woman peeled out, and we rocketed off into the future in a 1974 light blue Pinto.

Chapter II

The futuristic vehicle that looked suspiciously like a '74 Ford Pinto chugged through the streets of wherever the hell I was with the speed and grace of a 1974 Ford Pinto.

"Is this a '74 Pinto?" I asked my savior.

"No," she said. "It's a '76 Pinto—2076. Brand new."

Of course, that didn't make any sense. Who the hell would resurrect the Pinto? But there seemed to be some validity to her claim since the dashboard looked like something straight out of an alien spacecraft. The world speeding past the Pinto confused me as much as the car. There was no way the depressing concrete cesspool outside the car could be Hyattsville. There wasn't a single patch of green anywhere and the gray coating over everything reminded me more of Beijing.

Eventually, the Pinto slowed to match the speed of the other vehicles on the street. I turned, expecting to see Mustachio sprinting after the car Terminator-style, but there didn't appear to be anyone giving chase.

"I think we're in the clear," my captor said. "I posted a false description of the vehicle that you jumped into on a dozen message boards and posted several other false reports on *Savage Sightings* sites all over the interwebs."

That seemed impossible considering she had been driving the entire time we had been together.

"Well … thanks."

"Don't mention it."

She closed her eyes and released the steering wheel. In a panic, I reached for the wheel but realized the car drove itself, driving as straight as a roller coaster on a track. With the illusion of safety slowly sinking in, I took a moment to study my chauffeur. She appeared to be in her late-twenties. Atop her head sat dozens of strawberry-blonde Slinky-like curls. She wore the same tan tunic—plain and baggy—as the other women back at the station and a silly grin that grew in size every time she glanced over at me.

"I'm Klaryse," she finally said.

"Thanks for the help back there, Klaryse. By the way, I'm—"

"Oh, I know who you are." Her words tumbled out of her mouth so quickly it sounded more like chipmunk chittering. "Ijustcan'tbe-lieveit'sactuallyyou!"

Then she squealed. Yes, a squeal. I had never been present for an honest-to-goodness, genuine squeal before, but that's exactly what this was. She sounded like a teeny-bopper meeting the lead singer of her favorite boy band.

The Pinto eased to a stop at an intersection lined on both sides by Walmarts.

"Where am I?" I asked.

"Hyattsville."

"That's not what I mean. Wait … this can't be Hyattsville. It looks like one of the seedier areas on the outskirts of D.C."

"This city has changed since you walked these streets. Things really started to go downhill back in the fifties."

"*Back* in the fifties? You mean this really is the future?"

"Of course not. You're looking at the timeline from a very egocentric point-of-view. The year 2076 is actually the current year. You actually exist in *our* past."

"But that doesn't make any sense. If someone traveled from this time into the future then the people in the future would consider *their* time to be the current year. So how can there be a *current year?*"

"Time travel into the future is impossible."

"Why?"

"How should I know? I'm not a scientist. Do you know how your—uh—your toaster works?"

It was a valid point. I certainly didn't know how my toaster worked or why an airplane doesn't fall out of the sky like a cinder block or how the Internet was even possible. It worked. That was all that mattered to most people.

Klaryse laid on the horn, only half paying attention to our conversation. The traffic light had switched to green, and yet the Apollo in front of us hadn't budged. She honked again. The car's four-ways lit up. Klaryse grumbled and took the wheel again, squeezing past the disabled car and speeding through the intersection.

"How'd you know where I was anyway?" I asked.

Klaryse's eyes transformed from emerald green to deep violet. She held up her left hand, palm up. A 3D holographic image of the Time Port appeared in the air above her hand. I watched myself running through the lobby like a scared rabbit.

"Word travels fast around here, 'specially when there's a celebrity involved."

"Ooooooookaaaaaay," I said. "I have some questions, but I'm not sure whether to start with the purple eyes or all the Walmarts or what the hell you mean by *celebrity.*"

The purple eyes were easily explained. iContacts had hit it big in the 60s and then evolved into iLids, optical computers that acted in a similar fashion to the transparent inner eyelids of alligators. They turned violet when in use so others knew when an individual was currently viewing the optical computer.

"And what did you mean when you said a celebrity was involved?" I asked.

The Pinto suddenly jerked forward and unleashed a disconcerting belch from its bowels. Smoke poured out from beneath the Pinto's hood, and it jerked back and forth like a bucking bronco. Klaryse pulled the Pinto onto the curb in front of another Walmart before we stopped moving altogether.

"Fiddlesticks," she said. "We got a breakdown." She looked over at me and smiled. *"I got an emergency here! I'm going to need you to pick me up. I'm two blocks from the Prole District on Burnett Boulevard."*

"How am I supposed to pick you up? I'm in the car with you," I said.

"Sorry. I'm not talking to you." Then she continued, staring right at me. *"Yes, now! I don't have time to explain. Just get over here!"*

"Is everyone in the future—or the present—or whenever *insane*? I never know what the hell you people are talking about!"

Klaryse looked at me, confused. Then she giggled and placed her hand on my shoulder, sending a tiny shock through my neck. "I'm sorry, Savage. Everything must seem new and confusing to you."

She leaned toward me and held her Slinky locks back. Embedded into the skin behind her ear was a tiny metallic dot the size of a Skittle. She explained that it was a Bradbury Implant, a device capable of simulating telepathic communication. All one had to do was think of a person and the implant would produce an immediate verbal and auditory link.

She released her hair, and the Slinkies sprang back into place atop her head. I caught a whiff of her shampoo, a mixture of strawberries and apricots.

"So much for asking for a girl's number at the bar," I said.

I laughed quietly at my own joke, but Klaryse was busy playing some kind of 3D word puzzle on her iPalm. Obviously, downtime was not her specialty. I exited the Pinto and popped the hood. I half-expected to find some sort of fusion reactor or something that ran on garbage, but it looked like the gas-powered engine of a 1974 Pinto—only worse.

The engine looked like it had been put together by a five year old. It was leaking oil all over the place and smoking more than a stoner at a drum circle.

There were dozens of people on the sidewalk, walking in and out of the Walmart. Being recognized wasn't a concern because every one of them had their eyes buried in their palms or overcast in violet. Most of the tunic-clad individuals leaving the store carried small pouches. Every few feet, they paused to pop what looked like some sort of candy into their mouths. They walked blindly along the broken sidewalks and into the street, sometimes bouncing off objects or other people and wandering aimlessly in a different direction.

One woman walked right past me with her eyes buried in her palm. A quick glance revealed she was watching a clip of my escape from the Time Port. Her hand moved mechanically toward her mouth and then I saw that it was a small red and blue pill, and not candy, she tossed down her gullet. A strange, vacant smile spread across her face as she stumbled off.

As I watched the woman disappear into an alley, a strange sight caught my eye on the horizon. I knew my eyes had to be playing tricks on me because what it looked like was a squad of Nazi soldiers goose-stepping in unison down the street. They were dressed in black uniforms with bucket helmets and armed with firearms that resembled paintball guns.

"Um … Klaryse," I called into the car.

Her eyes remained overcast in violet and her mouth was moving as if she were speaking to some unseen person.

"Klaryse!" I called again. "There appears to be a squad of Nazi soldiers marching this way."

Her eyes flashed back to emerald. "Nazis?"

There was a scream, followed by a flash of neon orange, and then a group of women exiting the Walmart exploded in a cloud of ash.

"Get down!" Klaryse screamed.

She jumped out of the car, knocking me to the asphalt. Streaks of orange light filled the air above us, and, with each blast, another person disappeared and was replaced with an ash cloud and a hailstorm of red and blue pills. Klaryse and I crawled under the Pinto as the assault continued. The Nazi storm troopers marched past the Pinto, firing their paintball guns into the crowd indiscriminately. Their concrete faces beneath their helmets showed absolutely no sign of remorse or pity. They might as well have been stepping on ants.

"Are they looking for me?" I asked over the blasts.

"No," Klaryse said indifferently. "This has nothing to do with you. Well, not really anyway. It's a random SS selection."

"A selection? Like during the Holocaust?"

"Kind of. It's our murderous president's *brilliant* plan to fix the social security system and improve the jobless rate. Instead of creating more jobs, he makes less people."

"The president uses Nazis to murder American citizens?"

"They're not *Nazis*. They're Secret Service. The SS."

"Aren't those the guys in charge of protecting the president?"

"Not anymore. Now they're his private security force. You'd be smart to avoid them at all cost. Now that you're here, *he's* going to be looking for you, and believe me when I tell you, he wants you dead *real* bad."

"Why would the President of the United States want me dead?"

But it was already too late. A curtain of violet lowered over her eyes, and she was back to playing her word game. This clearly wasn't her first rodeo as far as the whole government-endorsed public execution thing went. She reached over and placed her hand in mine. Usually, I hated being touched by strangers, but, oddly enough, my proximity alert never triggered. I watched the rest of the massacre hand-in-hand with Klaryse.

Eventually, the screams in the immediate area faded, and the streaks of light gave way to the usual smog cover. Klaryse's eyes flipped back to emerald. She crawled out from under the car and squinted into the smog. The blasts could be heard in the far distance, but there was no other sign the SS had been there except for the other individuals emerging from their hiding places. The survivors swept up the stray pills from the asphalt and continued on their merry way.

"C'mon," Klaryse said. "We're safe now."

Safe was not exactly how I would describe my general feelings after watching the president's private security force cut through a crowd with deadly paintball guns. As Klaryse and I slipped back into the Pinto, one thing became perfectly clear:

America 2076 was not a good place to be, and the sooner I could leave, the better.

Chapter III

The sights Hyattsville had to offer were less than engaging (unless you've got a hard-on for cinder blocks or smog) so I tried to kill some time by engaging Klaryse in small talk, but it was nearly impossible. Time and time again, she escaped behind her violet curtains or dove into the plasma pool of her iPalm. I tried to pump her for as much information as I could about the brave new world I had stumbled upon, but she seemed reluctant to answer any of my questions.

"Where are you taking me anyway?" I asked.

"To meet some very important people."

"And what's the deal with all the Walmarts?"

"Too complicated to explain."

"And why would the President of the United States employ Nazi storm troopers?"

"Because our president is a murderous tyrant who slaughters his own people like cattle!"

That subject she was not shy of discussing. The absurdity of the entire situation made me laugh, but I stopped immediately when I turned and spotted two dark eyes staring at me through the passenger-side window. The eyes were attached to a man with dyed black hair that hung low near his bug eyes.

"Relax. That's my big brother, Brian," Klaryse said. "Fair warning: He's kind of a dick."

Brian marched toward the driver's side door and threw it open. "I knew it! I knew you'd have him! I recognized all your ghost accounts with all that bullshit information. What the hell do you think you're doing?"

"Oh, Brian," Klaryse said. "Can you stop being my big brother for a second?"

He appeared to be a year or two Klaryse's senior, but his eyes belonged to someone much older. There was a shadow of pain in those bulging eyes that usually only appears after a few decades of getting one's ass kicked by life.

Brian shoved a finger in my face. "He cannot be here. We're in enough financial trouble as it is without a lawsuit from those nutjobs in the Historical Preservation Society."

It was starting to concern me that I had yet to encounter a single person who didn't already know who I was.

"I didn't *bring* him here," Klaryse said. "I'm just trying to help him maintain a low profile. What's the problem?"

"You're harboring an illegal time immigrant! Jesus, when are you going to start acting your age?" Brian's left palm blinked red and emitted a high-pitched *beep*. "Great. Now you've gone and cost me ten credits!"

I had learned long ago not to get in the middle of two squabbling siblings, so I stepped out of the car and left Klaryse and Brian to duke it out. Personally, I thought Klaryse was doing an excellent job of acting her age. She was rash and reckless and irresponsible like every other twenty-something I had ever known.

I returned to the hood and inspected the oily mess to occupy myself while the siblings decided my fate. It didn't look like a total loss. I certainly wasn't a mechanic or anything, but I had driven enough POS cars in my day to know how to get a beater back up and running (as long as the vehicle hadn't melted or turned into a pile of cheese curl dust). Eventually, Brian joined me at the front of the car.

"Jesus, this thing is a mess," I said.

His left palm flashed and beeped again.

"Careful! I'm not made of credits, caveman!"

Again, for my own sanity's sake, I ignored him and focused on the immediate problem at hand. "I think it might be a dead battery. It's just a cheap Walmart battery in there. Only a few months old, though. Or it could be the alternator. Simple fixes."

Brian's face crumbled into a look of disgust that would have been appropriate had I said I knew a prayer that would fix the engine. He grabbed my arm and dragged me away from the open hood.

"C'mon. We gotta go before someone spots you."

"But what about the car? Don't you want to call a tow truck or something?"

"Don't be stupid. The Scrapper will be by in a few minutes to junk the thing."

"But I thought it was brand new?"

He dragged me over to a banana yellow Gremlin and shoved me into the backseat. Klaryse was already sitting back there diddling with her iPalm.

"Brian agreed to take you back to our place until we can figure out what to do with you," Klaryse informed me with a squeal.

I had no idea whether that was good news or bad news.

Brian jumped into the driver's seat and pushed a button on the Gremlin's futuristic dash. He pressed it three times before the thing finally started.

"Sweet ride," I said to Brian. "My father used to drive one back in the 80s."

"Thanks. Got it at Walmart for thirty store credits."

And then we chugged off. We were only a block down the road when the earth seemed to quake and a loud rumble erupted behind us. I turned and spotted what could only have been The Scrapper. It was a huge metal beast, the size of a dump truck and the width of a tank. The front of the vehicle consisted of two huge metal jaws lined with dozens of metal shark teeth. The Scrapper rumbled toward the Pinto, opened its jaws wide, and devoured the vehicle in two violent bites.

We drove through the destitute streets, which were sparsely populated by pill-popping iPalm viewers and abandoned vehicles, without incident. The towering high rises that disappeared into the smog created an intense feeling of claustrophobia, which was only magnified by the complete lack of grass and trees. With each block, the buildings shrank and degenerated and grew more dilapidated. The number of smashed windows increased. The smell of sewage and old cabbage seeping into the car grew stronger.

The buildings gave way to shacks, and then the shacks to makeshift shanties, and then we were surrounded on all sides by ramshackle tents. This wasn't just a tent city, this was a tent metropolis! The tent empire was abuzz with activity: Children weaved in and out of the tents playing tag, men and women in rags sat around raging fires laughing and talking, and the dogs and cats seemed to be just as numerous as the humans.

"Why would you take us through the Prole District?" Klaryse asked her brother.

There was fear in her voice.

"It's the only place the camera drones don't have regular runs. If we're spotted with your troglodyte friend, we're finished."

"Why's it called the Prole District?" I asked.

"It's from some book or something. Don't make eye contact with *anyone*."

The denizens of the Prole District wandered aimlessly through the streets like wayward sheep, forcing Brian to slow to a near crawl. Finally we came to an abrupt halt to accommodate what appeared to be a highly competitive dice game in the middle of the street. Brian honked the horn, but the players in the street appeared indifferent to the car's objections.

"Goddamn street rats," Brian growled. "I'm tempted to just run these maggots down."

I tried to stare straight ahead—God knows I tried—but the entire shanty town was too damn interesting to ignore. My eyes got away from me, and as they scanned the hustle and bustle of the tent city, they made contact with the bloodshot eyes of a bearded man wrapped in a stained bed sheet. He sort of half-ran, half-stumbled toward the car, noticeably dragging one leg behind him.

Klaryse shielded her face. "OhmyGodohmyGodohmyGod!"

The bearded man smooshed his cheek against the window, pressing what looked like a debit card against the glass.

"Spare some credits, young man?"

"Drive!" Klaryse screamed. "*They're asking for things!*"

"I—I can't!" Brian yelled back. "They've got us closed in!"

Other derelicts quickly filled in behind the bearded man, all waving debit cards and dragging one leg behind them. Soon, every window was blocked by the dirt-encrusted face of a Prole and a debit card. I glanced from the debit card in their hand to their actual hands.

No iPalms.

I pressed my left hand against the window. "Sorry. Couldn't help even if I wanted to."

When they saw I was iPalm-less, the Proles scoffed and spat and quickly dispersed.

"*Shiiiit*," the old man said. "Ain't nuttin' 'ere but paupers in rich man's digs."

The mob marched off without so much as a stumble. A few children remained once the adults had dispersed. They were thin as twigs, their dirty tunics hanging off their frail limbs. One pointed to her mouth and made prayer hands at me.

"Do you have anything to eat in this car?" I asked.

Klaryse pressed a button on the dash. A bag of unsalted Walmart brand pretzels appeared from a tiny compartment in the back of the driver's side seat. I pressed a button on the door and the window evaporated. I threw the bag out the window to the children. The children became a hurricane of gnashing teeth and scratching claws as they fought for ownership of the bag. The bag exploded, sending the pretzels into the dirt. The children threw themselves to the ground and scooped handfuls of pretzels and dirt into their mouths.

"Hey! What did you do that for?" Klaryse asked. "Those were for you!"

"They looked hungry."

"They're Proles. They'll never learn to take care of themselves if you just give 'em stuff. Feeding them is pointless. They're going to die anyway."

"Not today they won't."

Klaryse suddenly burst out laughing. The outburst was so sudden I jumped. "Of *course* you would do that. That is *such* a Jonathan Savage move! Why am I surprised?"

"Yeah, he's an idiot," Brian said. "Now, we have to get out of here before the rest of these cockroaches think we're running some sort of charity."

He plowed through the roadblock of destitute humanity, nudging the rest of the Proles out of the way with his bumper.

We continued to roll through the Prole District, and it became clear just how desperate these people's lives were. There was an entire city block of nothing but overflowing Port-o-Johns. Lines fifty people long stretched out in front of vans serving some sort of soup or chili. A little girl carried the decapitated head of a doll.

"So much trash," Brian said, referring to the Proles. "Maybe if they got off their lazy asses and got a job, they wouldn't have to live in this squalor."

I was about to ask where so many people were going to work, but that's when I saw *IT*.

Looming on the horizon, surrounded by a thick curtain of smog, stood the largest structure I had ever seen. It towered high into the clouds and stretched out several football fields in length. With all the activity surrounding it, the structure could have been a gargantuan beehive, hundreds of people pouring in and out of multitudes of entrances and exits. Between us and the colossal monstrosity lay a half mile of asphalt. It took my brain several attempts to convince itself that this ocean of asphalt was a parking lot. The giant neon letters hanging on the front of the building made it fairly obvious what it was, but I still had to ask the question.

"What the hell is *that*?"

Klaryse glanced over, her eyebrows raised. "It's Walmart."

Chapter IV

Eventually, I was able to persuade Klaryse to provide me with an abbreviated history lesson on why Walmart was now the only commercial entity in the country. It was clear she was more interested in her iPalm than enlightening me about the world I had stumbled into, but she consented and dumped the cliff notes version of the past fifty years into my lap.

As she explained it, the Re-Recession in the 20's continued to deteriorate until the Trump administration eliminated all business regulations in 2029. A brief resurgence in prosperity known as the De-Re-Recession occurred until the economy totally collapsed in '31 (an event most referred to as the Re-De-Re-Recession) after China finally claimed victory in its decades-old trade war against the United States. After that, most Americans couldn't afford to shop anywhere but Walmart, so the retail chain flourished while other American companies went the way of the dodo. Walmart took over *everything*. Online retail, brick-and-mortar, the automobile industry, pharmaceuticals, *everything*."

"Wait … we *lost* the trade war with China? How could that happen?"

"Arrogance," Klaryse said. "We thought we were more important on the global stage than we actually were. Trump's diversion war with Iran dragged us further and further into debt. The United States sold China more and more of that debt, thinking their economy was linked to ours, but when those *emerging markets* we'd been talking about for so long finally emerged, they didn't need us anymore. China sold off the debt, interest rates skyrocketed, and the dollar collapsed. The yuan became the global currency, China continued to prosper by trading with the rest of the world, and we got left behind."

"That's awful."

"It got worse. China froze us out of the global market until the country was on the brink of total economic collapse. We dumped our remaining assets into winning the war in Iran until America finally went bankrupt. China agreed to bail us out but only if we agreed to become a Chinese province."

"America was a Chinese province?"

Klaryse nodded sadly. "For almost a decade. It was the first ever hostile takeover of an entire country. Those were dark days. I hated learning all those stupid little drawings."

"So what happened?"

"What always happens in a capitalist economy. The big fish kept swallowing the other big fish until only Walmart remained. Eventually, Walmart became so big it was able to buy the country back in the summer of '48. Without Walmart, we'd still be eating nothing but rice and performing well on standardized tests."

The city was suddenly cut off by a rusty ten-foot fence, surrounding a massive estate with an old, crumbling mansion set high on a hill. The estate grounds were the first place I had seen grass—albeit brown—since arriving in 2076. Brian pulled the car up to the main gate, where the name *Goldstein* was etched in rusted letters.

"This is home," Klaryse said.

The mansion dated back to a time when the Goldsteins and America were more prosperous, but it had seen better days.

"Some home," I said.

"Mommy and Daddy were fairly well off," Klaryse explained. "Unfortunately our funds are drying up so we had to let all the servants go. Brian and I maintain the place ourselves."

The gate seemed to creak open on its own. Brian drove the Gremlin up the long, winding drive, doing his best to avoid the minefield of potholes and cracked asphalt. We circled around the side of the house and parked at a back entrance.

Behind the mansion, a garden now grew nothing but weeds, and a three-tier fountain was crumbling beneath the watchful eye of a cherub with his tiny cock in his hand, but it looked like his cock had dried up long ago.

Klaryse dragged me toward the entrance, but Brian cut us off.

"Sister, do try to keep our guest's arrival quiet until we can figure out what to do with him. M'kay?"

"Mum is the word, dearest brother."

The back entrance led to a large, musty sitting room. Most of the furniture looked to be early 20th Century, which really messed with my mind because I was trapped in the future in a house trapped in the past. The lack of house servants was obvious, too. A thick layer of dust covered most of the furniture, and the paisley wallpaper was faded and peeling.

"C'mon," Klaryse said. "We spend most of our time on the lower level. It's a bit more modern."

Her hand found mine. Her soft skin melted into my palm, and I had to remind myself I was probably old enough to be her grandfather.

She led me down a long hallway lined with portraits of old men whose sideburns grew in length and intensity the further we traveled. Then there was a sharp left turn, and Klaryse threw open a door, revealing a metal spiral staircase leading down to what at one time probably used to be the servants' quarters. She shoved me forward, and I took the lead on the descent.

My footsteps clinked with each step down the spiral staircase. The basement was completely dark, so I let my hand glide along the handrail and guide me to the bottom. The only light was a soft glow behind me, which I assumed was coming from a flashlight, but, when I glanced back, Klaryse had her left hand raised and a soft glow was emanating from her iPalm.

"You forget to pay the electric bill or something?" I joked.

A chuckle from somewhere in the darkness erased my smile. We were not alone.

The room erupted in light. Half a dozen young women, shrieking at the top of their lungs, surrounded me, their voices crawling up my spine and testing the dexterity of my eardrums. They closed in, clawing at my hair and clothes, and I knew right then and there that I was going to be killed by a pack of wild Barbie Dolls.

The basement transformed into a garden of grabbing hands and quivering uvulas. I pushed through the shrieking horde but didn't get far. I was stopped by—*me*. The walls were covered, nearly wallpapered, in giant posters of my likeness.

There I was, decked out in a tux, holding hands with Millie in her wedding dress.

There I was, commanding the kitchen on my first big catering job.

There I was, brushing my teeth before bed.

"Jesus, what is all this?"

The palm of the shrieking girl closest to me blinked red.

"Oh—my—God! Jonathan Savage just cost me ten credits! How amazing is that?!"

"And he told a lame joke!" another screamed into my ear. "You forget to pay the electric bill? *Classic* Savage!"

I found Klaryse in the sea of shrieking estrogen, screaming and yelling as much as the rest of them.

"Klaryse, what the hell is going on?"

"I invited your fan club over!"

"What happened to keeping things quiet?"

"It's *only* the charter members."

The girls shoved me onto a piece of furniture that looked like an abstract artist's idea of a giant pink banana. I sank down into it like a beanbag chair and found that I sank so far down I couldn't get out of it on my own. The girls piled in around me, forcing me to sink even further into the banana.

One shoved a poster toward me.

"Can you sign this for me, Savage?"

Another shoved a car decal of my face into my actual face.

"Oh, can you sign this for *me*? Pretty, pretty please?"

I batted each object away as it came. "I'm not signing anything!"

A busty redhead pushed through the crowd and lifted her puke green tunic. "Can you sign *these* for me, Savage?"

"Anyone got a pen?"

Klaryse pulled the redhead away by her auburn locks and quickly asserted her dominance over the group. She scratched and clawed and bit and tore at the girls until they created enough room for me to finally breathe.

"Ladies, we need to control ourselves. There will be enough time for signing and photos and everything else. First thing's first, though. Savage, we have to get you out of those clothes."

The suggestion elicited a chorus of cackles from the girls and a long extended *Whoooo*.

I was still wearing my catering duds, which were about fifty years past their expiration date. I understood the point Klaryse was making (and it wasn't nearly as lascivious as the other girls took it). Everyone in the future seemed to be dressed in the same tan and puke green tunics and baggy parachute pants, so my outfit made my presence even more conspicuous.

Klaryse helped me out of the quicksand sofa and walked me into the corner of the room to a machine that looked suspiciously like an old-school popcorn maker. She called it *The Gopher*. A scan gun hung from the side of the machine, and inside the glass case where a kettle should have been, there was a metal disc that contained holes like a sieve.

"We'll just order you some clothes from Walmart," she said. "You'll fit right in."

She tapped away on her iPalm, and then scanned it with the scan gun. The machine buzzed into action. The metal disc flashed blue and what appeared to be a swarm of miniature gnats floated out of the sieve-like holes. The swarm buzzed around furiously inside the glass case, trailing what appeared to be silk webs wherever they went. It took me a few seconds to realize the material the swarm farted out was actually thread.

In only a few seconds, the outline of a tunic appeared inside the case and in another minute the outline was filled in, leaving a tan tunic like I had seen most of the men wearing at the Time Port. Klaryse pulled it out and handed it to me and then a pair of parachute pants was created in the same manner.

It felt strange to hold clothes that had seemingly been created from nothing. God lived in that popcorn machine. I wanted to ask how the machine worked, but then I remembered that I still had no idea how my toaster worked so I kept my question to myself.

"Nanobots," Klaryse said, answering the unasked question. "The machine uses nanobots to create whatever you order. The Gopher made online shopping obsolete. It's what Walmart used to put Amazon out of business once upon a time."

I retired to the bathroom to change away from the prying eyes of my fan club while Klaryse occupied the girls with the telescreen (whatever the hell that was). The uniform certainly had an Asian flavor to it. The shirt had a long, slender waist complete with big, metal buttons and a high collar. The pants were baggy and lacked a zipper. As I placed the tunic over my head, it seemed to wrap around my body, fitting perfectly to my frame.

I fully expected to be mobbed when I exited the bathroom, but Klaryse and her shrieking shrews were piled onto the banana sofa staring at the wall, which was projecting a picture like a giant television screen. The picture resolution was flawless, and the words that appeared on screen popped out as if in 3D. Neon yellow letters zoomed across the screen one-by-one until they spelled out *The Best of "Getting Savage with Jonathan Savage."*

Then the telescreen blinked into a very familiar living room. I recognized the interior of my home almost immediately. There was the familiar sound of a body slamming against a door thinking it would be unlocked, followed by the sound of someone fumbling with keys. The door swung open, and there I was, larger than life. Millie entered the picture, wiping her mouth with the back of her hand, her hair mussed and wild. TV Me shoved my coat into Millie's hands.

"Take this," TV Me said. "I'm about to shit my pants. That Chow's we had last night ripped a hole in my intestine or something."

The girls on the banana giggled while real-time me did my best to melt into the wall.

As soon as the sound of my footsteps faded, the closet door swung open and some suave-looking shirtless Spanish guy popped out and took my wife into his arms. Then Millie—my wedded wife—opened her mouth and the shirtless Spaniard shoved his tongue down her throat.

I watched all this in silence knowing that all this was going on with TV Me just a couple feet away, sitting on the crapper while my wife sucked face with a stranger.

"She is such a whore," the redhead whisper-yelled across the banana.

"Yeah, him, too," Klaryse agreed. "Although I like him better than Maurice."

"Maurice?" I said. "Who the hell is Maurice?!"

The slobberfest continued and even escalated to some heavy dry-humping through Millie's sweats until it was interrupted by a flushing toilet. Millie opened the front door and shoved the Spanish guy outside, doing her best to put herself back together before my return.

Unfortunately for me, I did return and delivered a line that I was well aware was coming (because I had been the one who originally said it), but there was no way to prevent it from coming. All I could do was brace myself.

TV Me entered the frame zipping my pants. "God, that Chinese has my asshole singing. I'm going to have to pitch a tent up there because I'm going to be living on that toilet tonight."

The giggling in the room reached ear-piercing levels.

Then TV Me leaned in for a kiss. I begged, pleaded, prayed for him to reconsider, but it was pointless. I already knew the ending to this story. TV Me leaned in and delivered a deep kiss to those same lips that, seconds before, had been licked furiously by some Spanish dude. As the two larger-than-life characters embraced, the camera captured a close-up of Millie's face and that bitch looked straight into the camera and winked.

"Enough!" I shouted. The girls whipped around and saw me standing there watching the wall. "Please, turn it off!"

The telescreen faded to black, but that wink remained, scarred into my memory.

"What the hell was that?" I asked. "I mean, it was me, but—"

"It's a clip from your show, *Getting Savage,*" Klaryse said matter-of-factly. "You're a huge star!"

"But that wasn't a show. That was my *life.*"

"But your life *is* the show. It's a reality show."

"But I don't even live in this time period!"

"It's a *historical* reality show. Lots of famous people from the past have one. George Washington, Martin Luther King Jr., Elvis. We send people from our time back to the past to mess with 'em. They're the most popular shows on television!"

As Klaryse explained, Millie was an actress sent back in time to make my life a living hell for other people's entertainment, a sort of Terminator in high heels.

One might think that playing such shenanigans in the past would have massive repercussions on the present, but that was not the case. Altering the past actually had no effect on the present. Changing anything in the past creates a parallel time strand that will then lead to its own, altered future completely separate and self-contained from the future the time travelers come from.

Since the act of traveling back to the past in itself represents an alteration, one could travel back to the past, step on the first fishfrog that crawled out of the primordial ooze and travel back to one's departure year without changing a thing. Time was just one giant playground one could mess with without ever suffering even the slightest repercussions … as long as one has the coordinates for the original timeline. Apparently, the first time-travelers found that out the hard way.

The science behind the whole production didn't interest me as much as the fact that my entire life was a lie, a sham, a mockery.

Klaryse walked me over to the banana sofa, and the girls huddled in close to comfort me.

"I'm a sideshow attraction," I muttered. "My whole life has been manipulated and controlled to make me look like a fool."

I tried to digest the fact that my life had been sabotaged for the entertainment of millions, maybe billions (I wasn't sure how popular I was), but each time I tried to swallow the information, I choked.

"I just can't believe you didn't realize what was going on," the redhead said. "I mean, it seemed pretty obvious at times. I thought for sure you were in on the whole thing."

"How the hell could I have guessed I was on a futuristic reality show?!"

"Yeah, but you had to know *something* was going on. How about that time you woke up in the middle of the night, went to pee, and found that naked guy hiding in the shower? You just went back to bed like nothing happened!"

"I thought I was dreaming!"

Red giggled. "That was no dream. Millie and Caleb were having sex in the bed next to you for, like, twenty minutes before you finally woke up!"

"Leave him alone," Klaryse said. "Of course he didn't know. He's a good person, a *trusting* person. It's totally genuine. I've seen it. He may be totally oblivious and painfully unobservant, but he's a *good* person. That's him. That's Jonathan Savage."

The more I thought about it, the more the whole thing did make a lot of sense. The random clouds of cologne floating around the house, the constant changing of the sheets, the naked guy hiding in the shower. The clues had all been there, but I couldn't see them—or wouldn't. Millie always accused me of being Mr. Oblivious, a passive observer of my own life. Maybe she had been trying to warn me.

"Wait," Red said. "Now that Savage knows about the show, does that mean the show is, like, over?"

"He did almost die a couple times," another girl said.

"I didn't like where the show was going anyway," Klaryse said.

I asked what she meant.

"Oh, the whole Julia storyline they were starting."

"Julia? I would hardly say she was significant enough to warrant a storyline."

Klaryse shared a look with the other girls, who instantly broke into another giggle tirade.

"She was a plant and an obvious one. Why do you think Millie was sex starving you? She was setting you up. You and Julia were going to continue your harmless flirting until eventually it would escalate, and, because you're so miserable with Millie, you'd bite. Millie would catch you in some compromising position, and you'd be her eternal bitch forever."

"You should listen to her," Red chimed in. "She called Millie's miscarriage a month before it happened."

The mention of Millie's miscarriage opened a deep wound. She'd had a miscarriage last year, and the loss had cut pretty deep. The casual mention of a subject I hadn't even shared with my parents felt like a kick right to the gut. Millions had watched me cry in the bathroom while I tried to summon the courage to force a smile and tell Millie everything was going to be OK.

And it hadn't even been real. The wife. The miscarriage. Any of it.

I held up my hand for a short reprieve, which, surprisingly, was granted. The circle of estrogen expanded, allowing me some breathing room. If I had known I was a popular television star, I would have shaved more often and eaten less Chinese. The realization that I was a joke across time rattled around in my head, but then an obvious question slapped me across the face.

"OK, wait," I said. "I get the whole historical reality show and everything, but all the other people you mentioned—Washington, MLK, Elvis—were famous. So why would a nobody like me have one?"

The girls' faces lit up, and they sang a chorus of *He doesn't know! He doesn't know!*

"Please!" I shouted over the shrieks. "Can someone please just tell me, for Christ's sake?!"

But the only answer I received was the basement walls exploding in a blast of cement and wallpaper. The gleeful shrieks transformed into shrieks of terror as SS poured into the basement carrying their very threatening paintball guns. The uniformed thugs pushed and kicked their way through the girls as if they were made of papier-mâché.

The SS agent with the fanciest uniform screamed something in German, and two SS thugs wearing contraptions that looked like vacuum cleaners on their backs grabbed me, one on each side. Then we were hovering over the basement floor and out the hole they had created when they first blasted into the basement. Outside was a rotorless helicopter hovering soundlessly just feet off the ground. The SS thugs tossed me inside and threw a black sack over my head, drowning me in darkness.

Not that it mattered. I knew exactly where I was going, and, if Klaryse was to be believed, I was being taken to the last person I wanted to see.

Chapter V

The hovercopter sped silently across the sky. From deep within my personal abyss, I called out for my captors to tell me why I had been taken, what the president wanted with me, and when I'd have access to a bathroom. They ignored me for the most part, and when they did answer, it was in German, which I did not speak.

My ride ended with the heart-in-my-throat feeling of a descent and then a slight thump as the copter landed. A sudden rush of air let me know the doors to the copter had opened, and then I was lifted and tossed through the air. I landed in a pair of muscular arms, and then arms on both sides carried me effortlessly at a steady pace while my feet dangled below. Doors opened and closed behind us after short exchanges in German. The change in the air temperature indicated I was indoors, and the hollow *clunk* of the boots on the floor confirmed my suspicion.

Finally, one last door opened and I was dumped onto the floor and freed from my restraints. The black hood disappeared. It took my eyes a few seconds to adjust to the light, but, when they did, I found myself in a room without a single corner: the Oval Office.

The room was, for the most part, just as I remembered it from my own era, except for a few key differences. The room was decorated in a purple and black motif that was very much to my own tastes, and, instead of any presidents' portraits adorning the walls, there were portraits of several

Bond girls—Honey Rider, Pussy Galore, Solitaire, Jinx Johnson—which was also much to my liking. The entire room was full of a strange aura, a feeling of history. Some of the most important decisions in history had been made in that room, and there I was in the thick of it.

I knelt a few short feet from the famous Resolute Desk adorned with the seal of the United States. The back of the desk chair faced me, turned so it faced the windows, but it was obvious the chair was occupied.

"Leave us," said a familiar voice from the chair.

The SS guards left, leaving me alone with the voice in the chair. I waited to be addressed or greeted or for pretty much *anything* to happen. When nothing did, I stood and continued to wait. The chair remained silent.

"Why was I brought here?" I finally asked.

No answer.

"What do you want from me?"

Again, no answer.

I assumed escape was not an option. The Nazi goon squad would be just outside the door. Besides, it was the freakin' White House! I figured it would be harder to get out of than a scuba suit. I accepted the fact that I was there until the president got whatever he wanted from me—or killed me.

"Who are you?" I asked.

"Ah, how existential," the chair said with a slight chuckle. Again, the voice sounded familiar, but I couldn't place it. "*Who am I?* The ultimate question."

"Is there a reason you brought me here?" I asked, trying to avoid philosophy 101.

"Eighth grade. The homecoming dance. Rose Tyler kept asking you to slow dance, and you kept telling her no because you had never slow-danced with a girl before. Finally, she dragged you out to the dance floor and you danced to "Chasing Cars" by Snow Patrol, but Rose danced so close you came in your pants halfway through the song."

"What?!"

"Yes, you came in your pants. Then you told Rose you weren't feeling well and left her without any further explanation. When you got home, you were ashamed but still managed to masturbate one last time before tossing the soiled boxers into a plastic bag and burying them in your mother's garden."

I stared at that chair in utter disbelief. After everything I had seen and experienced, one would think I'd be completely incapable of shock, but this shocked me more than any iPalm or insanely gigantic Walmart. The eighth grade homecoming dance was the single most humiliating moment of my entire existence, an event I had never spoken to anyone about—*anyone*. I had intended to carry that memory to my grave and even further if necessary.

"Have I been on television *that* long?" I asked.

"No," the chair said. "The reason I know about that mortifying encounter is—" the chair spun, revealing my own face staring back at me, "—because I, too, came in those pants."

I couldn't believe what I was seeing. It was like looking into a mirror, only the mirror added twenty years or so. The math made absolutely no sense, but neither did standing face-to-face with myself in the Oval Office. My brain raced to try to make sense of what I was seeing. I was the President of the United States—or maybe the President of the United States was me. Either way, there were two of me in the Oval Office, and one of them was very confused.

The other me moved out from behind the desk in the exact manner I would move out from behind a desk. As he drew closer, I noticed a large scar running diagonally across the left side of his face that I did not share. He stood in front of me, my mirror image, and then quickly smashed his right fist into his left palm, shouting, "Rock-paper-scissors-SHOOT!"

We both shot out our fists in the universal sign of *rock*.

"Rock-paper-scissors-SHOOT!"

Rock and rock.

"Rock-paper-scissors-SHOOT!"

Again, we both threw rock for a third time. We both laughed. The triple rock was a strategy I used back in elementary school to take down many a rock, paper, scissors challenger on the playground. My classmates used to think scissors was such hot shit, and *nobody* expected three rocks in a row.

My doppelganger (I'll refer to him as President Savage to cut down on confusion) and I shared a moment of perfect harmonization. The only feeling I can compare it to is when you look into a mirror and find you're wearing a little half-smile, and you shoot yourself a nod to let you and the reflection know you're both on the same team.

I studied his face and did the math for a second time, and, again, the numbers didn't add up to anything that made sense. He appeared to be in his mid-fifties, but he should have been well past his eightieth birthday.

"Not bad for 86, huh?" he asked, seemingly reading my thoughts. He shifted his face back and forth for my inspection. "Wish I could say it's *o-nat-ur-al,* but I had Fountain Surgery at 56. Old enough to reflect experience but young enough to avoid being labeled 'past my prime.' I'll have this face in my coffin."

He explained that Fountain Surgery was an extremely expensive vanity surgery invented in 2044 that froze an individual's outward appearance at whatever age they were at the time of the surgery and added ten to twenty years onto the average lifespan. Problem was that the surgery also made the recipient infertile, meaning people were sacrificing the next generation in favor of their own vanity.

"And the scar?" I asked.

"Assassination attempt. One of many."

We stared at each other, trying our best not to stand in the same position, but each time we adjusted we seemed to instinctively choose exactly the same stance. Arms crossed over our chest, then resting our weight on our right leg, then shifting to the left with our hands held behind our backs.

Finally, President Savage ushered me to the other side of the room, claiming we'd be more comfortable, but where he escorted me had no place to sit nor anything that would add to my comfort. He positioned me on a specific spot on the floor and then took a position five feet directly across from me. Then he clapped and a ping pong table rose up from the floor.

"Nice," I said.

Table tennis was kind of my thing back in high school. We had a table in the basement growing up, and I pretty much destroyed all my friends who dared pick up a paddle. Something told me, though, that the president and I would be fairly evenly matched. We played while we continued our conversation.

"This is all just so unbelievable," I said. "How can I possibly be President of the United States?"

"You're not. You're just some schmuck caterer."

"But isn't this my future? Isn't this what I'll become?"

The ball continued to *ping* and *pong* across the table. I knew exactly how the ball was going to come off the president's paddle, the spin that would be on the ball, and when he was going for a smash, and the president seemed to know every move I made before I made it. It had an eerily similar feeling to when I used to push the table against the basement wall and play against myself.

"Let's get something straight right from the start," President Savage growled. There was a change in the President's demeanor and suddenly I barely recognized him as my future self. "You are *not* me. And I am *not* you. And this is not *your* future. This is *my* reality. We are two separate entities that simply happen to share the same DNA make-up. Got it?"

The change in the president's tone was so surprising I surrendered the first point of the match. An alarm went off somewhere near the Resolute Desk, and the far wall lit up into a giant telescreen.

"Oh, excuse me for a moment," the president said. He had returned to his former, cordial self. "We're about to go to war in the Mid-Middle East."

"Oh, wow. Do you need me to step outside?"

"No, no. This will only take a few seconds."

On the telescreen, I expected to see tanks and jets and men in uniform, but the only thing on the screen was a series of numbers. It looked like a box score for a baseball game except where it should have listed hits and runs and RBIs it listed things like total soldiers, resources, and technology. The scoreboard was split in half with The United States on one side and The Mid-Middle East on the other. The numbers in the categories spun like a slot machine, and, a few seconds later, they stopped. Before I could make heads or tails of the numbers, a trumpet blared and the word *VICTORY!!!* exploded in red, white, and blue letters on the United States' side. Fireworks exploded outside the White House followed by loud, joyous marching band music.

"What the hell is that?" I asked.

"Victory parade."

"Victory parade?! You mean it's over? That was the whole war?"

"Of course," the President said. "You think these global conglomerates are going to allow millions of customers to go out and murder one another? Please. They just run the numbers in the United Nations supercomputers and they spit out a winner. Besides, the public doesn't have the attention span for long, drawn-out wars anymore so we've simply sped them up. These wars in the Mid-Middle East are good for a momentary diversion from unpleasant internal matters so we try to schedule one every now and then."

We returned to our game.

"I'm sorry. This is a lot to take in," I said. "I don't understand. How exactly could I—*you*—become president?"

The ball continued to *ping* and *pong* between us in perfect synchronization.

"Well, without spoiling too much of your life, it started with Trump's fourth term in office. Trump dropped the corporate tax rate to near 0% and jacked up taxes on small business owners and the middle class. He said he was protecting America's job creators. What he was really doing was eliminating their competition. My catering business went under. I had no job, no source of income. That's when fate came calling."

"What happened? Did you experience an existential enlightenment that placed you on the path of your one true calling?"

"Not exactly." He snatched the ball out of the air and held it, pausing for dramatic effect. "I got on TV."

It wasn't quite the earth-shattering revelation I hoped for.

He served the ball with some wicked topspin, and I barely managed to return it.

"I auditioned for a new reality show called *Who Wants to be a Congressman?* I had nothing else to do so I figured, what the hell? I was chosen to fill the 'pathetic white guy' trope and took up small business rights as the base of my platform. The winner of the show wasn't guaranteed a seat in Congress but would receive a million dollars of political support to run as a representative in the House. The exposure alone was enough to guarantee a victory."

"You got into politics because of a TV show?"

"It was better than sitting on the sidelines feeling sorry for myself. After Trump was elected president, there was little difference between politics and entertainment. My involvement on the show caught the attention of a small but vocal protest organization based in D.C. that opposed Big Business monopolies. They were called The Minutemen. Long story short, I won the competition, won a seat in the House of

Representatives and The Minutemen evolved into its own grassroots movement. We fought to preserve small business rights as mega-corporations like Walmart continued to swallow one another and consolidate power through Trump's fourth term and then into Don Jr.'s reign of terror. Of course, then the Chinese took over and everything went down the crapper."

"Yeah, but then Walmart bought back the country, right?"

President Savage laughed and his laughter grew and grew to the point I was able to sneak a point past him along the left side of the table.

"What's so funny?"

"Don't you get it? Walmart *is* the Chinese. Walmart buying back the country was a ruse to placate the American people. The American public may be obese, stupid, and naïve, but they are also proud. After nine years of Chinese rule, there were uprisings, riots, and civil unrest. For some reason, the metric system infuriates Americans and learning all those stupid little pictures? Forget about it! So to create the illusion of sovereignty, the Chinese partnered with Walmart and allowed Walmart to *buy back the country* and set up a puppet government. And the lie was just big enough to work."

President Savage served the ball back into play, and the shadow game continued.

"So, China and Walmart have been in bed together since the buyback?" I asked.

"Of course. Walmart's success meant millions of jobs for Chinese workers and became the cornerstone of their economy. China used its political influence to topple the other mega-corporations until only Walmart remained. America got Walmart prices and the quality to go with it."

"But why didn't the American public see through the facade of Walmart's buyback of the country? Seems like a fairly transparent scam."

"Because," President Savage said, "people were too busy staring into their phones to care. Once all the universities and public education were privatized and taken over by Walmart, that was the end of any semblance of intelligence in the country. Then the blanket legalization of narcotics in '52 became the final nail in the coffin of common sense. Basically what Walmart did was turn the entire country into a giant mining town. Because there was nothing but Walmart, everyone had to work for Walmart. Instead of paying people in dollars and cents, Walmart paid them with—"

"Store credit," I said, finishing my own sentence.

"Exactly. Not only is Walmart the only place anyone can work, but it's also the only place anyone can spend their money. Any money a worker makes gets recycled right back into the system, and then a large percentage of that money gets sent back overseas to the Motherland. Americans have become cattle, bred for the sole purpose of consumption."

My other self juked left but moved right and sent the ball rocketing across the center of the table for another point. Apparently, I had learned a few new tricks over the years. He tossed the paddle onto the table.

"C'mon," the president said. "I want to show you something."

He walked me back over to the Resolute Desk. He handed me a digital picture frame that showed a 3D video of my doppelganger standing on a stage in front of the Capitol Building. He stood sandwiched between a group of Chinese men and some dejected-looking white dudes.

"That's me and the Chinese Premier on the day of my inauguration. Saddest day of my life. To think that I was the only hope this country had for salvation."

There was a somber look in his eyes. I could tell our conversation was very therapeutic for him. These were things he hadn't been able to share with anyone before. It must have felt strangely cathartic to have an honest face-to-face with oneself.

"So how did Walmart's biggest opponent become the head of their puppet government?" I asked, trying not to allow him to wallow in the quicksand of his memory for too long.

"Well, like I said, the Chinese set up a puppet government after the Walmart buyback in '48. The Minutemen were forced to go underground. We developed a plan to infiltrate the puppet government, but in order to do that, I had to appear to betray The Minutemen. Unfortunately, the only way to appear to do that was to *actually* betray them. Several of our high-ranking officials were taken to The Tower of Walmart for … reprogramming."

"Reprogramming?"

"Don't ask. Anyways, I bided my time, served my Walmart overlords, and waited for my opportunity. Then I got nominated for president the same way candidates got nominated back in the early 21st Century: I made sure I appeared to be the least remarkable, least offensive, most brainless, and most loyal party member, and, once it came time for nominations and all the adulterers, drug addicts, inside traders, and pedophiles were weeded out, I was the only available candidate. Plus, it was one of the off years where they were electing white guys."

"Wait, are you a Democrat or Republican?"

"Neither. We did away with those party labels after the Chinese restructured the government. Now there's the Walmart Red Party and the Walmart Blue Party."

"What's the difference?"

"Not much really. Basically the Walmart Blue Party supports the use of in-store coupons and the Twalmart Red Party opposes it. Oh, and abortions. People are still crazy about abortions."

President Savage pulled out the chair behind the Resolute Desk and offered me a seat. "You wanna give it a whirl?"

It was an offer I couldn't refuse. I restrained the urge to run around the desk and walked briskly to join my older self. I lowered myself down into the chair and immediately felt the unbridled power surge through my ass cheeks. The view from that chair was one only a handful of individuals had enjoyed throughout history, and now the view was mine.

"Pretty nice, huh?" the president said. Then he continued his tale. "Anyway, I pledged my allegiance to Walmart and the Chinese, agreed to become their puppet, and they rigged the election to make certain I won. Little did they know that I planned to cut the strings. Shortly into my first term, I formed my own private military force from soldiers forced into obscurity after the Chinese disbanded our military and bunkered down here in the White House. That was back in '64. Been fighting to take back America ever since."

"Wait. Your own private military. You mean the SS?"

"Exactly."

"Can I ask you a question? Why do they look like Nazis?"

A smile spread across the president's face. "Because who's more intimidating than a freakin' Nazi?"

I thought it through and decided I was a genius.

President Savage plopped down in the seat in front of the desk so that we had essentially switched positions from earlier. The mirror had flipped.

"It all makes sense now," I said. "The reason everyone thinks you're such a homicidal tyrant. It's a frame job! Walmart is trying to turn the people against you. *They're* the ones behind the selection massacres!"

"Oh, no," the president said, "that's all me."

"Wait—what?"

I checked the President's pinkies to see if they were twitching, a tell I have when I'm bluffing. There wasn't so much as a flicker.

"Unfortunately, what I learned early on in my first term is that the American people are a liability. I tried to reason with them, win them over to my side, convince them that Walmart did not have their best interests in mind, but no matter what I said, Walmart could always yell *louder*. They control the media, the interwebs, the television stations. The people became the trees who believe the ax has their best interests at heart because it's made of wood. I couldn't compete with the money Walmart could throw around, so I decided to focus on a different kind of currency: fear. When the public started talking impeachment, I liquidated the Senate and implemented my population control selections. Not happy with the jobless rate? Well, then maybe what we need is fewer people because we sure as hell aren't getting more jobs."

"That … makes sense in a horrifying sort of way."

"Of course it makes sense. You get it. You understand. Everything I've done, I've done to take this country back from Walmart. The people wouldn't act so they needed to be punished. If the trees keep serving the ax, then I'll wipe out the forests so the ax has nothing to feed on. I've stripped the people of all their rights and wiped my ass with the Constitution. Most are too busy staring at their phones or popping pills to even notice. They've gotten exactly the kind of president they deserve."

"So, you—*I*—am the monster that people say?"

"Sometimes to defeat a monster, one must become a monster. Don't you see? If America is to be liberated, Walmart must be defeated and good is too weak and naïve to ever defeat evil. No, the only thing that can defeat evil is a greater evil, a cleansing evil, evil done for the right reasons. And I have become that evil."

My stomach turned in on itself. If I'd had lunch at any point over the past fifty years, I would have recycled it all over the Oval Office. My biological twin was a homicidal lunatic, which meant *I* was a homicidal lunatic. I couldn't even explain away his misdeeds by saying he was insane because that would mean admitting my own insanity. There was something dark inside me I had yet to uncover, and I wanted it out.

"There has to be another way," I said, flailing for something. "There has to be another way to unite these people against Walmart instead of *killing them?*"

He laughed deep and gritty. It was a stranger's laugh. "I wish there was, but the truth is that these red, white, and blue imbeciles *love* the Walmart. It provides them with the *things* they love so much. People gladly volunteer for slavery as long as they have their techno gadgets and their reality television shows and their medication to distract them from how miserable their lives are. As long as they're entertained, people will sit in their invisible chains for eternity. They've sold their souls to the gods of consumerism. The only thing you can do is make the public so afraid *not* to act that they're forced into action. The choice is simple: Rise up or die."

The comfort I had felt earlier staring into the face of my future had completely evaporated. This wasn't me sitting across the desk. Hell, it wasn't even someone I liked. I sat across from a complete stranger.

"I think I could use a drink," I whispered.

"I had Walmart over a barrel my first two terms," the president said, ignoring my request. "The public trembled in my presence. They were on the brink of rising up like a tsunami and washing Walmart into oblivion. But then early into my third term, Walmart unleashed its secret weapon."

"Are you not going to get me a drink?"

"How about some entertainment instead?"

The president snapped the fingers on his left hand (which did not have an iPalm implant) and the screen blinked back to life.

And there I was.

I stood in the kitchen with Millie. She held a milk carton in her hand. The sound was muted, but it was obvious from her body language she was upset. She threw the milk carton on the kitchen floor and stepped on it, sending milk splattering all over. I stared at the mess on the floor for a few seconds before grabbing a dish rag and dropping to my knees to clean it.

I remembered the argument well (I had lived it, after all). Millie had been upset because she had asked for 2% milk and I had brought home 1%.

"Pathetic. Absolutely pathetic. What you've allowed that woman to do to you. It's sad."

And then it all made sense—why I was a reality show star, why I was famous, why anyone would bother to go out of their way to take a dump on my existence.

"I'm the secret weapon. The show, my life. It's a political smear campaign."

President Savage touched his finger to his nose. "A reality show helped me rise to power, and now Walmart is using another reality show to steal it from me. Your reality show was created to make you look like a joke so the public would, in turn, think that *I* was a joke. Without that fear, my control over the masses is in jeopardy. Hell, the public's calling for an actual election this year! For the past three years, my grip on this country has been weakened each time Millie promised you sex on your birthday and pretended to fall asleep, each time she forced you to skip poker night to give her a foot massage, each time she deleted one of your Bond movies."

I wish I could say I took the news well, but, more accurately, I took the news like a sledgehammer to the gonads. The fact that Millie had been introduced into my life with the sole purpose of humiliating me was bad enough, but now that I knew the whole thing actually had nothing to do with me, it was even worse. I was a pawn in a game I wasn't even playing.

When I looked up, the chair in front of the desk was empty. The president stood near a hollow hole in the wall housing a Gopher machine like the one Klaryse had back at the mansion. The Gopher unleashed its microwave *ding,* and the President retrieved whatever it was that he had sent for. His body obscured my view so it was impossible to tell what it was.

"I wish I had never come here," I said. "Even if the show continued and my life was miserable and I didn't know about it. Not knowing would have been better."

"It's too late for that now," President Savage said with only a tinge of disappointment in his voice. "If it's any consolation, that show has been the bane of my existence, as well. I watched the fear I had worked so hard to instill in the American people fade, to be replaced with pity and shame. Then something strange happened. That pity turned into love. The more Millie came to humiliate and berate you, the more they admired you. But not me. You became your own entity, something separate, and the more they grew to love you, the more they despised me because you were humble and generous and loving and I ... wasn't. Finally, I realized there was only one solution."

"What solution?"

President Savage sighed. "Suicide."

"You tried to kill yourself?"

He turned back to me, my slightly older mirror image. In his hand, he held some sort of ray gun.

"No, you idiot. I tried to kill *you.*"

Chapter VI

The Commander and Chief approached, ray gun held firmly in his hand—*my* hand. I scrambled out of the chair and backpedaled toward the windows that faced the White House lawn. Walmart's smiley face logo grinned back at me from the side of the firearm.

"You should feel honored," he said. "This is the first time I've ordered something from Walmart in almost thirty years. Of course, we have to have your death traced back to those smiley-faced bastards for this whole thing to work. In the game of politics, everything has to be spun in one's favor, even one's own death."

"Wait," I said. "You can't kill me. You'll screw up the time stream continuum … or something."

The gun rested comfortably in the president's hand, like he had done this before. "Please, you know as well as I that any effect on the past has no consequence on the present. Hell, I don't even think me killing you is against the law. At least no one has ever been prosecuted for his own suicide."

"Man, I turned out to be a real asshole!"

The president paused in front of the Resolute Desk. "You know, I was excited when I thought I was going to get to watch you die on live television, but this is soooo much better. Not many men get to be present for their own deaths and live to tell the tale."

And suddenly it all made perfect sense.

"*You're* the one who sent Mustachio back to kill me!"

"Mustachio? You mean Booth?"

"Is Booth the mustachioed psycho who's been trying to kill me for the past fifty years?"

"You don't realize who he is, do you?"

I shook my head.

"When I was trying to decide how to kill myself, I figured the best man for the job would be someone with experience in presidential assassinations. That left me with a very short list of potential applicants."

"No way ..."

President Savage flashed his eyebrows. His pinkies remained still.

"You mean to tell me that the man trying to kill me is—" I studied my doppelganger's face to see if there was any hint of humor. "—John Wilkes Booth? I'm being hunted by *John Wilkes Booth?*"

"Hey, I figure if you want a job done right, you gotta hire the best. So I sent my men back in time to recruit Booth, convinced him that Abraham Lincoln would eventually be reincarnated 200 years in the future, hooked him up with some more modern weaponry, and sent him on his way. Of course, he's done nothing but botch repeated attempts to blow you up and disintegrate you, but what he lacks in skill, he certainly makes up for in persistence."

I couldn't help feeling a sense of pride knowing that the same man who assassinated one of the greatest presidents in history was also attempting to take my life. At least I'd be in good company.

"Looks like I'll get a refund from Mr. Booth considering I'm doing the job myself. I was going to write it off as a job expense anyway."

He raised the ray gun and pointed it directly at my chest.

"Wait," I begged. "Don't do this. I never asked to be involved in any of this. All I ever wanted was to live a simple life and maybe get laid biweekly. Is that too much to ask?"

"Sitting on the sidelines doesn't make you less guilty, it just makes you a coward."

His finger caressed the trigger.

"Wait, wait, wait. What about this? You can't kill me unless you tell me what number I'm thinking of right now."

"It's 39."

"Damn it! I mean, no, uh, it's *not* 39."

President Savage suppressed a smile. "I never was a very good liar until I became a politician. I'm sorry, Jon. Consider yourself canceled."

As if being killed wasn't bad enough, the worst part of the whole thing was that that cheesy line was going to be the last words I ever heard.

The president pulled the trigger. The gun unleashed a blinding light that filled the Oval Office, and then I felt myself being hurled through space and time—falling, falling, with an ear-shattering *crash*. A cool breeze swirled and embraced my corpse like a blanket. Then that sudden feeling of falling just as suddenly and violently halted. My back slammed hard against a solid surface, crushing the air from my lungs.

I existed in silence, waiting for the cold embrace of death to clutch me tightly to its bosom. But that's when I realized my eyes were closed. I opened them and stared up into a gray abyss, and I knew I was dead. Then a crow flew directly overhead and crapped on my cheek, and I knew I was still alive.

I managed to roll over and look around. I was lying flat on my back on the White House lawn. My chest was smoking, and there was a hole burnt into the fabric of my tunic, but my skin and organs were exactly where I had left them.

I glanced back toward the White House. President Savage stared down at me from a hole in the shattered window.

"Damn it!" he yelled down to me. He tossed the still-smoking ray gun onto the lawn. "This cheap piece of shit was supposed to completely disintegrate you!"

"You get what you pay for!" I yelled back.

"That's true. Stay right there. I'm going to send some of my men down to get you and we'll try again, all right?"

My first instinct was to do exactly what he said, but then I realized how insane that would be and got up and hobbled off the White House lawn toward Pennsylvania Avenue. The cheers and big band music from the victory parade was faint and far off in the distance.

I expected the street outside the White House to be crowded with hordes of tourists snapping photos and vendors selling tiny American flags (made in China), but instead I found a deserted street. There wasn't even a fence separating the White House property from the street anymore, almost as if the president was daring someone to trespass. It confused me until I realized that fear is a better defense than any gate, wall, or moat.

I took off running and didn't stop until I reached a busy intersection on a street called Kardashian Avenue. The parade wasn't there, but the traffic was. A loud explosion erupted from somewhere back near the White House. I ran from taxi to taxi, praying one of them would open its doors to me, and then one did. Klaryse stuck her head out and waved me inside.

"Get in, Savage!"

The whole experience created a strong sense of déjà vu, but I eagerly jumped into the backseat since I was strongly opposed to dying. I fell in a heap onto Klaryse's lap and scrambled into the empty seat.

"Drive! Drive! Drive!" I screamed to the cabbie.

The cabbie did not drive, drive, drive, though. Instead, he turned around and examined me like someone had just dropped a deuce in his backseat.

"Watch your shoes on the seat, man," the driver said. He wore a tan newsie cap on top of his greasy hair. "You lucky Lady Klaryse made me stop for you o' else I kick your ass right outta this cab fer messin' up my seats."

"I'll buy you a whole new damn car. Just drive!"

"Where you 'spect me to go, boy?"

I immediately saw his point. Traffic was at a standstill. There was absolutely nowhere to drive, drive, drive to. We were trapped.

"Who the hell is this guy?" I asked Klaryse.

"Oh, this is Benny. He used to be our chauffeur until we had to let him go. I pay him to drive me around when Brian is being a dick and won't let me borrow his car."

I sat up and stared out the window back toward the White House. A swarm of SS marched down the street. I knew if they got to the cab before we drove off, Benny's cab would be my yellow coffin. The SS marched straight out into traffic and stomped down the avenue, scanning the interior of every vehicle they passed.

I realized what a fool I had been to actually think I could escape the tyrannical President Savage in his own backyard. His goons were going to find me and disintegrate me, and I'd be the first victim of unwanted suicide in the history of mankind. I slunk down in my seat, accepting my fate.

Klaryse and Benny didn't seem to understand the gravity of the situation. They sat patiently, bopping slightly to the music seeping into the cab. Klaryse was already busy typing away on her iPalm.

Benny glanced over his shoulder and saw me slouched down in the backseat. "What's your problem?"

"Oh nothing. Just expecting my impending death as soon as those SS reach this cab and turn me into sawdust."

Benny let out a raucous guffaw that filled the cab. "We see 'bout that." His fingers danced over the terminal in the center of his dashboard.

"What are you doing? Are we gonna fly out of here or something?"

"Ain't nobody gonna fly! Just sit tight. 'Ol Benny's got you."

In spite of Benny's assurance, I was still fairly certain I was a dead man. An SS guard held up traffic at the intersection ahead, and a team of goose-steppers were inspecting the car behind us. I closed my eyes and clicked the heels of my shoes together and prayed to wake up anywhere but 2076.

When I opened my eyes, I was still in Benny's cab and there were two SS agents outside the window, one standing on each side. The agent on the passenger side stared me directly in the face, and I couldn't help staring back. I waited for him to pull open the cab door and drag me across the hot asphalt.

But he didn't.

A look of disgust crossed the guard's face. He said something to the other guard in German, and then they both moved on to the next car. I couldn't believe my luck.

"They didn't see me," I said in astonishment. "They didn't see me!"

"Course they didn't," Benny said. "I got dis baby tricked out with a cloakin' device."

"Cloaking device? You mean we're invisible?"

"Not 'nvisible. You know how messed up you get drivin' 'round in some 'nvisible car? No, we ain't 'nvisible, we camouflaged. To those people out there this cab look like a minivan driven by a fatass woman eating a turkey leg with three kids hootin' and hollerin' in the backseat covered in their own shit, and ain't *nobody* wanna mess wit dat!"

He laughed, deep and hard, and this time, I joined him. A few minutes later, we were through the intersection, waved through by another SS guard, and on our way out of central D.C. It wasn't until we were safely out of downtown D.C. that I realized I had been holding my breath. I released it, and the joy I felt at still being among the living overwhelmed me.

"You came back for me," I said to Klaryse. I could barely believe it. "You saved my life!"

I threw myself across the backseat and planted a kiss on Klaryse's lips. It was only meant to be a quick thank you kiss, but then her lips found mine, then her tongue, and soon I was lost in a haze of strawberries and apricots. Eventually, I remembered I was kinda-sorta married and tried to pull away. Klaryse caught my lip in her teeth, drawing blood, and it took some effort to wrench it free.

"I just wanted to thank you," I said.

"Wow. Oh wow. You can't imagine how long I've dreamed of that moment." She wiped my sweat from the side of her face. "It was much sweatier than in my dreams."

I was ripe with my own stink, but it didn't matter. I was *alive!*

"How the hell did you know where I was?" I asked.

"After the SS crashed our party, it wasn't hard to figure out, but I did have some help." She reached under what was left of my tunic and removed a small black sticker from under the left armpit. "It's a stalker bug. Crazy girlfriends and suspicious wives use them to keep tabs on their men. I figured it might be a good idea to keep track of you. I'm just glad you found us because I had no idea how we were going to get you out of the White House. Most people who go in there never come out."

"And here I was thinking you were just some spoiled brat who wanted to show me off to her friends like some sideshow freak."

Klaryse laughed nervously and dipped her eyes back into her iPalm. "Well, I guess I feel kind of responsible for you now."

"Thank you. You've saved my life three times now. After how you snubbed those Prole children, I thought—Well, that doesn't matter because I was wrong. You're a good person."

Klaryse's fingers froze on the liquid screen. "What did you say?"

"I said you're a good person."

She seemed confused by this. "I'm a good person?" The words crackled on her tongue like Pop Rocks. "I've been called a lot of things in my life: a rich bitch, a spoiled brat, and an old nag, but no one has ever called me a good person."

"An old nag?" Now it was my turn to be confused. "Forget what other people say. You didn't have to come back for me, but you did, so thank you."

She didn't seem to know how to respond, so she didn't.

"Not to inta'rupt, but where 'xactly we headed?" Benny asked. "I figure we bouncin' outa downtown, but I can only go so far out before I need to start going into sometin' else."

Klaryse had clearly already thought about this because she had an answer immediately. "The only place that is off limits to the president and his goose-stepping thugs. We're going to Walmart."

Chapter VII

The Mecha-Walmart rose up huge and horrible on the horizon, its central tower disappearing into the smog. It seemed even more monstrous after passing through the meager dwellings of the Prole District. There were still questions to be answered—like why Klaryse had failed to mention that the homicidal president she so despised was my future doppelganger or why she was taking me to the evil empire that had sponsored my very public humiliation.

Still, I gave her the benefit of the doubt. After all, she was my savior … and she smelled like fresh strawberries and apricots.

The line of cars backed up nearly a mile from the entrance of the store so Benny dropped us off in the middle of the vast ocean of asphalt. He didn't even charge us for the ride. All he asked for was an autograph for his wife on his iPalm. I happily agreed. I had signed my name hundreds of times throughout my life, but that signature (my first as a celebrity) felt different. Now, there was weight to those scribbled, loopy letters. Now, my name meant something. Benny also provided me with a digital business card that automatically contacted him if I pressed my thumb on a sensor.

"Just in case you be needin' some wheels," he explained.

Klaryse and I became just two more bodies in a human landslide oozing toward the massive palace of consumerism. I immediately felt exposed among so many people since I was a national celebrity and had a giant hole burnt into my tunic, but most of the pedestrians' eyes were hidden behind the violet curtain of iLids or drowning in the liquid pool of iPalms. The problem was solved when a box literally fell out of the sky at our feet. I looked up in time to spot a drone buzzing back toward the building. Inside was a brand new tunic.

"On-the-go Gopher-free delivery," Klaryse explained. "Slow but still effective."

"So much for two-day delivery," I said.

"Two days?" Klaryse laughed. "Anything more than ten minutes is considered a crime."

I changed right there in the parking lot, and we continued our hike through the asphalt desert.

"What makes you think I'll be safe here?" I asked after we had traversed nearly a quarter mile in silence.

I had to repeat the question before Klaryse, who was also lost in her own iPalm, answered.

"The SS won't encroach onto Walmart's turf. It's kind of an unspoken agreement."

In my peripheral vision, I caught sight of a restored VW bus creeping through the crowd a few dozen yards behind us. While we were back in Benny's cab, I thought I had seen the same VW bus following us, darting through lights to keep up and every now and then, weaving behind stalled out vehicles to stay out of sight. Still, it was possible the people just happened to be heading to the Walmart, too (as most everyone else seemed to be).

By the time we were within half a football field's length of the store, my new tunic was saturated with sweat, and when I went to wipe my face, my hand returned smeared with blood. My nose was bleeding. The air quality around the store was horrendous. The air was thick, humid, and moist. Giant smokestacks sticking out of the top of the store vomited thick plumes of black smog continuously into the air. Many members of the mob even wore surgical masks as deterrents from the smog. Klaryse, I noticed, wore a small tan strip of plastic on her nose that seemed to be acting as some sort of filter.

"The air quality around here is shit. Doesn't the EPA exist anymore?" I asked.

"Sure." She pointed to the left side of the Walmart. "Level seven of building E."

We eventually reached the main entrance. The front of the store consisted of about a quarter mile of automatic doors. Hundreds of people entered and exited in a perpetual cycle of motion. The trademark smiley face loomed over the entrance like the sun, only the eyes were a bit more narrow and sinister looking than I remembered. And the coup-de-grace, standing in front of the entrance, greeting customers as they entered, was Jesus Christ himself.

Well, it wasn't really Jesus. It was some guy in a giant inflatable costume that was supposed to be Jesus in effigy. He looked like a Major League Baseball mascot one would find dancing on top of the dugout. He had a robe and beard and carried a sign that read, *Save Us ... from high prices!*

"What ... uh ... is Jesus doing here?" I asked.

Klaryse's iPalm lit up red and spat out a high-pitched *beep*.

"Shh," she commanded. "You can't say that."

"What?"

"Jesus," she said. *Beep!* "Great! Now you made me say it!"

"But why can't I say ... that guy's name?"

"Because Walmart owns the likeness rights to—that guy. He's their official mascot so they charge you even for saying his name aloud."

"They charge you for saying *Jesus*?"

Beep!

"Urgh! Yes! And since you don't have an iPalm, they're charging the closest person in proximity—me! Now, shut up! You just cost me thirty credits!"

We joined the mass of moving bodies entering the store at a steady ooze. Jesus shot me a big thumbs up as we passed, but I was more interested in the VW bus creeping toward the store reflected in mascot Jesus' big plastic eyes.

As soon as we stepped through the automatic doors, I realized that this Walmart was no mere store. No, it was the biggest damn commercial monstrosity I'd ever seen. The lobby made the Time Port look like a child's diorama.

An entire platoon of greeters welcomed us as we approached the central hub of the store. Most were in wheelchairs or hooked up to ventilators or could only move one half of their bodies. One of the greeters was actually lying face down on the floor, motionless. Besides the greeters, everything else in the store appeared to be automated.

The mob pushed us past the line of greeters and into the central hub where digital signs pointed shoppers in every possible direction—left, right, up, down, diagonal—toward an infinite number of products and services. There was an entire wing of the store dedicated to low-income housing (Klaryse described the apartments as basically coffins implanted into the wall). Instead of departments like *Furniture & Appliances*, though, the signs read things like *Automobiles*, *Emergency Room*, and *Mortgages* (all sub-captioned in Chinese, by the way).

Following the signs led to multiple elevators, escalators, movable walkways, and trams and trolleys. The entire interior of the building was a perpetual motion machine fueled by human beings.

"Do you mind if we do some shopping while we're here?" Klaryse asked. "I need to pick up a new car."

Instead of waiting for an answer, she grabbed my hand and dragged me in the direction of the *Automobiles* department. We were carried through the store on a moving walkway as wide as a freeway for a couple hundred yards. The walkway branched out every fifty yards or so in what appeared to be off-ramps to different departments. We passed departments like *Lawyers, Firearms,* and *Narcotics.* We took a ramp to an oversized elevator labeled Elevator 3-Z, which took us up eight or ten stories, and then dumped us onto another movable walkway.

While we were cruising along the movable highway, I caught Klaryse staring at me.

"What?"

"It's still so strange seeing you here in my world," she said. "You're different than I thought you'd be. Can I ask you a question?"

"Sure."

"Back in the Prole District, why did you give those kids that bag of pretzels?"

I thought maybe she was joking, but she wasn't. She wanted an actual answer.

"Because they looked hungry."

She shook her head in disbelief as if I had said something absurd. "You know, I thought maybe your whole *altruism thing* was just for the show, but it's genuine, isn't it? That's really you."

"How could it be for the show? I didn't even know I was on a show!"

She shrugged. "I've been thinking about those kids, ya know? They made me feel kind of bad."

"You should feel bad. That entire craphole you call the Prole District should make *everyone* feel bad."

I studied her face to see if what I was saying was making sense, but all I saw was the color drain from her cheeks.

"Hide your face!" she whisper-shouted at me.

I did. I held up my left hand in front of my face like I was staring at an iPalm until Klaryse told me it was safe to look up.

I glanced behind us. Two jacked up Asian dudes dressed in blue uniforms slipped into the distance on an opposing movable walkway. I spotted yellow smiley face patches on the sleeves of their uniforms.

"Store Security," Klaryse explained.

"I thought store security guards were old guys with beer guts and pepper spray."

"These guys are Chinese ex-military and not very nice. Now, c'mon! This is our exit."

We exited through a large corridor below an oversized *Automobiles* billboard, and then entered the car department, and, believe me, there was no need for a sign. The place was the size of an airplane hangar.

Five huge glass towers, stocked with six rows of automobiles (mostly 70s and 80s models) stretched from the floor to the ceiling. An automated elevator zipped around in each tower, retrieving the vehicles, and delivering them to their new owners basically like a giant car vending machine.

The ancient vehicles had confused me since I first stepped foot inside Klaryse's Pinto, but it was starting to make sense. Competition breeds innovation. Without competition, Walmart had simply begun to recycle older models from previous decades, reintroducing a different era's models every few years to create the illusion of progress. Why create anything new when you're the only show in town?

I stood, mouth agape, staring at the vehicle vending machines towering over me. Klaryse walked over, placed her fingers delicately under my chin, and closed my mouth.

"Remember, we're supposed to be hiding out—and shopping."

While Klaryse scanned the inventory on her iPalm, I was forced to use my inferior, non-digital eyes. The glass towers were rife with Gremlins and Hornets and Vegas and Pintos, and I even spotted a Plymouth Cricket three rows up. There were a few floor models scattered throughout the department, so I went to inspect the wares for myself while Klaryse staggered after me. Being the cheap bastard that I am, I went right to the digital sales tag on the window for a price on a Buick Apollo and what a found made my tightwad heart sing.

"Eighty credits?! This car costs eighty credits?"

Klaryse shrugged. When she looked up from her iPalm, her eyes were bathed in violet.

"I'm glad to see they finally got inflation under control."

"It's not that great of a deal considering you'll have to pay that much to fill the thing with gas for a week."

"These things still run on gas?"

"What else would they run on?"

"I don't know, hydrogen or garbage or dreams or something? We were transitioning away from gas when I left."

Klaryse giggled at my naïve ideas of innovation. "Walmart's top scientists proved that all that environmental nonsense—climate change and global warming—was nothing but politically-charged propaganda. A total hoax. Besides, now that we can travel back in time, we have access to all the natural resources we want. We just go back and steal them from the past. Problem solved."

She wandered around to the other side of the car to check the interior while I continued to scan the vehicle's vitals. I wondered what kind of warranty one got for eighty credits. Unfortunately, I never got that answer. I was too distracted by the two SS agents less than ten feet away, scanning the area. One lifted his gloved hand and danced his fingers across his left palm. A *beep* rose up from every customer's iPalm simultaneously in the department.

As the SS agents turned toward me, my ankles were squeezed together, and I fell to the floor and out of sight behind the vehicle. Klaryse lay under the vehicle, motioning for me to join her. I scrambled under the car just as the SS emerged into view. Klaryse held a finger to her lips and showed me her iPalm.

It was a picture of my face with the word **FUGITIVE** printed above it. We remained hunkered under the Apollo as the Secret Service agents continued to prowl through the department, scanning customers' faces with their iPalms.

"You said we'd be safe from the SS here," I whispered.

"I thought we would be. The SS *never* come into Walmart. The president must want you dead *real* bad."

"How did they know we were even here?"

"It would be a miracle if they didn't. There are cameras *everywhere*. Plus, they're probably tracking my iPalm now that I think about it. Fiddlesticks. Come on."

We slipped out from under the Apollo and duck-walked to the next floor model, a Fiat 127. We hunkered down behind the car while the SS agents marched to the far end of the hangar. A short Hispanic man walked by and glanced at us hiding behind the car.

I quickly whipped around to hide my face, but I turned too quickly, tripped over my own feet, and fell back into the car. A loud car alarm erupted from the Fiat, and then the first row of cars in the glass tower answered its call. The alarms climbed to the second level, then the third, until the entire tower of automobiles *beeped* and *buzzed* and *whooped*.

The SS guards turned, and there we were, in the middle of the chaos. They immediately stomped toward us. Klaryse took my hand and it was off to the races. We escaped the automobile department, shoving our way onto the nearest on-ramp and rejoining the traffic on the self-propelled freeway. We sprinted down the movable walkway, reaching almost superhuman speed.

The world through the windows was nothing but a gray blur as we raced past startled customers, many of whom seemed to be recording the incident on their hands. A steady *thump, thump, thump* thundered behind us, propelling us forward. A dozen yards up the walkway, two more SS guards ran against the flow of the walkway, and we hurtled straight for them.

"This is our stop," Klaryse said, latching onto my arm.

She dragged me over the railing and onto an adjacent walkway, sending us rocketing off in the opposite direction. I stood up just as the pursuing SS guards passed on the original track. One made a clumsy grab for me, but I ducked at the last second, and the guard ended up clotheslining his partner. They fell to the walkway and then bowled over the other two SS like human bowling pins.

Klaryse led us down an off-ramp, down two escalators, and then off two more off-ramps before we even dared turn around. We were in a nearly deserted part of the store (appropriately some of the departments we passed were *Antiques* and *Outdated Technology*), and the few customers we passed had their eyes buried in their palms. The SS were nowhere in sight.

Klaryse danced her fingers over her palm and sighed. "Snickerdoodles. They *are* tracking me. My screen's locked."

"Is there any way to block the trace?"

She shook her head as we continued to drift down the walkway. "'Fraid not. As long as you're with me, you're in danger."

"But you can't leave me! Where will I go?"

"It's better I not know." She smiled sadly and ran her hand—her iPalm hand—down the side of my face. "Do you remember your compliment from earlier? About me being a good person?"

I nodded.

"I wish I deserved it," she said.

She shoved me square in the chest. I stumbled backwards onto an off-ramp. From my derriere, I watched Klaryse drift down the movable walkway, offering a pathetic little wave as she disappeared from sight.

Chapter VIII

As soon as Klaryse was out of sight, the panic set in. It was the first time since I had exited the Time Port that my fate was in my own hands (always a dangerous scenario). The movable walkway was in control of my destiny now. The department sign I passed underneath read *Support Groups*.

The off-ramp dumped me into a section of the store that looked more like a white collar office than a retail store. There were very few cameras in the area, so I assumed it was not a much-frequented department. A long hallway was dotted with doorways on both sides with loud voices pouring out.

I passed by one of the open doors and peeked inside. The room looked like a small college classroom with stadium seating. Two dozen audience members filled the seats—and I mean they *filled* the seats. All of them were extremely obese individuals, some easily flirting with the 400-lb. mark. A semi-obese woman at the front of the room spoke to the audience. I slowly backed away from the door and noticed a digital sign next to the door frame displaying the words *Overeaters Anonymous*.

I slowly turned from the door and found myself staring at a portly man in a sweater vest over his tan tunic.

"You lost, lad?"

The man appeared to be in his early 70s. He sported a white, fluffy beard just below his pudgy bulldog cheeks. The man's eyes narrowed and his bulldog cheeks quivered.

"Say, don't I know you from somewhere? You look awfully familiar—"

I laughed nervously, doing my best to look like someone he didn't know. I backed away, stammering like an idiot. Surprisingly, his left hand wasn't equipped with an iPalm, so I hoped maybe he wasn't aware he was conversing with a wanted fugitive.

The sound of heavy boots echoed from the off-ramp, drawing near. I tried to keep my eyes locked on the old man's, to refuse to allow them to wander to the off-ramp, which I was certain would give me away. But my eyes listened to me as well as my television wife.

Not only did they glance over at the off-ramp but they remained there. The footsteps drew nearer. I raised my left hand to wave off the old man as an apology for running off, but then the old man grabbed my wrist and patted me hard on the back.

"I see," he said, as if I had offered some enlightening information. "What you're looking for is right in here, lad."

He led me toward the room, and, for some reason, I let him. There were about a dozen other people already seated in a semicircle of plastic chairs. At the head of the semicircle was what looked like an old desktop computer resting on a table and an unmanned podium. The best feature in the room, however, was the complete and utter lack of security cameras. Sweater Vest led me to an empty chair in the semi-circle and eased me down onto the plastic. He smiled and took his place behind the podium.

Out of the corner of my eye, I spotted two SS agents stomp past the doorway and continue down the hall. I did my best not to look, not to betray myself. The problem was that there was a door on the other side of the room, too, so I had to keep an eye on both entrances.

From the front of the room, unaware of my impending doom, the sweater-vested man cleared his throat and spoke in a low, baritone voice, which was much more intense than the one he had greeted me with.

"My brothers and sisters, I welcome new and old alike. It takes a lot of courage to walk through that door. Sitting here today, you're all heroes in my book. Give yourselves a round of applause for being here today."

The request was met with chuckles and nervous laughter. I joined in, not really getting the joke, throwing a quick glance toward the door and the empty hallway.

"For those of you who are new to the group," Old Man Sweater Vest continued, "my name is Dr. Zimmerman. I teach history of technology courses at Walmart University 127. And for those of you wondering, no, I am not just someone who studies the negative effects of technology on society. Like many of you, I know the cruelty of our day and age far too well."

He lifted his left hand high into the air, and his index finger jerked up and down like a piston. The skin color on the hand was just slightly off from the rest of his body. It was some sort of prosthetic. Taking a quick survey of the room, he wasn't the only one.

Several of the audience members had prosthetic hands or hooks or stubs where their left hands should have been—there was even one guy who appeared to have a spoon jammed into the club of flesh on his left arm. I was one of only three people with intact hands, but none of the intact hands included an iPalm accessory.

A digital sign near the entrance helped explain things. It read: *Tech Rage Support Group.*

"Technology is the new religion," Dr. Zimmerman continued, growing more passionate with each word, "but it is a false prophet. Man has extracted his *soul* and replaced it with *megabytes!*"

Dr. Zimmerman paused and composed himself before continuing. The speech had certainly roused something in the audience members, too. The fellow with the spoon for a hand was rocking back and forth like a deranged mental patient. Unlike everyone else I had seen so far in the future, the spoon fellow seemed to be dressed in the height of fashion in his black tights and an overcoat with built-in shoulder pads. On his neck was a small tattoo of a spider.

"But we must be better than the machines. Technology is not going away. We must learn to coexist with technology as best we can. We must accept that which we cannot change."

Heavy footsteps out in the hall pulled me out of Dr. Zimmerman's verbal hypnosis. Somewhere in the maze of hallways, the SS were still actively continuing our store-wide game of hide-and-seek.

While I was distracted, Dr. Zimmerman had started some sort of confirmation. He spoke, and then the audience members repeated his words.

"Technology is a part of the modern world."

Technology is a part of the modern world.

"I must accept technology for all of its benefits and detractions."

I must accept technology for all of its benefits and detractions.

Dr. Zimmerman strolled along the inner circumference of the semicircle leading the incantations. He paused in front of me (probably because I wasn't joining in the choral response) and didn't move until my voice joined the monotone drone.

"I am better than the machine."

I am better than the machine.

"Technology is not the master of me."

Technology is not the master of me.

The rolling thunder of the SS boots boomed over the chorus of affirmations. I glanced toward the doorway, and there they were. Two guards paused at the doorway. They spoke softly in German, turned … and then walked straight into the overeaters anonymous meeting across the hall. I knew it was only a matter of time before they found me among the mutilated members of Tech Rage Anonymous.

"Being tech-free does not make me any less of a human being."

Being tech-free does not make me any less of a human being.

"I am flesh and blood and bone—and that's all I need to be."

I am flesh and blood and bone—and that's all—

Without warning, the guy with the spoon erupted from his seat and attacked the computer at the front of the room. He grabbed it with his good hand, tossed it on the floor, and stomped the holy hell out of it with his oversized military boots, stopping periodically to stab at it with his spoon. Apparently, that was the ancient computer's reason for existing. It was the unattended pack of cigarettes left in the presence of the nicotine addict. It was there to be resisted.

Zimmerman and several of the other one-handed anti-technites ran to restrain the lunatic, but he seemed possessed with almost superhuman strength. All the noise seemed to catch the attention of the SS guards across the hallway. One glanced over to see what all the fuss was about, and that's when I decided it was time for me to exit stage left.

I ducked down behind the crowd and crept to the exit on the far side of the room. None of the anti-technites seemed to notice my departure. I turned toward the door and walked smack-dab into a brick wall of two store security officers.

I glanced up from the yellow smiley face patches and automatic weapons to the hardened and unsmiling faces of the Asian security guards.

"Mr. Savage, your presence is requested upstairs," one said.

They each latched onto an arm and dragged me down the hall to make sure I was aware that I had absolutely no choice in the matter. I glanced back toward the Tech Rage Anonymous room. Dr. Zimmerman stood peeking out from the doorway, watching the guards haul me off. The look of sorrow on his bulldog-cheeked face made me realize my terror was absolutely justified.

Chapter IX

The twin gorillas dragged me to a private elevator and tossed me inside. One waved his iPalm over a sensor on the control panel, and the elevator immediately shot up like a rocket. It climbed and climbed until I was sure when the doors opened, we'd step out in front of the Pearly Gates.

Instead, I found myself in a spacious private office with high ceilings and decorated in gold and cream … but mainly gold. There was gold in the wallpaper, gold sewn into the Persian rugs, and gold cherubs hanging from the ceiling. A massive marble fireplace stood out as the centerpiece of the massive office. The room seemed to be a villainous lair ripped straight out of a James Bond film.

"You know, my legs do work, guys," I informed my two-man entourage.

They ignored me and carried me across the room like an infant.

"Shoes!" a voice called out.

The security guards made a U-turn, returned me to the elevator, and removed my shoes. They turned to carry me over the Persian rugs, but the voice screamed, "Shoes!" again, forcing another U-turn. The security guards grumbled under their breath as they lowered me to the floor and untied their boots. When they were down to their socks, they picked me up again and carried me across the Persian rugs. I didn't bother to fight. After doing so much running around, it was nice to be carried again.

They dumped me in front of the desk, and then took their posts in the corner of the room. The desk was so massive, even on my knees, I couldn't see over it, especially since it was covered in clutter. Stacks of papers, file folders, and a veritable Post-It mountain. Plus, there were more Sharpies than any one individual would ever need in a lifetime. I had to struggle to my feet to finally get a good glimpse of the back of the cream desk chair.

"Welcome, Jonathan Savage, welcome," the familiar voice said. "Tremendous to finally get to meet you face-to-face. Just tremendous."

"Can you just turn around so I can see who you are? No need for the dramatic reveal. You're not going to top the last one."

"Hey, you don't tell me what to do! I do what I do when I want to do it. Believe me. Now, I'm going to spin around ... not because you told me to but because I want to. *My* choice. Here I go."

The cream chair spun around to reveal ... Donald J. Trump.

Yup.

I thought that discovering my future self was the President of the United States was a shocker, but this ... didn't make any sense. Trump should have been long dead, Fountain Surgery or not. Doing the math put him at around 130 years old, yet the Trump in front of me seemed to be in his early 50s. This was prime Trump.

"That look," Trump said. "I see that look often in this office. You're impressed. I designed it myself, you know. You wouldn't *believe* what the gold cherubs alone cost. Very, very expensive."

"How can you exist? Aren't you, like, one-hundred-thirty years old?"

Trump ran a hand through his wheat chaff-colored hair. "You've mistaken me for my father. Common mistake. Happens all the time. That loser is long dead."

The Trump at the desk wore four gold rings on his left hand. Each one was engraved with a single letter. The letters spelled out T.W.I.T. across his knuckles.

"Tiberius Winston Ivanhoe Trump?" I said. "You're Trump's ... son?"

"In the flesh. This must be a great honor for you to meet me."

"But you look *exactly* like him."

It was true. The pursed lips. The orangy skin. The weird hair that could be a wig but I guess isn't. The likeness wasn't uncanny, it was exact.

There were rumors back when Tiberius was born that the birth had not been natural. An 80 year-old man procreating with a 24 year-old female seemed a little unrealistic. Still, how to breach such a sensitive subject ....

"I'm a clone," Trump said in answer to the unasked question. "The first successful human clone in the United States. I'm kind of a scientific marble. Those other tube mutants were losers. Real lightweights. Diet Coke?"

He pushed a button on his desk and a Diet Coke flew out of a pneumatic tube into his hand. I declined, but he had no problem slurping it down while I watched.

"It's strange to see you sitting here in my beautiful, beautiful office," Trump continued once he was finished. "I know you better than you know yourself, but I have to remind myself we've never met before." He paused, waiting for me to respond. When I didn't, he continued. "When my surveillance guys—top guys by the way—informed me that you were in the store, I knew it was meant to be. I have a deal for you that you're gonna just love. It's really terrific."

"All right, let's table that for a second because I'm still confused." I tried to wrap my head around what I was seeing, but the whole thing still didn't add up. "I'm a little confused as to why you're here. Isn't Walmart a front for the Chinese? And weren't you—I mean, your father—battling *against* the Chinese in the trade war?"

"*Gyna?* I love Gyna! My father didn't love Gyna, and look where it got him. Dead! The Chinese bumped him off—or maybe it was Putin.

Or maybe he just ate too many hamberders. I don't remember anymore. And the less said about my loser siblings, the better. That thing with Eric? Very bad … very, very bad. No, I'm it. The last of the great Trump line …."

There was a far off look in his eyes. I thought maybe he was reminiscing, but then I realized he had just spaced out.

"You were talking about Gyna—I mean, China."

"Oh, yes. Irregardless, the point is that my father forgot where true power lies in this country. Not in the White House but in the boardroom. So, when Gyna came to me and proposed uniting America's two most powerful brands—the Trumps and Walmart—I did the smart thing. I took the deal. That's why I'm a stable genius. Come here. I want to show you something."

He circled around his desk and wrapped his arm around me. As conjoined twins, he walked me across the office and paused in front of the wall opposite the fireplace. The wall turned opaque, revealing a stunning view from the very top of the Walmart complex.

The tower where we stood looked out over the Walmart store, the asphalt ocean, the Prole District, and then the endless stretch of Washington in the background. We could probably have seen all the way to the White House had it not been for the smog blanketing the sky.

"Take a look. This all belongs to me," Trump boomed. "I'm the American CEO of Walmart and worth an amount of money you've never even heard of. Really, really extravagant. But do you know what I consider my greatest accomplishment? It's making you a god."

"I'm pretty sure gods don't have holes in their socks," I said, glancing down at my feet.

"A god lives forever, and I'm the one who made that happen. I've raised you up to be worshiped by billions of people around the world, and now you have the opportunity to repay your fans."

I didn't feel very loved. All anyone had done since I had arrived in 2076 was attempt to murder or capture me. Trump must have read the cynicism on my weary face.

"Don't believe me? Perhaps you'd believe someone more familiar?"

He released his grip on my shoulders and motioned back toward the desk. There, poured into Trump's desk chair like Chardonnay into a wine glass, sat my lovely bride, Millicent Savage, except this wasn't the Millie I was used to coming home to. The sweats and the sideways ponytail had disappeared and been replaced with a slinky black dress and curls. She was wearing make-up, too, something I hadn't seen on her since our wedding day. There was something different about her eyes, too. It was difficult to explain, but her eyes always made her look like she was up to something. It was a subtle change but noticeable. Her eyes looked sincere for the first time.

My memory flashed back to my living room where Millie was talking to a shadowy figure on the television. Now I knew why that voice sounded so familiar.

Millie touched her index and middle fingers to her lips and then waved them at me. "Hello there, darling. It's good to see you on my turf for a change."

Even her voice was different, more sensual and alluring.

"Well isn't this a nice, happy reunion?" Trump asked. He circled back around the desk to join Millie. A chair rose up from the floor in front of the giant slab of desk, and he motioned for me to take a seat, which I did and was happy to do. I was pretty damn tired.

"My *wife* is the last person I want to see right now," I said.

Millie leaned back and crossed her bare legs on Trump's desk, showing off her fuck-me heels. They only remained there for a second before Trump swept them off and checked for scuff marks.

"This isn't your *wife*," Trump said. "This is your co-star! And I'm the man responsible for bringing you two crazy kids together. *Getting*

Savage with Jonathan Savage was my creation. It was my baby! You wouldn't *believe* what it takes to get these historical reality shows off the ground. Truly state of the art stuff. And the ratings? Ratings through the roof! Number one across all demographics. That's gotta be some kind of record."

"So it was you?" I asked. "You did this to me?"

"I did this *for* you. And now I want to do something else for you. I've brought you here today, Jon, because I have a terrific deal for you. Truly fantastic. You're going to love it."

"If it's all the same, I'm going to have to pass. I prefer to stay as uninvolved in pretty much everything as much as possible."

Millie shook her head in disgust. "Such a simple Savage."

"You're going to want to hear my offer," Trump said. "Only a loser would walk away from a deal like this. Believe me."

"The only thing I really want is to go back home."

Trump's face lit up, turning the dull orange to neon. "And that's *exactly* what I was about to offer you!"

"Perfect."

"On one condition."

"Anything," I said. "Just as long as you don't want me to continue the reality show."

"I want you to continue the reality show."

"You can't be serious."

But he was. This man who was responsible for making a mockery of my existence for political gain and then broadcasting it to billions of people was seriously asking me to voluntarily step back inside the hell that was, once upon a time, my life.

"Why would I want to go back to living a lie?" I asked. "I know the entire show is a political smear campaign. Why would I volunteer to be your pawn?"

"I know you met with President Savage or *Little Hitler* as I like to call him. He's a bad man. Very bad. Everyone says so. Tell me, what was it like meeting your future self?"

"Well, he tried to kill me, so I wasn't all that crazy about *that*. And I must admit I don't particularly agree with his stance on killing everyone who disagrees with him."

"Don't you feel responsible for his actions? Wouldn't you want to assist in putting an end to his reign of tyranny?"

This time the answer wasn't so simple. I did feel responsible for my—President Savage's—actions. I knew if I did manage to escape to the past that guilt would remain with me. After all, he was what I was capable of becoming.

When Trump saw that I had no intention of answering, he continued. "I'm offering you a chance to make things right. But, more importantly, I'm offering you the chance to be a star! People *pray* for the kind of fame you've been handed. You're a beloved celebrity. Think of the fame and the fortune—"

"Fame and fortune?" I interrupted. "Until today, I didn't even know I was famous. And Millie's endless shopping sprees have me so strapped for cash I have to buy used toothbrushes. The only thing I've received for my involvement in your show, Mr. Trump, is an evil harpy for a wife who has spent every waking minute of her existence making my life miserable and a permanent case of blue balls!"

I made the mistake of making eye contact with Millie. She blew me a kiss through the air.

"She was simply portraying the role we hired her to play. Millie was sent back to add some much-needed—*spice*—to your life. Of course, she wouldn't *have* to be such a nasty woman. We can change that."

Millie rose from her seat and ran her hands down the sides of her curves, smoothing out the wrinkles in her dress. She walked around the desk and stood over me, her eyes burning into mine with a look I had long forgotten. The look was in stark contrast to the usual look of disgusted indifference that usually resided there. This was desire. This was longing. This was general horniness.

"I can be anything you want me to be," she whispered. She lowered herself down into my lap. "I can be obedient. I can be doting. I can be…" she lowered her lips to my ear, "a slut."

Her hot breath dancing in my ear got me thinking about all the things I might want Millie to be, but, unfortunately, while I was thinking those dirty thoughts, I forgot I was holding her and accidentally dumped my pseudo-wife on the floor. She scrambled back to her high-heeled feet, and, suddenly, the woman standing in front of me was my wife again, good 'ol Millicent Savage.

"You idiot!" she roared. "Do you even have a brain rattling around in that empty melon?!"

And before I could stop myself, I heard myself chanting my husband mantra: "You're right. I should know better. I don't know what I was thinking."

We both stared at each other, the realization that perhaps we were too ingrained in our previous roles to ever alter them. I realized that the part I most wanted Millie to play was that of my ex-wife.

Trump chuckled. "Perhaps you two have been married long enough. I don't blame you for being sore with the 'ol ball and chain. She's been a nasty woman to you these past three years. Very, very nasty. So, forget her! We'll write her off the show."

"Hey!" Mille protested. "But … it's as much my show as it is his!"

Clearly Trump was free-styling here. Millie's face reddened and she trotted back behind the desk and whispered something in Trump's ear, but he shook his head and shrugged.

"Sorry, Millie," he said, looking at me while he said it, "but Johnny here is our real star. What can I say? That's show business."

He dismissed her with a wave of his hand, similar to how one might dismiss a disobedient dog. She shot a death glare at me, mouthed the word, "Asshole," and then stomped over the Persian rug toward the open elevator doors.

"Take it easy on that rug with those heels, sweetheart!" The elevator doors closed. Trump smiled, and then turned his attention back to me. "Now that it's just us boys, let's cut the bullshit. What can I do to get you back on the show? What if we set you up with that hot number from your catering gig?"

"Julia?"

"Yeah, Julia. What if you came home to those smiling tits every day? Great set on her. Really terrific ya-yas. We had plans for her character, but we can go in a different direction. And I think we can do a little better than that catering gig, too. You name it, I'll make it happen. Hell, you wanna play quarterback for the Redskins, say the word and I'll have you on the roster by next week."

And right there on that desk was what every single human being desires: complete control over one's existence. Tiberius Winston Ivanhoe Trump was offering me the opportunity to write the script for my own life. It sounded like a dream.

Still—

"What you're offering sounds amazing," I said, "but I think what I'm looking for is something a little more … real. So thank you, but I'm afraid I'm still going to have to pass."

Trump pounded his fist on the desk and shot up to his feet. His salesman smile had vanished. "You ungrateful, little prick! You're a prick just like your older self! We tried to set him up with a cushy office job, and that stupid prick betrayed us. Both of you are too stupid to know a good thing when it's handed to you. You know what that makes you?"

"Ummm … a prick?"

"Exactly! Security! Take this lightweight to the place where there is no darkness!" Then to me he said, "A prick like you can scurry around all you want but all roads lead to the place where there is no darkness, and that is where we will meet again."

Unfortunately for my good pal, Tiberius Winston Ivanhoe Trump, store security never had the chance to act on his cryptic orders. Instead, the translucent wall exploded, blasting a giant hole into the office. Three SS guards flew through the hole wearing their vacuum cleaner contraptions on their backs and armed with laser cans. They landed and spread out in the room, their weapons trained on me. Through the gaping wound in the wall, I spotted the hovercopter hovering silently a few yards from the building.

The store security goons rushed to the center of the room to meet the intruders with their guns drawn, doing their best to look intimidating in their white ankle socks. A stand-off ensued, Secret Service on one side, store security on the other, and me smack-dab in the middle.

"Damn it!" Trump screamed. "That was my favorite wall!"

One of the SS guards yelled something in German.

"You're gonna have to speak English," Trump said. "I don't speak Spanish."

The SS guard rolled his eyes. "We have a presidential order to detain this man and transport him directly to the White House."

"President Savage knows his loser thugs don't belong in my store," Trump said.

"The president is aware of the treaty, but the capture of this time fugitive is a top priority. Now, are you going to give us the fugitive or are we going to have to take him?"

Fingers on both sides of the room caressed the triggers of their firearms (or cans). Trump seemed to ponder the decision. How this was all going to end was apparently his decision. Personally, I wasn't sure which side I wanted to come out victorious. My life seemed to be in danger no matter who won. I certainly didn't like the sound of *the place where there is no darkness*, but I knew a visit to the White House meant instant death at my own hand.

While I was pondering exactly whose side I was on, the looks in the room changed. The change was subtle but certainly noticeable. Everyone was still looking at me, but instead of everyone looking at me like a deer in the crosshairs, they were looking at me like a naked trapeze artist entering a church—that is to say, they looked confused.

Then I looked at me and realized what the confusion was about. I was growing translucent! I could see the Persian rug through my hand and my entire body was fading more and more by the second.

Trump seemed to realize what was happening because he yelled out, but it was too late. A few seconds later, I was gone.

Chapter X

I blinked back into existence amidst total chaos. My best guess was that I was still inside the Walmart, but now I appeared to be in the distribution center. The room stretched out over a football field in length with metal shelves stacked with boxes of all shapes and sizes towering over me.

On the far end of the hangar-like warehouse was a small runway where small unmanned drones zoomed off stocked with cargo. None of that seemed important, though. What did seem important were the dozens of people wearing black ski masks sprinting past carrying cartons of cigarettes and beef jerky. There were screams and explosions all around me. It was clear I should run, but in which direction was the real conundrum.

One of the ski-masked individuals paused in front of me, cigarettes and beef jerky pouring out of his cradled arms.

"Savage, listen to me very carefully—"

Then there was a flash of green and the ski-masked individual's skin seemed to expand and then—*BOOM*! He exploded in a shower of blood and internal organs, soaking me in his innards. His removal from my line of vision did finally solve the problem of which way to flee. Standing on the far side of the distribution center were several store security guards shooting firearms that spat out green, snake-like projectiles into the herd of fleeing ski masks.

I turned and joined the mass exodus. Everyone seemed to be sprinting toward a raised loading dock bay door. My legs pumped like pistons beneath me, but, since I still wasn't wearing any shoes, I was having trouble gaining traction. No matter how fast I ran, I couldn't seem to outrun the green serpents. With each stride, another ski-masked sprinter in front of me exploded into a torrential downpour of spaghetti sauce. Soon, the herd was just me and the green snakes. To make matters worse, a siren sang out, and the bay door began to slowly close.

It just wasn't my day ... or year ... or time period.

I ran side-by-side with the green blasts as the door lowered, threatening to imprison me with the deadly serpents. With only a few more feet to cover and only inches before the bay door closed completely, I hit a sweet James Bond dive and safely emerged on the other side. I emerged outside the building in a loading area where a white passenger van sat idle with its doors flung open. There seemed to be only one choice to make, so I made it.

I jumped inside.

Someone shouted, "Drive! Drive! Drive!"

Then someone else shouted, "Spoons! Spoons! Spoons!"

The van rocketed away from the loading dock with a *squeal* and the smell of burning rubber. It darted off the asphalt of the Walmart parking lot and onto a dirt road heading straight for the shacks and tents of the Prole District. The desperate ride tossed me, two other masked vigilantes, and several boxes of beef jerky and cigarettes from one side of the van to the other and back again. The van swerved hard to the left, and, somehow, I got smacked in the side of the face by a spoon. The driver was a portly masked fellow, but he drove with a restrained urgency of someone who was no stranger to life-and-death situations.

"We got company!" the driver shouted.

I managed to brace myself against the ceiling of the van and glanced out the back window. A bright yellow military Humvee tailed us a few hundred yards back. I could just make out the giant smiling face painted on the hood. We rumbled along the dirt roads through the Prole District with the Humvee gaining every second. The van weaved around shacks and tents and finally entered a stretch of road littered with disabled vehicles, a virtual car graveyard.

The driver knew the area well because he navigated through the junkyard with relative ease and quickly left the Walmart Humvee in the proverbial dust. The van entered a straightaway and picked up speed, heading straight for a row of Porto-o-Johns.

"Watch out for those crappers!" I warned.

The van accelerated, and we barreled toward the toilets without any hint of slowing down. I imagined the spectacular explosion of cheap plastic and shit the second we hit the row of toilets, but the shitty impact never happened. Instead, a few feet from the crappers, the earth seemed to open up like a book, the Port-O-Johns tilting back as if stuck to the ground with glue, and a ramp led underground. The van descended down the ramp and entered an underground tunnel. We slowly decelerated until we came to a complete stop in an open room lined with sheet metal.

The doors opened, and the passengers poured out of the van, pushing me out in the process. The driver, who I realized was wearing a sweater vest, raced over to what looked like some sort of periscope hanging down from the ceiling and jammed his face into the viewer.

"Where the hell are we?" I asked.

One of the other passengers raised a spoon to my lips. A few tense seconds passed as the driver scanned the area with the periscope. Finally, he withdrew and released his breath in a single whoosh.

"They're gone," he said.

The others finally released their breaths and removed their ski masks. I recognized both of them from the Tech Rage meeting, especially the one with the spoon jammed into the nub of his arm. You tend to remember a thing like that.

A metal door swung open, and a dozen or so men, many with hooks or claws instead of left hands, marched into the room. Again, I recognized several faces from the Tech Rage meeting. That's why it was no surprise when the portly man at the periscope finally removed his mask to reveal Dr. Zimmerman, the Tech Rage guru.

"What the hell is going on?" I asked.

Everyone in the room filed into rank behind the good doctor. Our previous encounter had been brief, but Dr. Zimmerman's kind eyes studied me as if an old friend had been resurrected from the grave. The rest of the group looked like Elvis had been resurrected in the middle of Las Vegas. Many had tears in their eyes and instinctively raised their left hands as if to snap a photo before they realized they were trying to take a picture with a metal hook or a claw and lowered the deformed appendage down to their sides.

"I can't believe it's actually him," one of them whispered.

"The shadow of the tyrant," said another.

"Spoons," said the young guy with the spoon for a hand.

"Welcome to the Morlock Lair, Young Savage," Zimmerman said.

"What the hell is a Morlock?"

"We are the Morlocks," he said, motioning to his posse. "We are an underground revolutionary group working to reclaim mankind's humanity."

"Huh. How about that? I'm out of here."

I turned to leave, but the spoon guy stepped forward, shoving me against the wall, and raised his spoon in as threateningly a manner as a spoon can be raised.

He was halted by a cry of "Spoonz, no!" from Zimmerman.

Spoonz slunk back, holding his spoon at throat level, ready to strike if the need arose. He retreated back into rank behind Zimmerman. The old man snapped his fingers, and everyone, including Spoonz, seemed to fall into autopilot, forming an assembly line and unloading the boxes from the back of the van.

"My apologies for my young friend," Zimmerman said. "Spoonz can be *reckless* at times, but the lad means well. Please, Young Savage, come with me."

He wrapped his arm around my shoulders and the combination of the man's girth and the sweater vest was like slipping into a warm bath after a busy day of people trying to kill me.

He walked me to the side of the room, where we watched the rest of the Morlocks empty the van of its bounty of beef jerky and cigarettes.

"My apologies for not recognizing you right away, Young Savage," Zimmerman said. "You're the last person I expected to run into at the Walmart. I didn't want to say too much for fear of attracting attention to myself and my comrades. It was a miracle the extraction was successful."

"Yeah, what happened back there? One minute I was in Trump's evil clone's office and the next—I wasn't."

Zimmerman reached behind me and removed a small metal device the shape and size of a paper clip from my back. I was so bruised and battered I hadn't even realized it was there.

"Matter transporter," he explained. "They're typically used in the distribution center to transport goods from one side of the DC to the other. I managed to slip one on you before Trump's goons escorted you to the penthouse. We coordinated your transport with the food raid to mask your escape. Unfortunately, the transporter only works at limited distances, and typically human transportation is frowned upon since the transporter struggles with the arrangement of internal organs, but you seem to be no worse for the wear."

Now that he mentioned it, my liver did feel slightly more to the left than usual.

"I'm sorry," I said, "but am I supposed to know you?"

Dr. Zimmerman seemed to ponder this question much longer than necessary.

"No," he finally said. "Not yet, anyway. But come. We have much to discuss."

We followed the Morlock assembly line through a side door and down a long corridor lined with sheet metal. The corridor led to another large room, but this room was full of boxes of canned food items and boxes of tampons and cigarettes.

The Morlocks added the distribution center booty to the piles to be sorted. Everyone moved mechanically around the room without any verbal orders. Zimmerman led me over to a fruit crate and instructed me to take a seat.

"I can't tell you how pleased I am that the Fates have brought you to us at the turning of tides," Zimmerman said. "You're a very important man, Young Savage."

"That's what people keep telling me. Everyone seems to want something from me."

"And what is it that *you* want?"

"Just to return to my own time and forget about all this."

The statement made Zimmerman visibly upset. His bulldog cheeks jiggled and reddened. "You don't seem to recognize the unique opportunity you've been awarded. You can erase mistakes you've yet to make. You can seek penance without being blackened by the sin."

Spoonz reappeared with a strip of beef jerky hanging out the side of his mouth and a cigarette dangling out the other. He dumped a package of beef jerky, a pack of cigarettes, and a small can of sliced peaches into my lap as a peace offering.

"I apologize we can't offer you more," Zimmerman said, "but, as you witnessed, our meals come at a high price."

Spoonz removed the spoon from his clubbed left arm, but I politely declined, choosing to slurp the peaches from the can sans utensils. Zimmerman allowed me to enjoy a few slurps of peach chunks and strips of dried beef without interruption. I must have looked as hungry as I felt.

"What's with the spoon anyway?" I asked, trying to ease the awkwardness of these two strangers watching me eat canned peaches and beef jerky.

"Spoons," Spoonz said.

"I'm afraid Spoonz is a victim of our times," Zimmerman explained. "He learned to text as a toddler and never properly learned vocalization skills since he could simply text his needs to his parents. I believe at one point he was identified as the fastest texter in the country under the age of ten."

"Spoons!" Spoonz said with pride.

"But the technology didn't advance as quickly as his skills, and what he perceived to be the limitations of the technology quickly drove him mad—to the point he severed his own iPalm from his body. Not an uncommon occurrence." He held up his own prosthetic. "When asked whether he wanted a hook or a claw or a prosthetic, the boy's obvious answer was a spoon, since that's the only word he knew. Spoonz and I found each other through the support group, a cover I've been using to recruit like-minded individuals to our cause."

He handed me another can of peaches. I thought about refusing it, knowing how many starving people there were above us and how many people exploded to bring that can of peaches to me, but, in the end, my hunger overpowered my compassion. I slurped its contents greedily.

"Don't feel guilty," Zimmerman said. "Although our people don't have much, they would gladly sacrifice every scrap of food they possess for you, Jonathan Savage. Our people love you. One of the few pleasures they have is watching you on whatever telescreen they can scavenge. Your humanity and your struggles have inspired billions. They've watched you suffer day in and day out for the past three years, and if you can continue despite life's constant humiliations, so can they."

"Gee, happy to help."

The Morlocks began to form a pile of boxes in the center of the room filled with various food items. They took great care in selecting what went into the pile. It was obviously reserved for someone special, but even this pile was meager by most standards.

"This is the reality of the world for the Proles," Zimmerman said. "That raid you just took part in? That's the only way much of the population can get a decent meal. Not everyone lives in latent luxury like some of your *friends*."

My thoughts wandered to Klaryse and her mansion and its fence, fighting off the approach of the dilapidated buildings surrounding it.

"Yes, your friends, the Goldsteins. Word in the District is they were the ones parading you around Hyattsville like a shiny, new toy. Their father served on Walmart's board of directors during the Chinese occupation. He became a billionaire by betraying his country. The Goldsteins are as much products of that store as anything with a price tag inside."

"Honestly, I can't say I know much about Brian, but there's no way Klaryse is a Walmart stooge. She saved me more times than I can count."

The idea that Klaryse could be working for Trump and the Walmart Machine was ludicrous. She had protected me. Until I fell into the hands of the Morlocks, she had been the only person in 2076 to show me even an inkling of kindness.

"Tell me," the old man said, "how is it that you ended up in Walmart, in the dragon's den, in the first place?"

I had to admit that Klaryse had brought me there. Perhaps she *wasn't* as innocent as she appeared. Although her final words before we parted rang in my ears, I chose not to share them with the good doctor. I didn't want to believe that another woman in my life was a liar, a fake, a charlatan. She was the only person I had met in the future up to that point who hadn't asked me for anything, which made me wonder what this elderly professor and his spoon-wielding lackey wanted.

Several Morlocks gathered around the special pile of boxes, looking anxious and excited. A side door opened and the VIPs scampered into the room: a dozen Prole children. The kids ran immediately to the boxes in the center of the room and rummaged through the contents. While the children picked through the boxes, almost all of them kept throwing sideways glances at me, trying not to make it obvious they were staring at me but doing a piss-poor job of it.

"You sacrificed a lot to get me here," I said to Zimmerman and Spoonz. "Let's cut the shit. Tiberius Winston Ivanhoe Trump wants me to be his puppet, and President Savage wants me to be his corpse. What is it exactly *you* want?"

Zimmerman glanced over at Spoons, who rubbed his spoon over his spider tattoo.

"What we want," Zimmerman said, "is for you to be our leader. We want you to run for the office of President of the United States."

The offer hung in the air like a half-inflated balloon no one wanted to acknowledge as it floated around, rubbing up against us. No one spoke. No one moved. The only sound in the room was the laughter of the children as they traded canned goods, small toys, and cigarettes.

"Correct me if I'm wrong," I finally said, "but aren't I already president?"

"I'm not speaking of the murderous tyrant currently in office, I speak of you, Jonathan Savage circa 2026. You represent what our current president was *before* being corrupted by power, what this country was *before* selling its soul to Corporate America. You are the perfect symbol of the past, which is exactly what we need to push our particular agenda."

"You want me to run against myself?"

"The timing couldn't be more perfect. President Savage ran unopposed the last election and looked like he would do so again in 2076. Walmart has attempted to run a few stooges against him, but President Savage has them killed, and anyone with any integrity is too afraid to run or lacks the appropriate star power. You have something no other candidate has had, and that's the support of the people. They love you. They're waiting for someone to save them, to lead them."

"If you can keep me alive until November."

"Correction. We only need to keep you alive until the end of August. The president changed Election Day to coincide with his birthday. A brilliant move, really. Who's going to vote against someone on his birthday?"

"That's … actually pretty smart."

Call my other self anything you wanted, but the guy was no dummy.

"Listen," I said. "I'm flattered people have enjoyed watching life kick my ass on television for the past three years, but that doesn't mean I have any business being president. I know *nothing* about politics. I'm just a clown from a crappy reality TV show!"

"So was Donald J. Trump when he was elected in 2016. His presidency changed everything. It was the beginning of the Age of Politainment. Politics are *boring*. Modern humans don't have the attention span for it. They want to be *entertained*. They want a larger-than-life character with an engaging story. What could be more engaging than a man who traveled fifty years into the future to do battle with his evil doppelganger for the honor of leading the American people to the Promised Land? That's something we can sell!"

I had to admit, it made for one hell of a story. It would make for a killer novel, one that made lots and lots of money and that everyone should buy.

I stopped before I got too carried away with visions of grandeur. "You have the wrong guy, Dr. Zimmerman. How about you? You seem to be doing an OK job of running things here. You run!"

Zimmerman sighed sadly. "An army of lions commanded by a deer will never be an army of lions. I certainly have a head for politics, but I lack the charisma to be the figurehead we need to topple The Tyrant.

That destiny is yours."

My immediate response was to laugh in the old man's chubby-cheeked face, but my guilt kept my tongue silent. Maybe I *was* responsible for the president's actions, even if it wasn't me who had committed them. Was it possible to pull a presidential do-over?

"What would be the endgame?" I asked, trying to avoid giving a straight answer. "You want President Savage out and Walmart toppled? Seems impossible."

Zimmerman furled his brow and tilted his head.

"Spoons?" Spoons asked.

"Walmart's extinction would prove disastrous for the country," Zimmerman said. "Our economy dances on a knife's edge as it is. No, Walmart is not the tyrant's accomplice in our despair."

"Then what is?"

"*Technology,*" Zimmerman said, spitting out the word. "During his first term, President Savage repealed the laws banning technological implants as a means of distracting the population. That single edict opened the floodgates to our enslavement. People were too busy staring into their palms and blinded by iLids to notice when the tyrant liquidated the Senate and had his own vice-president assassinated. They cast their eyes in violet to avoid looking at that stain known as the Prole District where children starve to death in the streets. We need to set people free of their technological chains, to look at what this country has become!"

I thought maybe the anti-technology thing was a front but apparently not. So, President Savage wanted Walmart gone, Walmart wanted the President Savage gone, and now the Morlocks wanted President Savage *and* iPalms gone but not Walmart. It was getting difficult keeping track of who was against what.

"Seems like that genie is out of the bottle," I told Dr. Zimmerman. "People aren't going to be willing to part with their precious technology.

You can't turn back time— Well, you know what I mean. Besides, technology didn't create that hobo village above us. Walmart did!"

"I once shared your beliefs, but I've learned that Walmart is simply too gargantuan to fail. It's a necessary evil. They're the only employer and supplier of goods remaining in the country. Perhaps, at one point, they could have been stopped but not now. Without it, our economy would cave in on itself like a dying star and take the country with it."

One of the children foraging through the boxes, a young blond boy about seven or eight years old, darted away from the other children and sprinted toward us. His mother tried to stop him, but he easily dodged her clumsy attempt. When he reached us, he held out his bare left palm and handed me something that looked like a pocket knife.

"Looks like someone wants an autograph," Zimmerman said.

I inspected the strange object I had been handed. "What is this? Some sort of digital pen?"

I pressed a button on the side of the handle and a six-inch blade emerged. The boy offered the flesh of his palm, hoping. I immediately retracted the blade and searched for a less grisly alternative to send the boy away happy but I had nothing to offer. In the end, I carved my initials into a box of cigarettes and handed the box to the boy. He returned to his friends, smiling, waving the box above his head.

"You see?" Zimmerman said. "These people love you. Once you declare your candidacy, your tyrant doppelganger won't be able to kill you because he would know that, if he did, the people of this once great nation would rise up and wash him out of the Oval Office like the rat he is. These people believe in you, Young Savage, and perhaps it's time you ask yourself what it is *you* believe in."

You had to give it to the old man. He was a hell of a salesman. Even I was starting to believe I was capable of great things.

"I'm sorry," I finally answered. "All I really want is to go home and feed my dog."

"Spoons," Spoonz said, a hint of disappointment in his usual response.

"It's just … it's not my fight. Hell, it's not even my time period. I can't be held responsible for the sins I committed in another lifetime. Besides, I'm just one person. What difference could I possibly make?"

"You underestimate yourself, Young Savage. It only takes one man to save the world—or destroy it."

He smiled and wrapped his big bear paw around my shoulders, thus ending our conversation. He offered me a new pair of shoes and then ushered me to a small barracks filled with other Proles doubled up on cots. He ushered me to an empty cot tucked away behind a shower curtain in the corner of the room. It was clear these were the finest accommodations the Morlocks had to offer, and I accepted it gratefully, knowing full well that I could not repay them for their kindness with anything but gratitude.

Chapter XI

I woke early the next morning after a restless night of bizarre acid dreams involving Millicent, Dr. Zimmerman, Tiberius Winston Ivanhoe Trump, and President Savage taking turns driving me into the ground with a giant mallet like an insane game of whack-a-mole.

I snuck out of the Morlock barracks while most of Zimmerman's crew slept and exited near the secret Porto-o-John entrance without being noticed. The lack of security in or outside the facility led me to believe that Zimmerman was running low on manpower and resources and the presidential proposal last night was a Hail Mary. Unfortunately, *Back to the Future* rules prevented me from interfering in the timeline. I wasn't sure exactly what might happen, but I was pretty sure Doc Brown would disapprove.

I emerged from the bunker into the pale morning sun, which was lying snug behind the blanket of smog. In the distance, the giant smiling Walmart glared down on the Prole District with contempt. I wandered back into the District where the early risers were cooking bacon on skewers over open fires (I didn't even want to guess where the meat had come from). I wandered down the main dirt road leading out of the Prole District. I knew I had to find a way to the Time Port and back to my own time. After that, I'd have to figure out how to piece my life back together.

A few beaters chugged out of town, most likely traveling to jobs hustling in the city, scraping together whatever credits were available outside the shadow of the Walmart. A banana yellow Gremlin screeched to a halt next to me, sending up a cloud of dust. When the dust cloud cleared, Brian stuck his head out the driver's side window.

"Oh, Brian," I said. "What are you doing here?"

"Looking for you," he said. "Get in."

He didn't seem that surprised or happy to see me. He wore the same expression as the giant smiley face towering over the Walmart store.

"Where's Klaryse?" I asked, doing what I could to delay the decision of whether or not to accept the invitation.

"She's waiting for you. Get in and I'll take you to her."

"I'm really trying to get back to the Time Port," I told him.

"Sure, sure. Klaryse wants to get you back to your own time where you belong. Just get in the car, and I'll take you to her."

I paused, glancing around again for a friendly face, but all I found were strangers.

"Can't help you unless you get in the car, friend," Brian said.

I realized I didn't have any other alternative. If anyone could help me, I assumed it was Klaryse, as long as she wasn't in bed with the enemy. Either getting into that Pinto was going to lead to my salvation or my coffin.

I wasn't even all the way inside the Pinto when Brian peeled out and raced down the dirt road, leaving the Prole District behind. He weaved in and out of traffic, speeding through the city, dodging stalled vehicles and the occasional Scrapper. He didn't even stop for red lights.

"Sooooo, where is Klaryse anyway?"

"We'll be there soon."

"She's something, isn't she? Your sister, I mean. She's—"

Brian whipped around and glared at me with those big, creepy eyes. "Do NOT talk about my sister, caveman."

Since my fate was in Brian's hands, I figured it best not to piss him off. The brick buildings and small market Walmarts blurred one after another as the Gremlin raced through the city. Finally, the buildings thinned and we drove under a giant metal gate that reminded me of the gate welcoming prisoners to Auschwitz.

"Where are we?"

I heard Brian growl under his breath.

As soon as we cleared the gate, giant towering mountains of garbage rose up on all sides of us and a pungent odor leaked through the pores of the vehicle. Large automated bulldozers tore through the mountains of garbage, pushing everything toward the center of the dump as hovering magnets sorted it into piles. In the very center of the junkyard sat a giant metal contraption that looked like a giant cannon mounted to a fifty-foot base. Attached to the base were several humongous industrialized vacuums that slithered and swayed with minds all their own.

"What is that thing?"

Brian parked the car at the base of the largest garbage mountain.

"Just wait. You'll see soon enough."

The vacuums suddenly choked off and fell to the ground like giant snakes being decapitated. The base of the cannon coughed and sputtered, and then emitted a low-pitched mechanical whine that slowly grew louder and louder until it sounded like the entire structure would explode. And then *BOOM*! It did explode!

The mouth of the cannon coughed a cloud of dark smoke, and then a giant ball of condensed garbage shot out of the cannon and rocketed through the sky, slowly growing smaller and smaller until it disappeared from sight. A light drizzle of cans and banana peels rained down on the dump before dissipating completely.

At that point, I had no right to be surprised by anything, but I honestly couldn't help it.

"Did—did that thing just shoot a ball of garbage into outer space?"

"Welcome to the Walmart Space Fill," he said. "I know during your time they used to just bury the garbage in the ground like animals, but our scientists came up with a much better solution." He made a gun with his hand and shot an imaginary ball of garbage into the air.

"And what happens when the balls of garbage show back up in our atmosphere?"

Brian smiled at my ignorance. "The first garbage comets won't return for another couple hundred years, and we'll all be dead by then. Let the people of the future worry about it."

"What a completely American thing to say."

Brian didn't seem to get my meaning and, instead, focused his attention on his iPalm.

"This is where Klaryse wanted to meet?"

Brian didn't answer.

I glanced through the rear window, then the sides, then back through the windshield. No Klaryse. Besides the bulldozers and hovering magnets, there was no movement at all. When I pointed this out to Brian, he shrugged and assured me she would reveal herself as soon as I stepped out of the car.

"Aren't you coming?" I asked.

"Oh, sure, yeah. Let's go."

I threw open the door and stepped outside, but, as soon as I was out of the vehicle, the Gremlin shot forward and sped out of sight.

My modern instinct sent my hand immediately into my pocket to retrieve my phone to send off an angry text, but then I realized I was unarmed in the phone department, and I started to recognize the convenience of having a phone embedded into one's hand.

The garbage cannon sputtered and coughed and whined so loudly I had to cover my ears before another ball of garbage was hurled into the stratosphere. A drizzle of garbage water rained down on me and immediately plastered my hair to my skull like glue, burning my scalp.

I had very little time to wallow in my newfound state of disgust because, at that moment, a dozen SS men emerged from behind a garbage mound, goose-stepping in perfect formation. They formed a semicircle with me as its epicenter, pointing their laser cans directly at me. The SS man at the center of the formation wore a fancier uniform and seemed to be in charge. He shouted something in German that sounded very threatening and aggressive, as most things in German do.

"Damn, you guys are impressive," I said, unable to withhold the compliment. "I mean, the goose-stepping and the German. You've got the whole Nazi-vibe down pat."

The head Nazi rolled his eyes. "By the order of the President of the United States, we place you under arrest."

The SS agents closed in, goose-stepping slowly for dramatic effect. I knew being taken by the SS meant a one-way ticket back to my mirror image, and, this time, he'd make certain to perform the coup de grace with a weapon above Walmart quality (so perhaps a rusty nail or shard of glass). I was so tired of running all over the future I almost welcomed the hovercopter ride and impending death that was sure to follow.

But before the SS agents could close in, a shout rose up from behind another garbage mound and a dozen members of Walmart's store security force emerged and filled in the rest of the circle around me.

"Tíngzhǐ!" the head store security guard shouted in Chinese. "We've been instructed to take Jonathan Savage into custody."

"Under whose authority?" the head SS shouted back.

"Under the authority of the Walmart Corporation. You goose-stepping bastards are on Walmart's private property, so stand down."

The store security guards took a step closer, tightening the circle around me.

"We're under orders from the President of the United States, and presidential authority trumps all other authority."

The SS goose-stepped closer, tightening the circle yet again.

The store security guards started yelling in Chinese and the SS screamed back in German. Store security raised their weapons. The SS did likewise, and, all of a sudden, I was in the middle of an international standoff.

And just when I thought things couldn't get worse, a great cry of "Sic Semper Tyrannis!" rose up from a nearby garbage mound, and John Wilkes Booth (a.k.a. Mustachio) emerged from the mound like a prairie dog from its den. Attached to his arms were what appeared to be two miniature chainsaws that rotated with a muted buzz, similar to the incessant buzzing of a mosquito. Booth raced toward me and filled in the last missing piece of the puzzle to create a perfect circle of death.

The SS and store security glanced over at Booth and then, unimpressed, turned their attention back to each other. The SS screamed for store security to stand down (which they ignored) and store security screamed for the SS to do the same (they were also ignored). Their fingers quaked on the triggers of their weapons. Sweat cascaded down their faces in sheets. Booth's mustache twitched in anticipation of the slaughter to come. He seemed to be unaware that he was outnumbered in this three-way dance of death. Not that it mattered. They could slice me into three equal parts and all go home happy if they really wanted.

Then the eyes of the men on both sides grew wide as they accepted the only logical conclusion to the face-off. And then *POW!* The first shot was fired and immediately answered. *Zip!* I hit the ground immediately and attempted to log roll out of the epicenter of the action while the futuristic weapons continued to erupt all around me.

Pow! went the Walmart pulse rifles.

Zip! answered the SS laser cans.

Pow! Pow! Pow!

Zip! Zip! Zip!

Sic Semper Tyrannis!

A Swiss cheese security guard plopped to the ground next to me. I scrambled away from the corpse, performing a strange crab walk/baby crawl that carried me away from the orgy of destruction. The ground beneath me rumbled with a terrible tremor I assumed was a result of the firefight, but then one of the automated bulldozers rumbled by just inches from my head. I scrambled to my feet, stumbled backwards, and landed in a pile of ancient technological devices from my own time: old smartphones and tablets and even ancient laptops.

The bulldozer drove through the heart of the firefight, collecting all the combatants, alive and dead, in a single scoop. The humans, nothing more than piles of meat, blended in perfectly with the rest of the garbage in the scoop. The firing continued even as the bulldozer pushed the entire mess of humanity toward the garbage cannon.

Pow! Pow! Pow!

Zip! Zip! Zip!

Sic Semper Tyrannis!

One of the slithering serpentine vacuums opened its voracious jaws and swallowed the entire pile, humans and garbage alike, in a single gulp. The vacuum choked off and fell lifeless. The base of the cannon coughed and sputtered and then emitted a low-pitched mechanical whine that grew louder and louder until finally—*BOOM!* A great matzo ball of garbage sprinkled with human beings exploded out of the muzzle and tore through the sky, shrinking with each second until it finally disappeared, not to return for a few hundred years.

I pulled myself out of the pile of obsolete technology and stumbled back toward the site of the standoff. As the bulldozers rumbled off to other parts of the dump, I welcomed the newfound silence. The stillness stood in stark contrast to the chaos that reigned over the dump just seconds earlier, full of laser blasts and cries of pain and agony. The sudden silence made me feel totally and utterly alone in an unfamiliar world and a voice deep within the hollow of my chest ached for someone, anyone, to break the chains of solitude.

As if on cue, a tiny buzzing snapped the chains. At first, I thought it was one of the many flies buzzing around the dump, but then I realized where the noise was coming from. I glanced over at the neck of the vacuum snake, and a rotating blade cut through the soft exterior, as if someone was dissecting the great beast from within.

Two hands reached through the slit and tore open a larger hole and then that slithering serpent gave birth to my oldest and dearest associate from the past, present, and future, Mustachio himself, John Wilkes Booth.

"Goddamn, you're one persistent sunnavabitch," I said.

In response, Booth buzzed his arm chainsaws back to life.

"Sic Semper Tyrannis?" I asked.

"Sic Semper Tyrannis!"

Instead of staying to continue the conversation, I took off running in the opposite direction. I had no idea where I was going, but I knew I had to get as far from Booth as possible. Luckily he was limping pretty badly so I got a decent head start on him. I ran blindly down a corridor made up entirely of crushed cars, but that ended in a dead end. I climbed over one side of the wall of twisted metal and landed in a pile of scrap metal. I waded through the metal bramble as the buzzing of Booth's chainsaws grew louder.

Suddenly, the metal all around me began to quiver and shake. Then a metal rod flew straight into the air. A tire rim struck me in the side of the head on its ascent. Then a jagged piece of sheet metal leaped into the air, cutting through the flimsy fabric of my parachute pants and slicing the side of my leg. A great shadow passed overhead as one of the giant hovering magnets passed over me. I scrambled to safety as the rest of the pile shot up vertically, but the gash in my leg sent lightning bolts of pain shooting through my calf.

I had every intention of sitting there and bleeding, but Booth's sudden appearance put an end to those plans. I scrambled to my feet, but I could barely put weight on my injured leg. What followed was the slowest chase scene in the history of chase scenes as I limped through the dump while Booth limped after me.

As I weaved between mountains of garbage, a bulldozer blasted through a giant pile of DVDs and parked directly in my escape route. With a bulldozer in front of me and Booth directly behind, I had no choice but to climb one of the mountains of garbage to my left or right. I chose the one on my left.

My choice turned out to be a poor one (as usual). The mountain was composed entirely of old paperback novels, their covers ripped and torn or missing entirely. I struggled to gain my footing, and each inch I climbed sent an avalanche of books cascading down toward the mountain's base.

I slipped on a copy of *1984* and almost fell directly into Booth's lap, but I managed to catch myself just as he made a clumsy swipe at my legs with his tiny chainsaw. Each step I took was agony. I scratched and clawed my way to the top of Paperback Mountain, but by the time I reached the summit, I was spent. And worse yet, there was nowhere left to run.

I collapsed onto the peak. Booth's head appeared over the side of the mountain. I swept half a dozen books into my arms and chucked them at my pursuer. A discolored copy of *Brave New World* struck him in the side of the head. *Fahrenheit 451* grazed his shoulder. *A Clockwork Orange* bounced harmlessly off his chest. But there was no stopping him.

I collapsed onto my stomach and used a copy of *Slaughterhouse Five* as a pillow. Booth's boots appeared at my side, but I didn't even bother to turn over. The chase was finished. The only consolation was that I'd share something in common with one of the greatest U.S. presidents in history, and I was glad it wasn't the gross mole.

"Sic … semper … tyrannis," Booth hissed above me.

The buzz of the chainsaws echoed in the valley of garbage. I knew

Booth was waiting for me to turn over, to face him, to stare into the face of death itself, but I refused to oblige. Lincoln took it in the back of the head. I figured it was good enough for me, too. The buzz of the chainsaw was washed out by the sound of my breath going in and out. I wondered what it would feel like to not have to choke out another breath, to not pump another milliliter of blood, to not think another thought—ever again.

Trapped there on top of a mountain of garbage in a future I wanted nothing to do with, I awaited the blow that would finally jettison me from this year back to my present and beyond, back to a point when time no longer had any significance.

I waited … and waited … and waited some more.

I knew Booth must have wanted to savor that moment, but it got to the point where it bordered on the ridiculous. There was savoring the moment and then there was milking it, and my mustachioed foe had crossed that line. Then I realized his chainsaws had fallen silent. I turned over, expecting the death blow to come the second I did.

But Booth was gone.

I sat alone on the top of Paperback Mountain with nothing but the paper cuts along the side of my face to keep me company. It was as if Booth had been plucked from the earth by God himself.

Then it became clear that's exactly what happened.

A soft buzz danced down from the sky to the peak of Paperback Mountain. The shadow of a giant magnet passed overhead. I shielded my eyes from the glare shining down through the blanket of smog and recognized a familiar silhouette kicking and screaming above. Booth hung from the magnet, his arms extended above him. The tips of his arm chainsaws clung to the magnet, and his feet kicked beneath him in a tragically comic sort of way. I couldn't help but utter a short, exhausted snort at the expense of my rival.

"Sic simper tyyyy—" his voice trailed off as the magnet carried him far into the distance.

There was no time to celebrate my good fortune, however. I wanted out of that dump before anyone else showed up who wanted me dead. I rolled toward the edge of Paperback Mountain and allowed an avalanche of literature to carry me to the bottom.

My story wasn't finished yet.

Chapter XII

As I sat resting against the metal post of the sign outside the Walmart Space Fill, a Chevy Chevette rumbled along the dirt road heading straight for me. I didn't have the energy or the will to run so I just sat and watched the Chevette stop directly in front of me. The driver's side window lowered, and Klaryse stuck her beautiful face out.

"There you are! Get in!" she said.

I didn't move. My leg was throbbing, but I had tended to it as best I could with a half-filled bottle of antiseptic and some old band-aids I found in the trash piles (Disgusting, I know, but I was desperate). I strained to lift my eyes to meet those of my alleged savior. I stared into those green emeralds, trying to read her thoughts.

"Get in!" she repeated, this time more forcefully.

I still wasn't sure if Klaryse could be trusted, but I realized I would rather be in the company of Judas than hanging on the cross by myself. I slowly rose to my feet, willing every aching muscle into action, and limped into the Chevette. Without another word, Klaryse sped off down the dirt road back toward the city.

As soon as we were back among the towering high rises and shredded tricentennial American flags, she put the car on autopilot and leaned over to kiss me. And I let her. I tried not to enjoy it, but her lips were so soft and felt so good and everywhere else on my body sang of pain and suffering.

She finally pulled away and returned her attention to the road. "Thank God you're all right."

"Do I look all right?"

She seemed to think about this before she rephrased her statement. "Thank God you're alive."

"No thanks to your brother."

"Whaddaya mean?"

I studied her face to try to detect any deceit written there. It revealed nothing.

"Your brother dropped me off in the dump. He said you were waiting for me."

"That's right. He called and said he found you in the Prole District, so I told him to take you there, but by the time I got there the Walmart goons were all over the place so I took off."

"Walmart *owns* the Space Fill," I said. "Why wouldn't they be there?"

"Yeah, but they own *everything*. Usually their presence is minimal so they must have intercepted my conversation with my brother."

I couldn't make heads or tails out of the whole debacle. Were the Goldsteins in bed with Walmart? Or with the president? Or both? Was Klaryse innocent in all this? Was I ever going to get a decent meal? It was all very confusing and uncertain.

"So, is it true?" Klaryse asked. Her voice contained a hint of restrained jubilation. It was obvious she was doing her best not to squeal. "Because if it is, you have to tell me. Is it true? Is it? *I*havetoknow!"

"I have no idea what you're talking about."

She pressed a button on the dash, and the entire windshield lit up into a telescreen. The telescreen was divided into several screens, all news channels discussing the same topic: my candidacy for the presidency of the United States.

"The news was all over the interwebs this morning," Klaryse chittered. "I mean, oh my God! You running for president against The Tyrant?

That would be amazing!"

Ugh. This was Zimmerman's doing, a final attempt to guilt me into agreeing to his ludicrous plan. The old man was right. He was a hell of a politician. He might have been onto something, though. All the news channels had polls showing that, in a head-to-head match-up against myself, nearly 90% of voters would support the younger of the Savages.

"Is it true?" Klaryse asked.

"Hell no! All I want to do is go home!"

She turned off the windshield telescreen, grabbed the wheel, and made a sharp turn to the left that smashed my face against the passenger-side window.

"You're absolutely right. You need to return to your own time. You're not safe here."

"You don't get it. I'm in—Wait. What did you just say?"

"You should leave," Klaryse repeated. "The sooner, the better."

The about-face confused me a little, and I'd be lying if I said it didn't sting a little, too. Although the coward in me was packing my bags, other parts were making the argument to stay. I assumed Klaryse, of all people, would object to my cowardly exit as any charter member of my fan club should. As I was trying to figure out what prompted Klaryse's change of heart, she seemed to have another one and slammed on the brakes, making an illegal U-turn at an intersection.

"Stay!" she said. "Forget what I said. Run for president. Let me take you back to the mansion so we can figure out our next move—"

"No! There is no *our* next move. Every time I'm with you I end up running for my life. The last time I listened to you I ended up in Donald Trump's evil clone's office with my 'wife' and let's not forget about my little field trip to the White House where I was almost blasted into the afterlife by the president—who is *me*! Did you forget to mention that little chestnut? That I'm the genocidal leader of the free world?"

Her face crimsoned, but it was not from shame. "I didn't tell you because I knew you wouldn't understand. That awful man, President Savage, that *isn't* you. Do you have any idea why your show is so popular? Why so many people love you?"

"Because I make them feel good about their lives in comparison?"

"No. It's because Trump and his Walmart goons do everything in their power to make your life miserable, and you just keep trucking along, no matter how many times life shits all over you. You give people hope. President Savage provides people with nothing but despair. You are the person everyone wishes *he* was. You are kind and generous and you look out for those who are less fortunate. Trump started the show to make President Savage look weak, but all it did was make *you* look strong."

"Just because you've peeked through the bushes into my life doesn't mean you know a thing about me. I am not this savior everyone is trying to make me out to be. I'm just a guy who wants to go home. Now, take me to the Time Port."

I glanced over for a reaction, but Klaryse didn't say or do anything. Then she jerked the wheel hard to the left, sending my face bouncing off the glass again. She put the car on autopilot and allowed the violet curtain to fall over her eyes.

"If that's what you want," she said.

We raced through the city in silence, the Chevette stopping to catch its breath every so often, but, eventually, the gas would catch, and the car would continue speeding through the city until we reached the Time Port, the place that had chewed me up and spat me out into this time period like so much stale bubblegum. I reached for the door handle, but Klaryse's annoyed voice froze my hand on the handle.

"You do realize how stupid this is, don't you?"

I answered with silence.

"You think you're just going to waltz in there and crawl back to your own time? You don't even have a time passport! The time portal won't activate without one, and, unfortunately for you, you can only get one through the government's Time Immigration Services, which the president will certainly be monitoring, or through the the head of Walmart's Time Entertainment division, which is Tiberius Winston Ivanhoe Trump."

Oops.

I had hitched a ride to 2076 so easily I hadn't thought about the difficulties of doing it in reverse. President Savage would never let me leave alive, and Trump would only allow me to go if I agreed to be his puppet. That time passport was my only chance of salvation.

Equally troubling was the fact that Klaryse had changed. This was not the rabid superfan I had met upon my unceremonious birth into the future. Now, she was judging me not as a personality on a television show but as a flesh and blood human being. It appeared she preferred her perception of me rather than the reality.

Still, it could all be a pretense—a farce, a sham, a hoodwink. Maybe she was on Walmart's payroll and had been playing me since the beginning, but oh how badly I wanted Klaryse to be genuine. I wanted someone to be exactly who they said they were for once in my miserable life because, after all, isn't that what anyone wants? Just some goddamn honesty?

"I've got to try," I finally said to Klaryse. "I need to get back home."

"But why? The life you knew is a sham. What is it you're in such a rush to get back to?"

I got her point. My entire life was bullshit. I couldn't think of a single reason for me to return (besides Seymour needing his worm pills). In the end I didn't say anything. I stepped out of the car, expecting that to be our unspoken goodbye.

The world outside Klaryse's car instantly seemed foreign and terri-fying. A miniature schnauzer trotted past on a leash attached to some sort of hovering automated dog walker. I walked along the sidewalk on the opposite side of the street from the Time Port, studying the people outside the building. Most had their faces buried in iPalms or remained vacant behind violet pupils, but any of them could have been undercover SS or store security. I stepped off the sidewalk, but the Scrapper rumbled past and chased me back to the sidewalk.

"OK," I said, to no one in particular.

"OK," a voice answered back.

Klaryse stood beside me on the sidewalk, her eyes shimmering with the same hint of fear I assumed my own betrayed. Just her presence there made the world seem far less foreign and terrifying.

"What are you doing?" I asked.

"I was there when you landed in our world, and I want to be there when you get off."

I flashed my eyebrows.

"Oh, fiddlesticks" she said, realizing her double entendre. "That sounded dirty."

We laughed, nervous and cautious, but the laughter freed us in a way. I extended my hand, and Klaryse took it. We stepped in unison off the sidewalk.

A VW bus immediately pulled up in front of us. Its door flew open and a half-dozen arms dragged Klaryse and me inside.

The entire incident happened so fast it took me a moment to realize we had just been kidnapped. The windows of the van were covered with black construction paper so it took my eyes a few seconds to adjust. I was in a van full of nerdy-looking old professor types and one Middle-Eastern fellow who looked rather disagreeable. The old nerd in the passenger seat (rocking a wrinkled dress shirt and bowtie) turned around and addressed me in a low, uncertain voice.

"Jonathan Savage, I'm afraid we require your assistance."

"Goddamnit," I said.

Chapter XIII

The inside of the VW bus was lined with shag carpet and reeked of cheap weed. The reflective cube dangling from the ceiling created a disorienting strobe effect as it bounced stray rays of light entering through the windshield around the interior. The light offered glimpses of posters of various historical figures taped to the walls of the vehicle: George Washington, Martin Luther King Jr., Elvis. I assumed Klaryse would look as scared as I felt, but her face revealed cool indifference. All in all, it was one of my more pleasant abductions.

"Yes, well, my name is Granger," the old nerd said from the passenger seat. "We've been tracking you for quite some time now."

"I don't care."

"My associates and I represent a group of—um—*preservationists* interested in historical preservation."

"Not my problem."

"We feel like you have been brought here for a purpose."

"Nope," I said. "Just followed my fake wife through a time portal and got trapped here. Nothing more to it than that. Now if you'll excuse me—"

I moved toward the door, but the Middle-Eastern fellow grabbed me and pushed me back onto the shag carpet. His expression didn't change during the assault. He was a man carved out of stone.

"You don't understand," Granger said. "That's exactly what we want for you."

I started to argue but then realized what he said. "Wait … you want to send me back? With no strings attached?"

"No strings attached," Granger said. "That's our organization's mission. We're historical preservationists. We oppose the use of time travel to interfere in the lives of past citizens. We create hundreds of different timelines and take responsibility for none of them. We believe the past should be, um, protected, much like nature preserves in your own time when they still existed."

I glanced at Klaryse for confirmation.

"They're legit. Walmart has condemned them as historical terrorists."

Granger eyed Klaryse carefully. His eyes widened as he recognized who she was.

"Umm … is it wise to discuss these matters in front of Miss Goldstein, especially considering her connections to Walmart? Do you trust her?"

I glanced over at Klaryse and looked her in her emerald eyes as I answered. "Absolutely I do."

It seemed to be enough assurance for Granger. He explained his organization's mission. Apparently, I wasn't the only historical figure being exploited by the reality shows. Hundreds of important men and women throughout history had been sabotaged and undermined for the entertainment of billions of futuristic couch potatoes.

"If you could please show him *The Cherry Tree*," Granger asked Klaryse since no one else in the van was equipped with an iPalm.

Klaryse danced her slender fingers across her iPalm and allowed me to view it over her shoulder. On the screen, George Washington stood in a long wooden raft full of soldiers that was slowly sinking into the Delaware River on a wintry December night.

"In this timeline, Washington's efforts are sabotaged, and America loses the Revolutionary War," Granger explained. "The United States is never born, and America remains a British colony."

I knew exactly how Washington felt as he splashed down into the icy waves of the Delaware. That the world was secretly conspiring against him. But I knew something Washington didn't; I knew he was right.

"What exactly do you want from me?" I finally asked.

"We want what you want. We want you back in your own time where you belong, unmolested and free to live your life as you see fit."

It was exactly what I wanted and it sounded wonderful (especially the unmolested part). They wanted what I wanted, and since I didn't have even a scrap of a plan of my own, I was willing to listen.

Granger outlined his plan as only an elderly man can: extremely slowly.

"We'll wait until the, uh, third shift change when Time Port security will be at its most, um, vulnerable. We've acquired TP tech uniforms, so we'll use those to covertly infiltrate the facility. Wing C-33 is currently closed for, uh, tech upgrades, but the time portals should still be functional. Mustafa here is our tech wizard, so operating the portal shouldn't be any trouble."

Mustafa was the Middle-Eastern fellow. He was dark-complexioned and had a strange hooked nose. He sat perfectly still, not even offering a nod of acknowledgement or a hint of a smile.

"What about the passport code?" Klaryse asked.

"Oh, yes, of course. Our operatives have provided us with a working passport code. All we've got to do is stroll in there and use it, and we'll have Savage back in time for dinner." He offered me a friendly smile. "Say the word, friend, and we'll get you back where you belong, and you'll be free to live a life of obscurity or whatever you wish to do."

It was exactly what I wanted so I gave Granger the only answer I could.

I said yes.

***

The moon's soft glow was already trying to push its way through the smog by the time Granger, Mustafa, Klaryse, and I emerged from the VW van wearing the gray uniforms and caps of Time Port maintenance workers. It took some convincing to get Granger to agree to Klaryse seeing me off, but, eventually, he relented and offered her one of the uniforms he had reserved for one of his nerdy thugs.

The four of us marched single file across the street and down the alley on the side of the Time Port, avoiding the crowds and security cameras at the front entrance. We marched until we approached a reinforced metal door with no handle. The door popped open, and a flat-faced man wearing a similar uniform to our own stuck the upper part of his torso out. The nameplate on his uniform read Bernard.

"Credits first," Bernard said to Granger.

He held out his iPalm, which displayed a number pad similar to an ATM. Granger shielded the number pad with his body and punched in a few digits. The iPalm beeped its approval. Bernard nodded and waved us inside, disappearing into the building. Mustafa held the door open while Granger ushered Klaryse inside. It was nice to see a semblance of chivalry had survived this far into the future.

Granger lowered his cap low over his eyes and instructed me to do the same. "Do try to keep your head down at all times. The last thing we need is attention from TP security."

I followed Granger through the doorway, but as I was passing Mustafa, his hand swung over my head and slapped me hard on the back of the neck as if swatting a mosquito. The assault froze me in my tracks. I turned to Mustafa, but he still wore the same look of indifference.

"Why'd you do that?"

"Do what?" His voice was gritty as gravel with only a hint of a Middle-Eastern accent.

"You just smacked me in the back of the neck."

"Did not."

"Yes, you did!"

Granger called for me to follow, so I had no choice but to abandon the discussion (which seemed to be going nowhere, anyway). I took one more glance back at Mustafa, and then followed Granger and the others inside.

Bernard led us through the backstage area of the Time Port. The hallways were narrow and lit with overly bright, sterile overhead lighting. A single blue line was painted down the center of the wall, and, every few feet, we passed a door with a scanner and a nameplate.

A Time Port security guard approached from the far end of the hallway. There were no turns or open doorways so we were forced to walk past him. I pulled my hat even further over my eyes and focused on Granger's feet in front of me. The guard's footsteps clicked closer and closer, and then I heard him say something.

Instinctively, I looked up and caught the guard's eyes. In that moment, I realized he wasn't talking to us at all but to someone on his Bradbury implant. He held my eyes for a solid three seconds before I finally forced them back to the floor. As we passed, I heard his footsteps pause. I prayed for the sound of the guard's footsteps on the floor to resume, to fade, to disappear, but all I heard was the distinct sound of our foursome's feet clicking in unison.

And then—footsteps. They were the guard's, but, thankfully, they were clicking off in the opposite direction. They faded and completely disappeared as Granger's feet led me around a corner and down another corridor. A hallway was sectioned off behind a plastic sheet and caution tape. Bernard pulled the plastic to the side and ushered us into Wing C-33.

We finally paused in front of a Time Portal on our left.

"This is it," our guide said. He waved his iPalm in front of the scanner, and the door slid open, revealing a room similar to the one where I had arrived. The only difference was that the counter had a control panel that seemed to activate the time portal instead of, you know, nothing. "The security feed to this room is cut, but that doesn't guarantee anything. I say you got five, ten minutes tops before someone notices something's up."

"That should be all we require," Granger said.

Bernard looked at me for the first time. "I thought you'd be taller," he said. He offered me his iPalm. "Would you mind?"

It was my second autograph, and I hoped my last.

Bernard disappeared with his autograph in hand (literally), and the four of us entered the room, the door sliding shut behind us. I approached the time portal, remembering the chaotic trip that had started this whole mess. I dreaded the French onion soup membrane bath I'd take on the other side of the portal, especially since there'd be no one waiting on the other end with a leaf blower, but being covered with placenta was a small price to pay to return to a timeline where Walmart was just one of many retail stores battling for world domination.

Granger ordered Mustafa to activate the portal and set the coordinates for the exact moment of my departure. While Mustafa fumbled with the buttons and levers on the control panel, I turned to Klaryse, knowing this was goodbye. She wore a sad smile, and I'd be lying if I said I was a little disappointed not to find the hint of a tear in the corner of her eye.

"You sure you can settle for mediocrity?" she asked. "After all, who wants to be a regular agent when you can be a double-oh agent?"

A James Bond reference. She was making this much harder.

"Trust me. Mediocrity sounds like heaven right now."

We met in the middle of the room, the soft *buzz* of the time portal mechanisms acting as the soundtrack to our farewell. We stood with only a few inches between us. Those inches might have even been fewer had we been alone, but we weren't. I hated that we had to share our final moment with Old Man Granger and Comrade Mustafa. Life doesn't always offer perfect season finales like on television.

I would miss Klaryse. In spite of her hardcore fan-girling and the possibility of her being a turncoat whose ultimate goal was my destruction, she made me feel wanted for the first time in my adult life. To Millie, I was a turd that refused to be flushed down the toilet. To Klaryse, I was a god.

I wanted to sweep her into my arms and press my lips against hers, delivering a kiss that would be remembered for the ages, the kind one always sees the handsome bachelor lay on one of the stunning women vying for his attention on one of those reality dating shows. But this wasn't a show. This was real life, and in the real world, I was an insecure, awkward man who didn't know much about women, and everything I did know were lies.

"I guess it's true what they say," I finally said. "You should never meet your heroes. You're destined to be disappointed."

I was hoping she'd tell me I was wrong, but she didn't. She shrugged and took a step back. "I just learned that you're human, like the rest of us."

Considering my future self was a mass-murdering tyrant, I considered being described as human a great compliment.

The roar of the machine continued to increase. The aqua blob appeared in the door frame and expanded, and the light above the door frame changed from red to yellow.

"I guess all there is left to say is … goodbye," I said.

"Listen," Klaryse said, "before you go, there's something you should know—"

A siren above the time portal interrupted. A loud humming, which I assumed was the time portal powering on, filled the room, but then it cut off and coughed like a car engine throwing a belt.

"Shit," Mustafa said, rising from behind the control panel. "Codes are no good."

Granger uttered a tiny whimper. "Oh my…oh my…oh my…"

"What does that mean?" I asked.

"I'm afraid it means you're not going anywhere," Granger said.

The door to the room slid open, and Dr. Zimmerman and his deformed sidekick, Spoonz, stepped inside like two knights on white stallions riding in to rescue the princess.

"Of course, he's not!" Zimmerman said. "And thank the good Lord for that!"

"Spoons!"

Then I was struck with the realization that I was the princess.

Mustafa abandoned the control panel and stood side-by-side with Granger. The four men met in the middle of the room with Klaryse and I trapped between them. It took a few seconds before I realized this was *another* stand-off, this one much nerdier than the last.

"What is going on?" I finally asked.

"This turncoat and his deformed friend are trying to prevent us from sending you back where you belong," Granger said. "And I deduce he's also responsible for the spurious codes!"

"You deduce correctly, my old friend," Zimmerman said. "I knew you'd bring him here if we fed you and your lackeys counterfeit pass codes, but Young Savage isn't going anywhere."

"Wait," I said, feeling the need to intervene on my own behalf. "Don't you *want* me to go back?"

"If that's what you wish," Zimmerman said, "but what I don't want is for you to unwittingly commit genocide."

"Genocide?!"

"Check the back of your neck."

Granger took a step forward, reaching out for me, but then pulled back and uttered a half-groan, half-sigh that trailed off into a string of unintelligible mumbling. He shuffled behind his associate, Mustafa.

I reached to the back of my neck and, sure enough, there was something small and circular stuck to my skin. It felt like a mole, but

I knew I was usually melanoma-free in that particular area so I tried to pick it off. It stuck, but, with a little force, I was able to remove it. I inspected the object. It was no bigger than the point of a pen and the same color as a watch battery.

"I'm so sick of people putting stuff on me! What is this?" I asked the Granger/Mustafa team.

Neither answered. Granger slunk lower behind Mustafa. The expression on Mustafa's face, however, did not change in the slightest.

"Give me a few minutes and I may be able to hotwire the portal," Mustafa said. He shoved Granger to the side and returned to work on the portal. No answers were coming from him.

"If I may," Zimmerman said, stepping forward and taking the object from me. He studied it briefly, but he obviously already knew what it was. "Ah, yes. It's a Bye-Bye Bug, a nefarious creation from Walmart's biological weapons department used to wipe out troublesome timelines."

"Spoons," Spoonz said, shaking his head in disgust.

"Once you're back in your own time, this device will release a fatal and extremely contagious disease that will immediately disable your immune system. That disease will spread to everyone you come into contact with, kill you, and most likely wipe out most of the human population of your time in a most hideous fashion."

"What?!" I turned to Granger. "Is that true?"

"Oh, um, well, yes. But we had a *very* good reason," Granger assured me.

"You had a good reason to kill me and everyone else in my time period?"

As far as ass-backwards reasons to kill an entire population go, this one was enough to make Hitler shake his head. The plan was to send me back, infect the entire population of my current day world, and force the people of the future to watch as the entire population rotted away from disease, leaving the viewers disgusted and appalled with how damaging interference from time travel can be to citizens of the past.

"Don't you see?" Granger said. "When viewers watch an entire population wiped out in a most hideous fashion, they'll demand an end to the historical reality shows. You could be your timeline's Christ figure. You could sacrifice yourself to ensure that no historical figure or past populations ever suffer through the denigration of outside interference from future generations ever again!"

"Yes, but Jesus *chose* to sacrifice himself. The apostles didn't trick him onto the cross!"

Klaryse's iPalm buzzed to let her know she had just been charged ten credits.

"Sorry," I said.

"If I may interject," Zimmerman said, "I believe there is a way both our agendas, those of anti-technology and historical preservation, could be furthered in a single stroke."

I knew this was the beginning of another commercial, and I just didn't have the patience. Behind me, the time portal began to smoke and quake. The aqua blob appeared on the outer edges of the door frame.

Zimmerman reached his hand out to me. "Young Savage, if I could have just a moment of your time—"

"I've had all the time I can handle. There's *nothing* that could convince me to stay here."

Klaryse flinched and took a step back.

"Please. There is something you should see in the hallway. It will be but a moment."

The time portal coughed and hummed. The aqua jelly began to fill the door frame.

"There," Mustafa said. "Should be able to get you home ... give or take a dozen years or so."

"A dozen years?!" I sighed and ran my hand down my face. I stepped toward Zimmerman. "Fine. Show me whatever you have stashed in the hallway and then … I'll procrastinate some more."

Zimmerman ushered me forward. I stepped past him into the hallway, and that's where I found … *everyone*. A great cry rose up the second I emerged from the room that shook the foundation of the building. The hallways to the left and right of the door were packed wall-to-wall full of people, and not just Proles. There were people of every race and every age, iPalm-equipped and iPalm-less, and they were all waiting for me. A single shout of my name quickly found its way onto everyone's lips until the walls quaked with the weight of it.

"SAV-AGE! SAV-AGE! SAV-AGE!"

My fear that the commotion was sure to attract the attention of Time Port security was quickly subdued when I spotted several security guards chanting along with the rest of the crowd. Near the front of the pack was the Prole boy who had requested my autograph back at the Morlock hideout. He raised his hand into the air to reveal the initials J.M.S. carved into his palm in bloody slashes.

The roar of the people took the fatigue I had been carrying around like a sack of bricks and transformed it into a dozen red balloons. My heartbeat fell into rhythm with the chants. I suddenly felt strong, like I could punch a hole through the wall with a whisper.

Klaryse appeared at my side. She stood beside me, allowing the chants to wash over both of us like warm bath water.

"No one has been able to bring the people of this country together like this since before the Walmart Buyback," she said. "All they need is a leader, a uniter, a voice for the voiceless."

I glanced back toward the time portal. The aqua gelatin tendrils reached out for me, calling me … somewhere. Home, The Renaissance, the Cretaceous Period, who knew? Maybe anywhere was a better alternative. Zimmerman and Granger had fallen back into their argument over which of their causes was the most noble.

They represented the problem with America. They were too busy duking it out with each other to realize there were greater enemies towering over both of them. The shadows of Walmart and President Savage loomed over the entire country, and the few minds capable of reversing the situation were too busy fighting each other about which fight to fight to fight the fight that needed fighting.

Klaryse was right. What they needed was a leader, a uniter, a voice for the voiceless.

I opened my mouth to speak, but Klaryse, sensing what was to come, yanked me back into the doorway.

"Before you say anything, realize you're not going to get another chance like this. If you don't leave now, you may not have another opportunity … unless you're in a position to grant yourself passport codes."

Her message was clear. This could be my last chance to get out of Dodge. After all, the only people who could grant passport codes were Tiberius Winston Ivanhoe Trump and, of course, the President of the United States.

The chanting had not lessened in intensity or volume when I reappeared in the hallway. The people surged forward to get closer to me, still chanting my name.

"I have an announcement," I said.

The hallway was instantly silent. Not a single pair of eyes were overcast in violet. Those equipped with iPalms faced them toward me, and I realized, at that moment, it wasn't just a hallway in the Time Port I was addressing, but the entire country. I glanced over at Klaryse for some support, but she had disappeared.

I was on my own.

I cleared my throat and spoke in a tone and volume I felt necessary for such a historic and monumental announcement. "I, Jonathan Milhous Savage, would like to officially announce my candidacy for the presidency of the United States of America!"

III

Election '76

Chapter I

Dr. Zimmerman stood behind a wooden podium, center stage, smiling softly into the screens of hundreds of iPalms belonging to curious members of the mainstream media, dirt sheets, streamers, podcasters, and members of the general public. Everyone was crammed into Walmart Indoor Stadium #354, a monstrous indoor structure that was the home of one of Walmart's professional basketball teams (they owned the entire league).

Things happened fast after my presidential announcement went viral. Surprisingly, there was very little red tape involved in starting a presidential campaign. I met all the basic requirements (I was a natural-born citizen, at least 35 years old, and I'd lived in the United States for at least 14 years … even if it was fifty years prior). My campaign team was a rag-tag all-star roster of pissed-off old dudes. Zimmerman was acting as my campaign manager (a position he claimed to have had previous experience in) and Granger and Mustafa immediately set off to drum up some much-needed financial support for my campaign, a herculean task considering everyone who had money to lend had already sold their souls to Walmart.

Inside Walmart Indoor Stadium #354, I stood off to the side of the stage with Spoonz, waiting for my cue. Zimmerman had decked me out in an ancient (and oversized) powdered blue suit for the occasion. It was the only non-Walmart formal wear anyone could find that came close to fitting me. It did, however, come with a digital tie that could display hundreds of different patterns. I went with a classic stars and stripes motif.

Everything had happened so fast I hadn't even had time to figure out what my platform was going to be—or if I had a platform. With the publicity my announcement had generated, I figured I might not even need one.

For the past three days, my name had been the top search item on all of Walmart's most popular search engines, and most head-to-head simulations had me defeating my older self in a landslide. If I could maintain my momentum for the three weeks leading up to the election, I'd crush President Savage beneath the avalanche.

The press conference had been Zimmerman's idea. He claimed we had to capitalize on the buzz while I was hot. It seemed to be working. Maybe that's why he seemed to be milking the moment to the last drop out there on the stage as he prepared to introduce me for my formal announcement.

"Ladies and gentlemen," he said, pausing for dramatic effect, "today, I have the privilege—nay, the *honor*—of introducing to you the man who will free this country from the iron grip of its current tyrant. A man who welcomed you into his his life every day for the past three years. Now it's time to stand with him in the great existential struggle of our time." It was a little much but effective nonetheless. "I introduce to you, the presidential candidate for the newly formed Morlock Party and star of *Getting Savage with Jonathan Savage* … Jonathan Savage!"

I knew that was my cue to enter, but my feet had forgotten. Applause drifted from the audience back to where I stood frozen, but the thunderous ovation wasn't enticing enough to get me one step closer to the podium.

"Spoons!" Spoonz insisted.

He jammed his spoon into my spine and shoved me out onto the stage.

As soon as I appeared in front of the audience, a roar rose from the back of the auditorium and built and built until it crashed over me like a tidal wave. An ocean of iPalms appeared as far as the eye could see. The people connected to those iPalms whistled and cheered and chanted my name.

The response nearly brought me to my knees. Usually my dog didn't even bother to wag his tail when I stepped through the door. The roar of the crowd reverberated through my entire body and settled deep in my core, warming me from the inside out. It was the same feeling I had experienced back in the hallway of the Time Port. Up to that point I wasn't sure if I had ever experienced *love* before, but if someone asked me to describe a moment in time when I felt truly loved, that moment in the auditorium was it.

My stride widened, and in three giant steps, I settled behind the warm embrace of the podium. Two jumbo screens displayed my face in horrifying size and clarity. The figure on the screen looked around, clueless, as an infant must view the world upon his grand entrance into the world.

I immediately attempted to regain control over my facial expressions, but that only made matters worse. The expressions on the screen morphed from holding back diarrhea to premature ejaculation to smelling cabbage. Finally, I managed to tear my eyes from the giant screen and refocus on the crowd.

The roar and catcalls continued, making it impossible to speak. Almost instinctively, I raised my hand for silence, and the noise instantly ceased. Another shot of euphoria raced through my veins faster than any needle could deliver. My hand—my palm and five digits—controlled the actions of hundreds of people. Again, I couldn't even make the dog sit on command, and now I commanded total and complete obedience.

Words started to appear in front of my eyes—the words of my campaign announcement. At first I thought I was simply remembering them so vividly they were appearing in physical form, but then I remembered the iContacts I had received from Dr. Zimmerman. The iContacts basically acted as a personal teleprompter that only I could see. The words Spoonz had written for my speech scrolled by in transparent letters in front of my eyes.

It was a brave new world.

I spoke in the most presidential voice I could muster: "My fellow Americans, I stand here humbly before you today asking for your support as I begin a quest to resurrect the very soul of this country."

It was a strong opening. Zimmerman claimed Spoonz was a brilliant speech writer, that words were sort of his expertise, but I remained skeptical (for obvious reasons) until I had actually read some of his work.

"Most of you have watched me over the years. You've become a part of my life. Now I am asking you to become part of my campaign as I, Jonathan Savage, seek the office of the Presidency of the United States."

I paused while the crowd applauded and pictures were taken. Spoonz had anticipated this and even added *Pause for Applause* in the text of the speech. Once the applause died, I continued, pleased with how well everything was going.

"I know the road I am about to travel will be littered with obstacles, but I also know, with your support, I will—" The giant screens overhead crackled, and my face disappeared, replaced with a picture of an American flag waving in the breeze. The National Anthem played loudly in the background. The eyes and iPalms of the crowd slowly drifted to the screens.

"What the hell is going on?" I asked before I realized I was speaking into the microphone.

A loud, booming voice spoke as the American flag continued to flutter. "Over the course of our history, America has been led by strong, decisive individuals with strong ideals and morals." Pictures of some of the great presidents of the past flickered over the screen: Washington, Lincoln, Kennedy, Roosevelt, George W. Bush.

"So," the voice-over continued, "in these trying times of global economic uncertainty, America needs a strong leader more than ever. Does this look like the face of a leader to you?" An image flashed on the screen of my face contorted in one of the expressions I had just been making minutes earlier—I think the one where I looked like I smelled cabbage.

The voice wasn't done berating me yet, though. "Do we want to trust our country in the hands of a man who couldn't even keep his own household in order?" A clip played of me leaving the house I used to live in with Millie. A few seconds later, some dude I had never seen before popped out of the closet and started tasting my faux-wife's tongue.

The video beatdown *still* wasn't done yet, though. Now, a still shot of illegal immigrants crossing the border filled the screen. "We don't allow people who aren't born in this country to run for the office of the presidency, so why would we allow someone not born in this timeline? Is that even *LEGAL*?" The word legal was said in such a way that it seemed to have venom dripping off it, and even I couldn't help wondering if my candidacy was legitimate.

"How can someone from America's past lead our country into the future? Does this look like a man who knows what's going on?" A video clip played of me standing behind a podium, staring up into the sky, and saying, "What the hell is going on?" into a microphone. It was a clip of me reacting to the start of the video package currently playing. The commercial finally ended with an image of my face superimposed over a burning American flag.

The jumbo screens fizzled back into giant projections of my face. My shock and shame were even more evident blown up to twenty times their normal size. The eyes and the iPalms returned to me. The entire crowd seemed to erupt into uncontrollable chatter and murmuring. I knew if I didn't get control of the room right away there would be no regaining their attention.

I raised my hand again for silence, but, this time, there was no reaction. The chatter and murmurs continued unabated. It was like pulling a gun only to discover it loaded with blanks.

I had lost them.

Not that I would have had them for long anyway. In the midst of the rabble, three Walmart store security guards stormed onto the stage. One made a beeline for me and shoved me away from the podium. The other two stood on each side of the podium like secret service agents. My protests were drowned out by the general chaos of the auditorium, but that chaos seemed like a whisper compared to the insanity that erupted the second Millie sauntered onto the stage and took my place behind the podium. She wore a figure-hugging puke green pants suit with a big, yellow smiley face pin on the collar. She wore her hair up in a sort of mini-beehive doo, a style I had never seen her utilize before.

The iPalms clicked, and the crowd surged toward the stage. Millie stood milking the anticipation, her coral lips turned in a wicked smile that appeared both seductive and deadly. After a full minute passed, she raised her hand and silenced the crowd as if flipping a switch. To see the power I had so briefly held in the hands of my wife angered me more than the hijacking of my announcement.

She lowered her lips toward the microphone and shot a glance toward the jumbo screens long enough that everyone knew she was admiring herself, but she was right so you couldn't fault her for the conceit.

"It looks as if, once again, my husband has come a little too early," she said.

As opening lines go, it was a killer. The crowd erupted in laughter (at my expense of course), and she had them—each and every single one of them with that first line—and all I could think about was why the hell Spoonz couldn't come up with a line like that for me.

"I was hoping to make this announcement closer to the election considering the short shelf life of most candidates," she continued once the laughter had died down, "but my husband's announcement has necessitated my being here today." She paused long and hard for dramatic effect. "I am pleased to announce that I have decided to throw my very fashionable hat into this year's presidential election on behalf of the Walmart Red Party." The room collapsed into a mass of Bradbury conversations and photos and general insanity, but, once again, Millie silenced the entire room with nothing more than a raised hand. "I'll be happy to answer all your questions at my official press conference. It'll take place out in front of the building in ten minutes."

The auditorium was empty in less than two. Millie adjusted her hair using the giant jumbo screens as mirrors and then marched to the side of the stage where a small army of make-up artists and stylists waited to fix up any microscopic imperfections that may have occurred during the walk from the podium to the side of the stage. And there, overseeing it all, was Tiberius Winston Ivanhoe Trump. He wore a shit-eating grin plastered across his orange-tinted face as he shot Millie a big thumbs up.

"Fantastic. Just fantastic," I heard him saying to her. "You nailed it. Had them eating out of the palm of your hand. Tremendous."

She turned and strolled back to where I was standing.

"Who's the star now, bitch?"

The store security guard holding me shoved me to the side as he left to accompany Millie and Trump out of the building. Zimmerman was already making his way to center stage followed closely by Spoonz. Neither one looked as concerned as I wanted them to.

"What the hell was that?" I asked. "That video—"

"Yes, the negative ads are starting early this year."

"Early? I wasn't even done with my announcement! And Millie! And Trump!"

"Yes, that was an unexpected twist," Zimmerman said dryly. "It's a brilliant move on Walmart's part. In a one-on-one race, President Savage would most likely have her killed, but he might actually need her to split the lower class vote between you and your wife. From Walmart's point-of-view, who better to run than the woman who's made a fool of you for years? She'll be the puppet they wanted your other self to be. Don't worry, though. This is all very typical."

"Typical?! This is typical for an episode of *Jerry Springer!* For those of you keeping score at home, I'm running against my future self *and* my fake wife in a race for the presidency of the United States! How is that typical?!"

"Political campaigns tend to be a tad more—*unpredictable*—than in your own time," Zimmerman explained. "They need to be or else no one will pay attention. Besides, the more attention, the more people who will actually vote, and the numbers are on your side right now, Young Savage. Keep your wits about you. This is just the beginning."

I watched Millie marching toward the exit accompanied by her army of stylists and advisors (and Donald Trump's evil clone) and realized what I must have looked like to her with my team of one gimp with a spoon jammed into the stub of his arm and an old dude in a sweater vest. Millie must have felt my eyes on her because she turned back and caught me staring. She puckered her bright, red lips and blew me a kiss.

Zimmerman was right about one thing: It was only the beginning.

Chapter II

The sweat swamps in my armpits were slowly expanding, creating natural wetlands over the majority of my torso. One thing about the future I was quickly learning was that it was hot as hell and the air quality was shit, most likely a result of Walmart's hands-off environmental policies. The outdoor venue of my public Q&A wasn't helping matters either. I couldn't complain too loudly, though. As far as historic venues go, one couldn't do much better than overlooking the reflecting pool on the steps of the Lincoln Memorial.

Of course, now it was the Lincoln/Kardashian Memorial. At some point, Americans had found it necessary to add America's favorite reality television family to the memorial. Now, it was Lincoln sitting on a couch among Kim, Kanye, and the rest of the Kardashian clan.

The poll numbers following Millie's entry into the foray were less than promising. The votes now being split three-ways certainly complicated matters. According to the polls, most of the lower class was still firmly behind me, while many of the wealthier, iPalm-owning folks had switched allegiance to Millie and the Walmart Red Party.

In the most recent mock election scenarios, 50% of the public supported me compared with just under 40% for Millie with President Savage settling for a little over 10%. Pro-Millie and anti-me campaign ads were running nearly 24/7 on the interwebs and telescreens across the country, and we didn't have the financial means of countering any of them.

We were still waiting on Granger and Mustafa to return from their fundraising tour. All the public support in the world didn't mean jack if I didn't have the financial means to grease my political machine. In the meantime, Zimmerman thought it might be a good idea to have a few meet the public events where I performed a little Q&A with the general public and let the voters know where I stood on key issues. The initial euphoria over my candidacy was starting to dissipate, so now I needed some substance to my campaign.

I had a few minutes before the event started, so I retreated to our campaign headquarters (which was nothing more than a beat-up Winnebago) to clear my head before I came face-to-face with the public. Unlike the auditorium setting with its bright lights and towering jumbo screens, this would be a much more intimate gathering, meaning there would be no place to hide.

Inside the Winnebago, I raided the fridge for a swig of water to moisten the desert that had sprung up in my throat but the only liquid refreshment available was Walmart brand bottled water, which was a weird yellowish/gray swirl with what looked like brown sugar floating around in it.

The door of the Winnebago opened and slammed shut. I expected to find Zimmerman entering for a last minute pep talk but, instead, found myself staring into a mirror. There I was in the flesh, my other self, President Savage, looking smug, decked out in a hooded tracksuit with the presidential seal on the breast. I searched for an escape route, found none (I was in a Winnebago for Christ's sake), and prepared for a purple laser blast to the face.

"Don't worry, I'm not here to kill you," the president said. "Sit."

He motioned for me to join him at the little plastic booth in the RV's dining area. We both sat, perfectly synchronized, facing one another. It was creepy how even performing a simple task like sitting down emphasized the fact that we were (at least biologically) the same person. We didn't do it similarly, we performed the act *exactly* the same. It scared me to have anything in common with a sadistic sociopath.

President Savage reached into the kangaroo pouch of his hoodie and pulled out a small wooden box. He set it on the table between us.

"What's that?" I asked.

"Just a little game."

"You don't you want to kill me anymore?"

"No need. Killing you politically is going to be much more effective. Now that you've entered my arena, you're not a celebrity anymore. Now, you're a *politician*. By the time I'm done with you, no one will care about you. You'll be irrelevant. And that is a death from which there is no return." He opened the wooden box. "Wanna play?"

Inside the box were four cups with dice inside.

"Liar's dice?" I asked.

Liar's dice was a game I used to play in college. It's a game where each player receives five dice and a leather cup. Players roll their dice and hide the results under their cup. After looking at their individual rolls, players take turns guessing (or bullshitting) the results.

For example, one could start by declaring there are two ones in play. However, someone can always call bullshit on the bid. When that happens, all the dice are revealed and either the bidder or the caller loses dice, depending on who's correct. Last player with dice wins.

"You know liar's dice is no fun with just two people," I reminded myself. "You need at least three to make it interesting."

"We have three. Zimmerman is going to be joining us. And trust me, it will be *very* interesting."

I was about to explain that the chubby professor wasn't present, but I followed the president's eyes back to the bedroom area of the Winnebago, and, sure enough, there was Zimmerman peering out from behind the curtain that served as the door. President Savage waved the old man over, and the good doctor obeyed, drifting over and cramming into the bench next to me. His eyes remained fixated on the president the entire time. It wasn't a look of fear or intimidation as much as the kind of hate-filled glare perfected over years of practice.

President Savage passed a cup of dice to each of us. We rattled the cups and slammed the dice down. I peeked under the cup (two ones, two fours, and a six), but it was the president who started things off with a safe bet at two ones.

"You've got a hell of a campaign manager," President Savage said. "I know he did wonders for me. What did we carry in my house election, Zimbo? Fifty-six percent of the vote?"

"Fifty-eight," Zimmerman said. He glanced under his cup. "Three twos."

"Wait," I said. "You and him? Three fours."

"Oh, yes. Zimbo and I go way back. He was one of the founding fathers of the Maryland Minutemen. Then he was my campaign manager when I ran for my house seat after my stint on *Who Wants to be a Congressman?* We were a good team once upon a time. Three fives."

"Until you betrayed us!" Zimmerman said. "After all we had been through! All the protests! Fighting the establishment! And you killed my wife! Five fives!"

"Bullshit."

"Wait," I said. "Bullshit to you killing his wife or bullshit to the five fives?"

"Both," President Savage said. "Zimmerman's wife died of plasma poisoning from a defective iPalm *and* there aren't five fives on the table."

We uncovered our dice, and, sure enough, President Savage was right. Between the three of us, there were only three fives on the table. Zimmerman lost one of his dice, and we rolled again.

"I helped you get elected, and you turned your back on me and everyone else who believed you were going to make things better. You were supposed to betray Walmart and give the country back to the people, not murder everyone!" Zimmerman said. "Debra was struck down not by a faulty iPalm but as penance for *my* sins helping put you in power. Human beings were never meant to be machines! Three twos!"

Things were now becoming clearer. Zimmerman was using me as a presidential do-over to replace the Savage he couldn't control with one he could. Add another name to the list of people who turned out not to be who they claimed to be.

"I apologize for my lack of openness," Zimmerman said to me, "but I wasn't sure how you would react when you found out there was history between me and your other self. Just know that my intentions are pure. I got you elected before, and I will do it again. I know all the dirty tricks you're capable of. Like that negative ad in the middle of your announcement. That had Johnny Savage written all over it."

"Guilty as charged. We both know modern politics isn't about making yourself look good, it's about making the other guy look worse. Three fours."

The president's motivations were fairly transparent. He was trying to drive a rift between me and my campaign manager, and doing a damn good job of it. I began to doubt my decision to stay. If I lost the election, I'd be stranded in the future, for as long as the president or Walmart allowed me to live.

"But it's not just me you have to look less worse than," I reminded the president.

"Oh, your little slut wife? She won't be a problem. I'll keep her around to split the vote three ways, but after you're out of the picture, I'll just have her killed."

Zimmerman shook his head. "You're a goddamn murderer. Two fives."

"You talk about killing someone as if it's as small a thing as stepping on an anthill," I said. "Three fives."

President Savage called bullshit on me so we uncovered our dice. I had two fives so I was certain one of them would at least have another, but, alas, my fives were the only ones on the table. I lost a dice, and then we rolled again.

"Like I was saying," I said, "you talk about killing someone as if it's as small a thing as stepping on an anthill. Two ones."

"Killing ants is easy. Ants don't keep you up at night. Killing people is more like operating a slaughterhouse. It's a messy business, but, eventually, you learn to view them for what they are: slabs of meat. That's the real difference between us. You think Walmart is the enemy, but Walmart is only a result of the true enemy's complacency. It's the people—the barnyard animals—who are to blame for this mess. Three ones."

"The people?"

"Oh, here we go. Three twos," Zimmerman said.

"Yes. They're idiots!" the president said. "That's the problem. They stood idly by while capitalism allowed the big fish to devour everyone and everything until they eventually devoured each other, leaving only one giant whale left. The reason 1% of the population is permitted to control the other 99% is because the majority consents to its own slavery."

"See. That's the real difference between us. I refuse to view people as *farm animals*," I said. "People don't want to be slaves. They could be lead to their own salvation, if they had a leader who was more interested in leading them than slaughtering them. Two threes."

President Savage chuckled and looked at me as if I was a small child insisting that the tooth fairy was real. Zimmerman was still at the table, but he might as well have been invisible. The president's eyes burned into mine.

"What's so funny?" I asked.

"Nothing. I just forgot how naïve I was at your age. I was wrong when I said you and I weren't the same. You're just me without all my experience. I saw you up on that stage before my little ad played the other night."

I attempted to wear my best poker face, but my pinky quivered, betraying me. We both knew exactly what he was talking about.

"Yeah, there it is." He made the same motion with his hand that I had made to silence the crowd. "You smelled a waft of the most alluring cologne known to man: power. It's what you've always secretly desired, and once you have it, you'll be no different than me. You'll realize there are some things that can't be fixed without wiping the slate clean. You'll be a butcher of farm animals, and not only will you not care, you'll enjoy it. Four sixes."

"Bullshit!" Zimmerman and I cried in unison.

It was an easy bullshit call, especially since I didn't have a single six under my cup. I glanced over at Zimmerman, and his eyes told me neither did he. That meant the president was trying to convince us that he had four sixes on his own—a statistical improbability.

"Are you sure you want to call me out?"

The question was for both of us, but he continued to stare me down. His pinky finger twitched ever so slightly on the table.

"Oh yeah," I said. "You're a liar, Mr. President."

"You sure about that?"

"Positive."

"Then let's make this interesting," he said. "If you're right and there aren't four sixes on this table, then I'll call off the negative advertising immediately. If you're wrong, though, I win this little game of ours and I double the money I put into making you look bad. You still wanna call me out?"

A quick glance over at my campaign manager elicited nothing more than a shoulder shrug. The decision was mine. So I pulled the trigger.

I flipped my cup over. Zero sixes. Zimmerman flipped his cup over.

Zero sixes. President Savage flipped his cup over—and there they were. Four sixes. The bastard had four sixes all by his lonesome.

Game over.

I glanced up from those four sixes, expecting to find a Cheshire cat grin spread across the bastard's face, but there was none. My older self stared back, and, if anything, he looked kind of sad. He stood and collected the dice and cups and returned them to his wooden box. Zimmerman and I didn't have the testicular fortitude to say anything.

"The thing I like most about politics," the president finally said, "is that despite the bog of lies in which it drowns, the truth always surfaces. I know what I am. I know what I've become. You need to start being honest with yourself, Johnny boy. The only way to save these people is to destroy them. When you accept that fact, only then will you become the savior this country needs. And then you'll become … *me.*"

I turned to Zimmerman, my eyes pleading for the old man to say something. Anything! To defend me. To put the president in his place. But soon, it became clear he wasn't going to say a damn thing. President Savage seemed intent to walk out of the Winnebago without saying a word in departure, but there was one last thing I needed to know.

"Does you not wanting me dead mean I don't have to worry about Booth?" I asked.

"It would … if we could find the son-of-a-bitch."

He put his hoodie over his head and exited the Winnebago. There were a dozen questions to be answered but no time for any of them.

"C'mon," Zimmerman said. "The barnyard awaits."

There was no doubt that Zimmerman had set up a truly memorable venue for my first public forum. Although it had seen better days, the Lincoln (and Kardashian) Memorial with its white marble columns still possessed much of its original splendor. There was a stage and podium set up at the base of the monument. Members of the public and press squeezed into the area surrounding the reflecting pool, and there was a microphone right up front where lucky individuals who had been chosen through a lottery would have the opportunity to ask questions.

From the busy and cramped confines of our makeshift prep area inside the monument, Zimmerman reviewed my prepared remarks and the procedure for the question-and-answer session to follow, but I was only half paying attention. I was still pretty steamed from the revelation that my campaign manager had assisted my other self onto the tyrant's throne. I guess, in reality, I was mad at myself for not being able to best my older self, but it was much easier to be mad at Zimmerman for his lack of honesty.

He handed me the iContacts, but I pushed them away.

"I know my speech by heart," I told him.

"You're still going to need the contacts for the question-and-answer session."

"These people are here to learn where I stand on the issues. They're not here to listen to some canned answers that have been carefully approved and vetted by my handlers. I'll just answer the questions honestly."

He looked as if I had just told him I was going to walk on stage and drop my pants.

"I would advise against that," he said simply.

"I don't want to play any more of your games, *Zimbo*. That's what's been wrong with American politics for the last hundred years. I'm going to go out there and do something no politician has had the guts to do. I'm going to go out there and tell the truth. Like I said before, the truth always rises to the surface."

"*You* never said that. President Savage said that and, again, I would advise against it."

"Well, considering you're the one who decided not to tell me you and my more homicidal self were best buddies back in the day, I'm not sure you're in the best position to tell me anything about honesty."

I turned and descended the stairs to my adoring public. I rode another tidal wave of cheers down the marble stairs to the makeshift stage and the waiting podium. In the outdoor venue, the sound quickly dissipated without staying to linger as it had done in the arena. This time, the cheers died of their own accord.

I sped through my written statement, which was mostly me spewing out the words Spoonz had written. It was all about bringing power back to the people and making America a global entity again and economic recovery and yadda yadda bullshit bullshit. Nothing about ending the corporatocracy that had transformed a majority of the population into relative peasants in what was once the most prosperous country in the entire world. I realized that if I was going to push my agenda, it would have to happen during the question-and-answer session. That would be my opportunity to truly connect with the people.

An overweight woman in a black and white tunic lumbered down the center aisle holding an overweight baby who looked more like a Shar-Pei than a tiny human being. She plopped herself in front of the microphone for the first question from the public.

"Are yooooou fooooor ooooor against in-store coooooupons?" she asked in a deep, slow voice.

I waited for more but no more ever came. That was the whole question.

"Can you elaborate on your question?" I asked, wearing a plastic smile.

She looked down at the baby as if it might have the answer, and then back up at me. "I coooome from a looooong line of pro-couponers, and I watch your show all the time and I'd looooove to vote for yooooou, but I can't well vote for an anti-cooooooupon man so which is yooooou?"

"Ma'am, I'd like to think that as a candidate I can't be pigeon-holed by my stance on a single issue."

The woman looked around uncomfortably. Almost instinctively, she pulled the top of her tunic to the side, revealing her bulbous breast and pressed the baby's greedy mouth to her nipple.

"But yoooou gotta be for or against cooooooupons," she said, drowning. "There's only twoooo parties. So, is you Walmart Bluuuuue or Walmart Red?"

"I am neither, ma'am. I'm running as an independent candidate. The two-party system is the biggest scam this country has ever perpetrated over the American people. It crams every politician into one of two boxes and claims—"

Zimmerman, who had situated himself in the front row, was rolling his finger, demanding I speed along to the next question.

"Look, ma'am, I think once you hear what kind of man I am and what I stand for, you'll realize I'm the best man for the job."

"Sooooooo," she said, "is you fooooor ooooor against coooupons?"

Zimmerman gave the nod and security escorted the woman and her suckling babe from the microphone and waved the next lucky member of the crowd ahead. This one was a skinny twenty-something man with a dirty beard that hung down to his clavicle and a faux hawk haircut.

"I'm (hehe) Ray," the man half-said, half-chuckled. His laugh sounded like a blend of a chicken clucking and a broken lawn mower.

He kept laughing like that for over a minute before he popped a pill into his mouth and continued. "It's—Wait (hehe). What I wanted to know (hehe) was if—Well, you know how there's, like, two of you here now."

"Yes."

"So, there's like two of you (hehe), and what I was wondering was if you would ever have a threeway, you know, with your other self?"

"What?!"

"You know, a threeway (hehe). 'Cause it would be, like, two of you and one chick, but really it would just be *you* and a chick. You could even play with your other self and it wouldn't be gay or nothin' 'cause, you know (hehe), it's like you're playing with your own stuff."

The man was quickly led away from the microphone and replaced by a younger and angrier looking man with a ring through his nose and his dyed green hair spiked in the appearance of horns. He breathed heavily into the microphone as he stomped his foot rhythmically on the grass.

"I just wanna go on the record of saying that I hate all politicians," he said.

"OK."

"What I wanna know is what you think the biggest problem in the country is—besides politicians?"

Finally. A semi-intelligent question.

"Well," I said, stepping up to the plate and preparing to knock one out of the park, "to me, the biggest problem facing our country is obvious. It's Walmart."

I waited for my answer to be met with a volley of applause, but I didn't even get a few stray nods.

"Walmart?" the man said, his brow lowering. "But that's where I get all my stuff. And I work there, too. Where would we get our stuff if we didn't have Walmart?"

This was going to be a harder sell than I originally thought. I glanced down at Zimmerman, but he turned to intentionally avoid my eyes.

"Sir, what you have to realize is that, back in my time, we had choices. There were lots of places you could purchase merchandise and a variety of places of employment. And having so many places available created competition, which is an integral ingredient for capitalism to function. That competition nurtured innovation, competition for customers, improvement in quality, and—"

"But now we only got to go to one place to work and to buy shit. It's better than running all over the damn place for every little thing."

The comment was met by a smattering of applause and nodding heads from the mob.

"I understand it's *convenient*, sir, but it's a monopoly. Without competition for employees, Walmart can treat their workers any way they want. They can pay you next to nothing, strip you of all your benefits, and sell nothing but cheap, ineffective products, and since they're the only game in town, you have to accept it. Don't you see the inherent problems in that?"

His brow lowered even further until it nearly covered his eyes completely.

"All's I know is that there ain't nothin' wrong with low prices, and Walmart has fed my family for the past twenty years. Who are you to bad-mouth'em? I thought you'd be different 'cause you're, like, on TV or whatever, but you're just like the rest of 'em. All politicians are crooks!"

This time, his comments were met with more than a smattering of applause, and the crowd was a sea of bobble-head dolls.

That's when I realized the truth. It slapped me across the face like a 9-lb. salmon straight to the kisser.

"My God, I was right," I said into the microphone. "You people are idiots."

The groan started with the man with the nose ring but quickly grew into one singular roar, hundreds of voices groaning as one. The boos rained down upon me like hail, cold and hard. The man at the microphone tried to rush the stage, but security was quick to restrain him.

A stray beer bottle missed my head by an inch or two. And within seconds, Zimmerman was there at the microphone, as if he had teleported there, telling the audience I was feeling under the weather and wouldn't be fielding any more questions. And then he was leading me up the stairs of the Lincoln/Kardashian Monument while the boos continued to nip at my heels.

As soon as we turned the corner into Lincoln's sanctuary and out of sight of the crowd, Zimmerman grabbed me by the collar and slammed me against the wall.

"What the hell do you think you're doing, lad?!"

"You heard them. He … *I* was right. They're idiots."

Zimmerman released his grip and turned his back to me. His index finger and thumb rested gently on the bridge of his nose, his head bowed, breathing slowly. Finally, he turned back to me and rested his hairy hand on my shoulder.

"Listen, kid, you gotta learn to play the game here. I know what I'm talking about—"

"Of course, you do. *You're* the one who put me in office the first time, remember?"

His eyes glassed over, but the sorrow was quickly replaced with rage. He leaned forward and pressed his forearm into my chest, pressing me firmly against the wall.

"I'm trying to make amends for what I did. And you wanna talk about idiots? Well, even a damn idiot knows where your numbers are headed after the shit you pulled out there."

He turned his hand into a plane and sent it on a trajectory straight into the ground.

And from the army of boos and curses charging up the stairs and settling at the feet of Lincoln and the Kardashian family, I knew my political career was on life support.

Chapter III

It had all gone wrong so very quickly.

Over the course of the next week, the clip of me criticizing the intelligence of the American public was shared over the interwebs more than a joint at a reggae concert. My numbers plummeted significantly in almost every sub-category except for the mega-fans of my show. Millie pulled ahead in most polls carrying nearly 60% of voters compared to my 30%. President Savage still lagged far behind near the 10% mark. Of course, he was known for committing mass murder on a regular basis, so how good could his numbers be?

The chants of love and adoration at the Time Port seemed like a distant memory. Being a celebrity had been easy. All I had to do was dance around like a trained monkey while people clapped and threw bananas. Being a politician was a bit more complicated. I still had to dance around like a trained monkey, but now these people *wanted* something from me. They wanted lies and false smiles and assurance I knew how to solve all their problems ... which I didn't.

In order to shock my campaign back to life, Zimmerman agreed to a three-way debate with Millie and President Savage (which I thought would please the perverted chuckling idiot from my question-and-answer session). It was the only way to keep my election hopes alive until Granger and Mustafa returned with some financial assistance.

Zimmerman piled the campaign team into the Winnebago, and off we rumbled to Walmart Outdoor Stadium at Walmart University #23B, the site of the triple-threat showdown that would decide the fate of the election, the country, and my chances of returning back home.

***

Prior to the debate, I stood in an isolated room in the bowels of the university arena reviewing the main points I wanted to get across during the debate:

End Walmart's corporatocracy.

Restore the country's sovereignty.

Resurrect the middle class.

Zimmerman appeared at my side with the iContact case. We hadn't been on the best of terms since the question-and-answer debacle, but we both knew the election teetered on the edge of a razor and the debate would save us or sink us.

"Here," he said. He handed me the contact case. "Things are going to move pretty fast out there. If you're in trouble, try to stall, and Spoonz will get you an answer as fast as he can. He's got some quality 'yo mama' jokes prepared."

I laughed, but Zimmerman didn't.

"Debates work a little differently than they did in your day," he continued. "Modern political debates are all about personal insults and spectacle and winning over the public without ever committing one way or another on any particular subject."

It sounded exactly like the debates back in my time.

"Just stay calm out there. If you start to panic just thank your supporters for their love and support and mention how you don't want to let them down and talk about how you love the constitution. People love that crap."

He let his plump hand plop down on my shoulder in an awkward sign of support. He kept it there too long, which only increased the awkwardness, and finally removed it, leaving me with a five-fingered sweat stain on my powder blue jacket.

I glanced around, looking for a familiar face to ease some of the pre-debate tension but found myself surrounded by strangers. Ever since I had started campaigning, Klaryse had been a virtual ghost. She claimed she didn't want to distract me from my campaign, but her absence was more of a distraction than anything else.

She'd appear at events super early and then disappear after a short while with some half-excuse and an assurance that she'd return in time for the event, but she never did. Despite the continual flow of Zimmerman's cronies following me wherever I went, her absence made me feel totally and utterly alone in a world that was not my own.

I popped the contacts into my eyes and said a quick prayer. There was no time to dwell on absent friends. My public awaited. The only problem was I didn't know if it was for public adulation or an execution.

The trek down the tunnel leading out onto the field was the single longest walk of my life, even longer than the walk to the altar on my wedding day. The echo of my footsteps was my only companion, holding my hand as my borrowed loafers clipped and clopped on the cement. The roar from the stadium thundered down onto the field and flooded the tunnel, creating the sensation of being underwater. I felt like a gladiator in ancient Rome preparing to do battle in the Coliseum (Is there a better metaphor for modern politics?).

A blinding light called me to the end of the tunnel, welcoming me into the roar. It grew brighter and brighter until it engulfed me and spit me out onto the field. The sight I beheld that day will forever shame anything I create in my tiny, meaningless dreams until the day I die. The giant stadium flood lights illuminated the field like the sun.

Since I was the first entrant, I stood alone on the field. I have never felt so small in my entire life. Jumbo video screens hung like God's personal flat screens on some sort of stationary blimp hovering over the stadium, which was jam-packed with thousands of screaming voters. Many of them carried digital signs that illuminated the name of their chosen candidate in the party's color.

Millie's name was illuminated in red for the Walmart Red Party, President Savage's in Blue for the Walmart Blue Party, and my Morlock Party signs shone in bright purple. The crowd was mostly peppered with red and purple fireflies, with a sampling of blue sprinkled throughout (the hardcore party members who would have voted for Hitler had he been resurrected and chosen as the party's candidate).

I stumbled to the stage set up in the end zone as a mixture of cheers and jeers hailed down upon me. Three vacant podiums sat on the stage equipped with microphones. My podium had been positioned in between the other two for maximum discomfort.

Millie's entrance immediately ripped the attention from me. Upon viewing my wife exit the tunnel, I realized I would not be getting it back anytime soon. Millie entered the field wearing a skin-tight black dress that plunged in a V in the back all the way to the usually forbidden territory where a woman's back blossoms into her derrière and a slit cut so high that I found myself holding my breath with each stride. Her hair was done up in a golden nest of curls cradled in a diamond headband. Forget the pants suit. She looked better than she had on our wedding day, and she certainly was showing more skin than I saw on our wedding night.

I tore my eyes away from Millie's naked back long enough to glance up at the jumbo screen, but it wasn't Millie standing gigantic for everyone to see. Instead, there were dozens of memes popping up on the screen. Most were of Millie in her dress with extremely inappropriate captions underneath but just as many were of my face with my jaw hanging down around my belly button. There were dozens of different captions, but my favorite was the one that simply said *BONERJAM!!!1* in all caps under my face.

I rolled my tongue back inside my mouth and failed miserably at pretending I wasn't fantasizing about being in bed with her at that very moment. I had to remind myself that I *had* been in bed with her for nearly three years, and none of those nights with her had ever even come close to reaching the absolute ecstasy I was imagining.

Millie's long, silky legs carried her onto the stage via a red carpet walkway that followed her with each step. She sauntered past without even glancing at me and stood in front, instead of behind, her podium. She stuck her bare leg out through the slit, placed her hands on her hips, and pressed her perfect tits tight against her dress. I could *feel* every iPalm in the place rapidly taking pictures like goddamn machine guns.

I stared out blindly into the crowd to avoid being caught on the jumbo screen gawking at my opponent. The bright lights seemed to be playing tricks on me because it appeared as if some of the purple signs in the crowd were blinking to red.

Millie finally drifted back behind her podium (much to the chagrin of the male members of the crowd), and then it was time for the reigning champ to enter. The opening baseline of my favorite song from back in my own time, a song by a German metal band called "Da Führer's Rage," filled the stadium, sending vibrations through the stage that shook the podium and sent a shiver of electricity through my hands.

I reminded myself that it should be no surprise we have the same taste in music. The drums kicked in next, sending the vibrations directly into my chest, wrapping a hand around my heart and squeezing. I knew exactly when the bastard was entering. In a few seconds, a face-melting guitar riff would tear through the air, and the evil tyrant Savage would ride those chords like black stallions into the arena.

I counted down in my head, *three ... two ... one ... now!* And, on cue, the tyrant emerged from the depths of the arena. The entire stadium in a single voice greeted the Commander-in-Chief with a barrage of boos. President Savage stood near the entrance, surveying the arena with a self-satisfied grin like he had just walked in on a surprise party being held in his honor. The man looked like he didn't have a care in the world, which scared me more than anything else he could have done.

The president took his time making his way to the stage. He'd walk toward one side of the stadium, which would boo him more ferociously and violently, and then raise his hand to his ear as if he couldn't hear them, causing them to grow even more insane with boos and shouts of anger. Then he'd venture to another side of the stadium and see if they could top the previous section. He seemed to be feeding off their negative energy, devouring it by the spoonfuls, and his appetite was insatiable.

He approached the front of the stage, rolled onto it, and then sprang to his feet, quickly claiming his position behind the podium to my right. He glanced over and gave me a little nod before turning his attention back to the crowd, shooting them a big, goofy wave that resurrected the boos. I knew I was in trouble the second he settled in behind that podium as comfortably as someone easing into the driver's seat of a Ferrari.

The moderator, some famous national news anchor who looked like he had a grin permanently etched onto his plastic face, took his place at a table set up on a smaller stage facing our podiums. He waited for the roar of the crowd to finally die until he went over the rules for the debate.

I tried to listen carefully to avoid any surprises, but my eyes began to water. I thought maybe it was just a result of the lights, but then my vision started to blur, which still wasn't that unusual. The unusual part came a few seconds later when my eyes filled with snow, the same way old televisions used to snow over when the cable went out. The snow was soon joined by a piercing pain like flaming needles being stuck in the back of my eyeball.

My first thought was that I was having some kind of nervous reaction, but then I remembered the iContacts. I immediately dug my fingers into my sockets and tore the contacts out, flinging them onto the stage. I wiped my eyes with my sleeves, trying to rub the vision into focus. The snow was gone, replaced by a darkness that slowly faded as my vision returned. I blinked rapidly, each blink producing a clearer version of the world. The first thing I saw once my vision returned was President Savage smiling at me.

Then my name boomed over the PA system, and there I was, larger than God, eyes bloodshot and blinking rapid-fire like an idiot for all to see. Luckily, the picture changed to the president's confident sneer. He waved cheerily as the thundering boos filled the arena again.

Then it was time for the battle royale to begin.

The moderator cleared his throat and spoke into the microphone. "We randomly selected the order before the event and Mrs. Millicent Savage will be starting things off, followed by President Savage, and Jonathan Savage will answer last. All the questions we'll be asking tonight are user-submitted questions from the interwebs. Here we go." His fingers danced across his iPalm, searching for the first question. I felt like a man standing in front of a firing squad, waiting for that first bullet to strike.

The moderator looked up at Millie and fired. "Our first question is from Logan Ruhn of St. Paul Minnesota. Mrs. Savage, what … is your favorite color?"

Instead of the shot from a rifle I was expecting, it was a shot from a rubber band gun.

"Ooh, great question, Logan" Millie purred into her mike. This was her sexy voice. "I would have to say that my favorite color is black since that's the color of most of my bras and other unmentionables." She giggled and leaned forward, offering the jumbo screens a beautiful view of her cleavage. "But I guess I'd have to say that I enjoy wrapping my bare skin in any color of the rainbow." She moved out from behind her podium and ran a hand down her slinky dress, and I'd be lying if I claimed I didn't feel a tug in my powder blue trousers when she did it. I was thankful for the podium more than ever.

I was certain the crowd would see right through her paper-thin answer, but the crowd erupted into cheers and cat calls. Again, it appeared as if some of the purple lights in the crowd were blinking into red, but then I realized that's *exactly* what was happening. Members of the crowd were changing their allegiance mid-debate. The entire stadium was a giant instant feedback machine.

The question moved next to President Savage. He wore a curt little smirk and stared directly at me as he said, "My favorite colors would have to be red, white, and blue because they represent the land of liberty we all call home," which was word-for-word what I was going to say, and the bastard knew it, too.

"But seriously," he continued, turning to the mob, "those colors and that flag still mean something to me, and over the past decade, I've done everything in my power—and sometimes beyond my power— to keep those colors burning bright. You wanted the country independent of Chinese control? I booted those rice eaters out of the White House. You wanted an end to the corruption in Washington? I liquidated the Senate. I've made a lot of hard decisions during my twelve years as president, and some of them haven't always been popular—like conducting selective exterminations of American citizens—but all those decisions were made with America's best interests in mind, and I stand by each and every single one of them."

Oddly enough, a few blue lights blinked into existence, even after he admitted to killing his own people.

The question bounced to me next, and, since the president had stolen my answer and the fried contacts left me flying solo, I had nothing. Thousands of eyes stared at me, waiting for me to say something intelligent or inspiring or halfway comprehensible.

"Well," I said, leaning too close to the mike and causing a scratch of feedback to fill the arena. "Oh, sorry. I guess I would have to say that, umm, orange is my favorite color?"

"Typical!" President Savage shouted into the microphone, thrusting a finger directly at me. "Scientific studies—by *scientists*—have shown that orange is the color most preferred by *serial killers.*"

An audible gasp filled the arena.

"This man," the president continued, completely unabated, "is not the dim-witted, lovable oaf that you've welcomed into your homes each and every single week. No, this man is a *monster.* He and I share the same DNA, and you all remember what I was like when I first took office. Well, my younger self will be even worse! You can change a man's experiences, but you can't change what lies deep inside his soul. He is as evil as I am but worse for his mind has been corrupted by this manipulative *Jezebel!*"

He thrust his other finger in Millie's direction so that he had both arms out, spread eagle, one finger thrust at me and the other at my wife. Millie only shrugged her shoulders and giggled, twirling her hair with her finger.

"His mind is warped and twisted," the president continued. "Elect him and there won't be anyone left standing to have another election. Why trade one tyrant for another? Isn't it wiser to stick with the monster you know rather than the one you don't?"

I was shocked to see a few dozen purple lights blink off, some replaced with blue lights. He had reached them somehow.

"Wow. Great stuff," the moderator said, scanning through his iPalm for the next question. "Next, we have a question from Audrey Randle of Newark, New Jersey. If you had the opportunity to have sex with any celebrity, dead or alive, who would it be and why?"

It was a question out of some third-rate dating game show.

"Wowzers," Millie said. "Great question, Annie. I have actually had sex with *several* celebrities, so this isn't really something I have to imagine, and I must say that out of the many, *many* celebrities I have shared a bed with—the complete list is on my Flittr page—every single one of them was armed with a higher caliber weapon than my husband over there, if you know what I'm sayin'."

The crowd erupted into a collective cry of "OOOOOOOOOH," and I distinctly heard a woman scream, "Oh snap!"

My eyes shot to the moderator, expecting some kind of chastisement, but he was saying, "OOOOOOOOOH" with the rest, so there was no help there. Claiming I was some sort of genocidal power monger was one thing but attacking the size of my genitals just seemed over the line.

"And, unfortunately for my other opponent," Millie said, motioning to the president, "I don't think size increases with age."

Another outburst of "OOOOOOOOOH!" and this one was followed by entire sections of the audience lighting up red.

"Please," President Savage said. He looked completely unfazed, almost as if he had expected that the size of his penis would eventually be brought up. "Just remember, Millie, baby, it's not the size of the boat but the motion in the ocean."

Another collective "OOOOOOOOOH" followed, and many of the newly won red lights blinked to blue. I wasn't sure what the hell was going on, but one thing was clear: I was losing.

"Let me tackle this one," the president said. "If I could have sex with any celebrity, it would be Lady Liberty because at least I would offer her the courtesy of lubing up before I bent her over and had my way with her, which is much more than Walmart has done."

I nearly toppled over my podium after that one. I scanned the crowd for someone—*anyone*—to look half as shocked as I was, but there was no one. Everyone acted as if this entire circus was perfectly normal. I thought maybe I could catch Zimmerman's eye somewhere from the sidelines, but the old polar bear was MIA.

"Walmart smiles in your face while it stabs you in the back," my alter ego continued. "At least I'm honest enough to stab you in the front. I'm a man of my word, and, with that in mind, allow me to make one thing perfectly clear. If you don't vote for me, the atrocities you've experienced up to this point will seem like a light spanking from your favorite uncle. I will lay waste to this entire country. By the time I'm done, you'll think Hitler was just a misguided German with good intentions."

A blue wave swept through the crowd, splitting the signs between red and blue with only a sprinkling of purple. I knew I had to do something and do it fast.

"Young Mr. Savage," the moderator said. "Same question."

"What kind of questions are these?" I asked.

The moderator glanced back down at his iPalm. "This one was from a woman in New Jersey who—"

"No, that's not what I mean. I mean, what the hell does any of this matter? What's your favorite color? Which celebrity would you have sex with? What do any of these have to do with leading the country?! What about job creation? What about education? What about national security? These are the kinds of questions people should be asking. That is the kind of stuff that matters!"

I paused to survey the crowd to see if anything I was saying was getting through. I hadn't turned any lights yet, but they were listening, and that was a start.

"This is unacceptable. You've got one candidate up here threatening you for your vote and another candidate basically promising to blow eight million Americans for their votes. This country doesn't need leaders like that. It needs someone who can bring us together for the common good. Together, we could change all this and create something that's worth having, something worth passing along to our children, but that's not going to happen until everyone realizes that politics isn't a cat fight outside of some bar. This country doesn't need more entertainment; what it needs is real answers from real leaders."

Silence.

I glanced around the arena, and, for the first time, the mob melted into individual faces. Men and women, young and old, white, black, Latino, and everything in between. They weren't chanting or laughing or cheering or booing. They were thinking. But that deep and insightful thought only lasted a few seconds before President Savage chimed in.

"That's all very well and good, but you're forgetting one thing Johnny Savage."

"What's that?"

"That your momma is so fat when she hauls ass she has to take two trips!"

OOOOOOOOOH!

The individual faces of the crowd quickly melted together to form one gelatinous blob of humanity all screaming OOOOOOOOOOH in unison.

"What?"

"Your momma is so fat she gave the hospital stretch marks."

OOOOOOOOOOH!

"This is ridiculous," I said. "We have the *same* mother."

"Yeah," Millie chimed in, "and she's so ugly her mirror contains a warning that says viewer discretion advised."

OOOOOOOOOOH!

"Oh yeah, well *your* momma is so ugly her birth certificate contains an apology," the president fired back.

OOOOOOOOOOH!

"Your momma is so old I told her to act her age and she died."

OOOOOOOOOOH!

"Your momma is so poor she washes paper plates."

OOOOOOOOOH!

I could feel the momentum slipping through my fingers as the insults sailed back and forth between President Savage and Millie. It was like playing Monkey in the Middle, and I was the monkey. I felt desperate to insert myself into the battle before the debate sped off without me.

I blurted out, "Your momma is so fat!" at no one in particular.

The entire stadium, President Savage and Millie included, instantly silenced. Eyes were on me. They waited. I waited. Finally a lone voice from the crowd yelled out "How fat is she?"

"Your momma is so fat," I said, thinking back to middle school arguments for some way to finish the sentence—any way really. "Your momma is so fat, she's … she's, uh, she's hard to buy shoes for?"

Silence.

No reaction at all except for the last sprinkles of purple in the audience blinking to red or blue.

President Savage broke the silence with a cry of, "Enough!" He kicked his podium in Millie's direction. It collided with her podium, tipping it over and knocking Millie onto the stage. She landed on her butt with her knees in the air. She glanced up, saw the cameraman shooting directly at her, and spread her legs wide to reveal she wore absolutely nothing under the dress. Most of the deep-voiced sections of the stadium lit up like a Christmas tree.

The president marched over to my podium and shoved me out of the way.

"I've put up with this charade long enough," he growled into the mic. "If these two assclowns even make it to the election, you peons better make the right decision or else I'll make every one of you very sorry. This debate is officially over, but don't bother getting up. I've got SS stationed at all the exits. There will be a selection immediately following the conclusion of the debate. Any audience member without a Walmart Blue sign will be eligible for the selection. Thank you for coming out tonight and drive home safely. God bless America!"

A tidal wave of blue flooded the arena until it had entirely erased all remnants of any other color. The president rolled off the stage and was escorted by SS guards back to the tunnel to be swallowed once again into the depths of the stadium. Millie pulled herself up and trotted over to my podium. She pushed me out of the way and cleared her throat.

"Walmart Red supporters, never fear. A fleet of hovercopters, provided free of charge by the Walmart Corporation, will be landing on the field shortly to airlift *my* supporters safely out of the arena. Meet me on the fifty-yard line, and I'll be glad to sign any iPalms or lingerie you may have brought with you tonight."

The blue tidal wave came down with a severe case of chickenpox as half the crowd's blue signs blinked red. Sure enough, hovercopters appeared over the stadium and slowly descended down onto the field. Half the mob started climbing down onto the field with their red lights flashing while the other half remained in the stands with their blue lights to be dismissed by the SS.

Not a single purple light remained in the entire arena.

Chapter IV

The Winnebago ride back to the Prole District was a quiet one. Zimmerman, Spoonz, and the rest of the campaign team sat near the front of the vehicle while I sat isolated in the back bedroom. When we reached the District, everyone filed out except for Zimmerman and Spoonz, who wandered back and stared at me for a few seconds without saying anything.

"What happened to the contacts?" Zimmerman finally asked.

"Not sure. They fritzed out."

Zimmerman nodded. He didn't seem mad or surprised or much of anything really.

"The president probably had 'em hacked. Knew you'd crash and burn flying blind."

I would have argued had he not been right.

The door of the Winnebago flew open, and in walked Granger and Mustafa, looking how I felt. They joined our pity party in the cramped bedroom.

"Tell me some good news," Zimmerman said.

"Oh, well, umm, I'm afraid I have none to share," Granger said. "Most of the big-time contributors are already in bed with one party or the other. The ones who were willing to jump ship were only willing to do so based on the results of the debate."

"Oh," Zimmerman said.

"Oh," I said.

"And, well, I'm afraid that's not the only bad news either."

"No?"

"No," Granger said. "Our organization is revoking our support of your candidate."

"What?!"

"I'm afraid it's true. The Historical Preservation Society is going to officially announce its support for Millicent Savage tomorrow morning."

"But she's part of the damn historical reality shows you oppose!"

"Yes, but she's leading in the polls, and we'd rather back a winner."

"I could still win," I said, sounding more like a jaded teenager than a serious contender for political office.

Granger looked directly at me for the first time since his arrival. He took off his glasses and studied me, squinting hard, apparently trying to peer into my soul and measure my worth. He didn't say what he saw, but the results didn't seem to matter.

"I think you believe that, young man, I do, but you must realize how many politicians have won major elections without adequate financial backing. You can count them on your friend's stub over there."

Spoonz uttered a sad, little "Spoons," and hid his stub behind his back.

Mustafa stepped forward and growled, "We would have been much better off sending you back as the human plague you were meant to be."

"Gee, thanks."

That sent Zimmerman off in a rage. I don't remember much of the argument that followed. I was aware of everything occurring around me, but I didn't seem to be a part of it. When it was all over Granger, Mustafa, and even Spoonz were gone, leaving just Zimmerman and me and a single question that demanded an answer.

"Now what?" I asked.

Zimmerman sighed long and hard, obviously trying not to become too agitated and freak me out which only freaked me out that much more.

"We keep fighting," he finally said. "That's the thing about elections. As they say, they ain't over until they're over. Remember, Donald Trump was caught on audio tape bragging about committing sexual assault … and America *still* voted him into office. Anything can happen. So hang in there, lad. Tomorrow is a new day."

He tussled my hair like a child and left me with my thoughts. I flopped down on the hard bed, which was like lying on concrete, and pressed my body as hard as I could into the mattress. I thought that maybe if I wished hard enough, I could sink down into the mattress like quicksand and simply disappear.

When that didn't work I closed my eyes tight, waited … waited … waited, then snapped them back open, half-expecting to find myself in my bed back in the past lying next to my indifferent wife, Millie, shaking off the last fragment of a horrific dream.

But when I opened my eyes, I found myself staring at the rotting ceiling of an ancient Winnebago.

There's no place like home … there's no place like home …

The Winnebago door slamming shut interrupted my fruitless escape attempts. I secretly wished it was Booth, coming to finish me off and put me out of my misery.

"Hey there," Klaryse said. "Mind if I come in?"

"Why not? Maybe you could kick me in the nuts and improve my day."

She wore a sleek, puke green dress with a giant ruffle around the neck. She sat down next to me, closer than I anticipated. We sat next to each other in silence, both waiting for the other to speak.

"Haven't seen much of you lately," I finally said.

"No. I've had … other engagements."

"Looks like you were at one of those engagements this evening."

I looked her up and down, letting my eyes linger too long on her exposed legs. "It wouldn't happen to be a fundraiser for the Walmart Red Party, would it?"

"Savage—"

"Or was it the Walmart Blue Party?"

"You have to understand my position, my family. We owe *everything* to Walmart—"

"You were playing me since the beginning."

"No," she insisted. "I'd die if I thought you actually believed that."

"Then you answer me this: Why did you take me to Walmart after I escaped from the White House?"

She sighed. "Because Tiberius Winston Ivanhoe Trump asked me to."

And there it was. Finally, some goddamn honesty, and the last thing I wanted to hear.

"It's not what you think," Klaryse said. "He said he could protect you. He promised he'd send you back home, which is what you seemed to want at the time. I would have told you, but Trump said you'd never trust him after talking to the president so he said it would be best if you getting caught by store security seemed like an accident."

"I should have went back when I had the chance."

I stood and stared out the window at the Prole District, illuminated by thousands of lights shining down upon Walmart's parking lot. Out there were my people, standing around flaming barrels, trying to stay warm while they watched old reruns of their favorite reality shows on ancient flatscreens hooked to car batteries. I hated them in that moment—all of them.

It was a terrifying realization since I knew my more homicidal self shared my sentiments, but I couldn't help it. I felt betrayed all over again. The autographs and the chants had seemed so real. Their love felt real. But it was as genuine as reality television.

"I don't get it," I said. "You *begged* me to stay and run for president."

"I know, and I want you to win, I do, but if I don't play my part for Walmart, then I'm going to find myself among the rest of your voter base in the Prole District. I'm a Goldstein. Things are expected of me. That's why I was so torn about you staying and running."

"So, you're willing to sell your soul to Satan because he keeps a roof over your head?"

"Don't you dare judge me." She shot to her feet and shoved a finger in my face. "I never lied about who I was. I was raised to be a wealthy Walmart brat, and that's exactly who I am. I have my vices, and you're no different. For me it's money, for you it's power. You didn't mind sticking around when everyone worshiped you, but now that you're finding your temples abandoned, all you want to do is escape."

"Excuse me for wanting to escape a world where everyone wants to kill me or make me dance around like their own personal puppet! Do you know what that feels like?"

Her eyes glistened in the flickering light of the old RV. "Yes. I do."

Her fingers danced across her palm, and she held the screen out to me. There she was in a photograph standing next to Tiberius Winston Ivanhoe Trump, who wore some kind of tan bathrobe that must have been the future's version of a tuxedo. Klaryse's most noticeable feature was not her curve-hugging dress or the elegant way her foot seemed to conform to the curve of her heels but her plastic smile that was all teeth and too carefree and indifferent to be genuine. Staring at that smile, I saw what no one else did. I saw pain.

"I know about your family," I said. "But you have to realize that winning this election is now my only chance of getting home. If I stay here, I have no future."

"And you have to realize I have obligations to maintain. If I openly side with you against Walmart, our funds go bye-bye. They'll take the mansion and end our line of credit, and Brian and I will just be another pair of poor white folks rotting in the Prole District."

She walked to the tiny bedroom window. She stared out into the slums of the District at the dilapidated tents and Swiss cheese shacks. Maybe she was imagining living in squalor with the other Proles who weren't lucky enough to come from Old Money.

I wish I could say that my thoughts were with her in that moment of quiet reflection, but, instead, they were busy riding the curves of her waist, her ass, her thighs. A sigh, heavy and dull, fogged over the glass of the window. Her slender arm rose from the side of her body, stretching the muscles of her back like a race horse's legs in mid-stride, and she pulled the shade down over the window. With a grand sweep of her arm, she pulled her hair to the side, revealing the bare nape of her neck.

I have this theory about women. I believe each one is the proud owner of one feature that sets them apart from every other woman walking the earth. It is God's signature on each masterpiece He creates. Usually it's understated parts like cheekbones, dimples, or the way a woman's hair cascades perfectly across her shoulders, the arch of her back, or the natural curve of her feet. Hell, I even had a girlfriend in high school who had perfect kneecaps.

For Klaryse, it was her neck. Her neck was as elegant and graceful as a hand-crafted Tiffany's lamp and stood as proof that, even in a world full of squalor and pain and suffering, God was still capable of creating something beautiful.

She reached back and pressed a brass button at the top of what looked like a zipper track without the zipper. The button lit up, and the dress opened like a flower opening to greet the morning sun.

Klaryse slid the dress off her shoulders and down her arms, letting it crumble in a heap at her heels. She carefully stepped out of it, her heels clicking on the tiled bedroom floor and turned to face me. She stood before me in her strapless bra and tan bikini-cut underwear, wearing no hint of shame.

I didn't even bother to attempt to corral my eyes. They wandered from the glories of her neck, traveled across the milky white hills of her breasts, across the plains of her stomach and down, down her legs, splashing down into her heels.

"You're perfection" I told her.

It might not have been as witty as a James Bond quip, but it seemed to have the desired effect.

"Time has been kind to me."

I couldn't help thinking time had wasted all her kindness on Klaryse and saved none for me.

She pressed her iPalm against my chest and pushed me back onto the bed. Her body melted into mine, the warmth of her pelvis pressed against my stomach and her chest brushing my nose as she leaned forward and offered her neck to my lips.

"What are you doing?"

"Apologizing."

She fell upon me like the ocean, crashing down all around me, and, sinking beneath her beauty, I drowned.

Chapter V

Waking up the next morning with Klaryse's hand draped across my chest was almost enough to make me forget I was also waking up inside a Winnebago parked in a sprawling hobo village in the shadow of a giant corporate metropolis that had used my life as a political attack on a future self that wanted me dead.

Almost.

I peeked under the sheets at Klaryse in all her naked glory and, after taking a mental snapshot, slipped out from under the covers. The sun seemed to have snuck through the smog blanket enough to shoot a few rays into the Winnebago's windows. The warmth of those rays wrapped around me and reminded me of the warmth of Klaryse's body.

I couldn't help but think that our night together most certainly destroyed the timeline somehow. After all, had I not traveled into the future, we most certainly never would have known each other in the Biblical sense.

I feared that our indiscretion would lead to some sort of New Jersey tsunami or the extinction of the muskrat or something else impossible to predict. I certainly had no way of knowing whether or not any of that was true, but I was pretty sure future generations would come to curse my name … more so than they already did.

The only thing I knew for sure was that I had to piss something fierce. The bathroom in the RV was inoperable so I stumbled outside in nothing more than my boxers into the District where the entire town was one giant toilet.

Imagine my surprise when I flung open the door and was met with a great cheer that rose from a crowd of what appeared to be hundreds of Proles gathered around the Winnebago. A few mobile iPalms clicked off photos and some of the poorer denizens snapped off pictures from what appeared to be digital cameras, a technology that I'm sure to these people must have seemed as ancient as a Polaroid.

An arm reached out from the mob and yanked me out of the Winnebago. The sea of humanity swallowed me and spun me around like a Piñata on a string, clicking photos and slapping me on the shoulder, the back, and even my backside.

A cry of, "Sav-age! Sav-age!" rose up from the crowd.

It was a miracle. They loved me again.

All those ill feelings I had felt the previous night instantly evaporated, dried up by the warm rays of admiration projected from the mob.

I fought my way back through the crowd while hands tore at my bare flesh like tree branches clawing the siding of a house during a storm. I managed to duck down and plow my way through the herd until I found the side of the Winnebago. I pressed my back against the vehicle so I was only dealing with my adoring fans on three sides instead of four.

The crowd pulsed forward like a collective beast and spit Zimmerman into the tiny space I had created for myself. The look of defeat had been completely erased from the old man's face. He looked downright jolly. He wrapped his arm around me and slapped me so hard on the chest he left a bright red handprint.

"Savage, my boy! Good morning to you, and what a glorious morning it is!"

It was difficult to hear him above the rumble and roar of the crowd.

"What's so glorious about it?"

"What's so glorious about it? Allow me to show you, my lad, what is so glorious about it. Spoonz show him!"

The crowd pulsed forward again, and, this time, it spit Spoonz into our half-circle of safety. My deformed companion shoved a mobile iPalm into my face.

"These were the numbers last night after the debate," Zimmerman explained.

The numbers on the screen showed a bleak picture. Millie and President Savage shared an almost equal percentage of the vote, with Millie holding only a slight advantage, while I had plummeted down to the point I was flirting with a single-digit share.

"And *these* are the numbers this morning," Zimmerman sang.

The next screen showed a more encouraging picture. Somehow, overnight, my approval rating had skyrocketed. The poll now showed me in almost a three-way tie with Millie and the president, trailing my alter-ego by only a few points.

I opened my mouth to speak but only a high-pitched squeak snuck out. Abandoning words, I fell into the warm, sweater-vested hug of Zimmerman, who squeezed me so hard my back cracked. When the old man finally released me, Spoonz held up his hand for a high five, but it was his spoon hand so I wasn't sure what to do.

I was saved from this conundrum by the arrival of Granger and Mustafa. Granger wobbled up to me and offered a sweaty handshake, and even Mustafa looked like he was trying hard to suppress a smile.

"Wonderful news!" Granger shouted above the crowd noise. "I've got donors coming out of the woodwork!"

"Of course, you do!" Zimmerman said. "Everyone wants to jump aboard when the sun's shining and the breeze is kind. Fickle, fickle, fickle. Doesn't mean we won't take their money, though, eh?"

The old men burst out laughing, throwing in plenty of back-slapping and shoulder punches to emphasize how happy they were.

"I don't understand," I confessed. "What changed between last night and this morning?"

All four men shared a look and laughed like four intoxicated men at a poker game.

"Only the two greatest words known to the political world," Zimmerman said. He counted them off on his pudgy fingers. "Sex … scandal!"

A sex scandal. No surprise there. Before we tied the knot, Millie had enjoyed celebrating milestones with a romp in the sheets—birthdays, anniversaries, Arbor Day—so it was no surprise she had celebrated her good showing at the debates with some inappropriate touching. Then again, it was just as likely to have been my doppelganger at the center of the controversy.

"So, which one is the perv?" I asked.

Granger's eyebrows rose, as if held by string, and remained high on his forehead. He glanced over at Mustafa, whose face curled in on itself like an old leather shoe.

"Well? Which one got caught doing the no-pants dance?"

"It was—Well, it was *you*," Granger said. "It's *your* sex scandal."

"What?!"

Spoonz held up the iPalm again and showed me the front page of today's iWashington Post. The headline read *Savage 'Sticks It' to Walmart*. Below the headline was a video clip. I played it, and there I was with Klaryse inside the bedroom of the Winnebago. She pushed me down onto the bed and climbed on top of me. The previous night I had a very different view of the same event.

"What the hell is this?!" I asked, despite the fact I knew exactly what the hell it was. I just didn't know how it was possible.

"An absolutely brilliant strategic move is what it is," Granger said. "I must admit, Young Savage, I've doubted your politic prowess to this point, but, after watching you pull *a Clinton*, I withdraw any and all doubts. The act of screwing that Walmart heiress is the kind of symbolism even *these people* can understand." He waved his hand toward the mob.

"Spo—ooo—oons," Spoonz agreed.

Granger, Mustafa, and Spoonz all seemed to be in agreement that I was some sort of political strategic genius. The congratulations continued with Zimmerman looking slightly uncomfortable, meaning he had the answers I wanted.

I dragged the old man back inside the Winnebago, slamming and locking the door behind us while the mob continued to crowd around the vehicle. After I pissed into an empty Walmart brand water bottle, it was time to get down to business.

"All right, speak, old man. How did Klaryse and I end up on the front page without any clothes on?"

It was difficult to sound tough in my underwear, but I think I pulled it off.

"I must admit that I may have had something to do with that."

"How much of something?"

"All of it actually. I planted a videosect in the bedroom hoping to catch you in a poignant moment, a moment of self-reflection after a stunning defeat—you know, a moment of pure humanity that could draw sympathy from the voters—but what that camera captured was far more valuable. You must understand, I had no choice in the matter. I had to do it. Otherwise, we would have been forced to concede."

"You thrust me into the middle of a sex scandal to *help me?*"

"Of course."

"I seem to be a little confused. How is being in the middle of a sex scandal going to *help* me get elected?"

Zimmerman laughed, a deep, hearty laugh that shook his enter sweater-vested chest.

"Sometimes I forget, Young Savage, you are not of our world. Perhaps a sex scandal was detrimental to a candidate's character back in your time, but no more. Now, that's what people want. The public doesn't want a leader who is morally superior and judgmental. No, now they want a leader who is flawed, who is just as disgusting and morally inept as the masses. Someone they can relate to and someone who can make them feel good about all their moral misgivings."

"This is not helping me feel better."

"It should. You've provided the Proles with what they crave most: entertainment. You've gifted them with something to gossip and hem and haw about for weeks and that's all valuable time they won't be bothered with their petty, mundane little lives. You've freed them from the bonds of their own mediocrity. You're Moses."

Let my people go.

In spite of the explanation, my first instinct was to thrust my fist into this old man's gut. He had taken the only good thing that had happened to me since I stepped through the time portal and turned it into something ugly, something … political.

"What happened last night between Klaryse and I, that had nothing to do with politics," I explained. "That was private. That was for me and—"

Klaryse.

In all the excitement of my sex scandal, I had nearly forgotten the other member of the tryst. I rushed back into the bedroom, but the room was empty.

Klaryse was gone.

***

It took a few hours for the crowd surrounding the Winnebago to finally disperse. Zimmerman, Granger, and the rest of my advisors were busy scheduling press conferences and television spots after my huge surge in popularity, so I used the opportunity to slip out of the Winnebago with a blanket over my head. I traversed through the masses of my supporters undetected and made my way to the edge of the District.

I had to see Klaryse. I had to assure her that I had nothing to do with the sex scandal and attempt to get her somewhere safe since Walmart would not be grateful for the morning's publicity.

I slunk to the edge of town with the blanket wrapped tightly around me like many of the other Proles. It was nice to have my anonymity back, if only for a short while. Sleeping in Walmart's shadow made me nervous so it felt good to be moving away from the giant commercial beast. As the tents and shanties grew less dense, I couldn't help but feel relief at leaving the slums and squalor of my voting base behind. I reached the agreed upon destination on the outskirts of the District and waited, praying the few people who passed wouldn't recognize me.

The five minutes I waited stretched out long and excruciating, but, eventually, a minivan full of screaming children pulled up to the curb. I approached the door, opened it, and stepped into the back of Benny's taxi.

"My, my, my," Benny said in a voice that seemed to echo off the cab ceiling and bounce around like a rubber ball. "Imagine my surprise when I git a call from de next president of dese United States! Where to, Johnny Savage?"

"The Goldstein mansion."

"Ahhh," Benny cooed. "Getting' in a bit of the 'ol in-out, in-out round two, eh?"

"Can you just drive please?"

We drove through the corpse of the city, weaving around abandoned vehicles that were now nothing but appetizers for the Scrapper. In a society guilty of reckless wastefulness, I couldn't forgive myself for using Klaryse like some cheap product to be tossed aside after one use. When people saw her they would think only of her lips and that neck and the sweet secrets she held below. I had helped transform her into rotting fruit.

An ocean of news vans and paparazzi surrounded the front gate of the Goldstein mansion, but Benny knew a secret entrance Klaryse's grandfather had installed to sneak his mistresses in and out of the mansion. He pulled up to the side of mansion where a hedge covered the fence. He pulled up to a specific spot, reached into the hedge, and pushed a button. A gate (and the hedge) opened and allowed us access. The cab drove slowly along the roundabout and came to a stop at the back entrance. He glanced back in the rearview mirror and studied me through squinted eyes.

"You sure dis where you wanna be, boss?"

"No, but this is where I *have* to be."

Benny let me slide on the fare. He didn't even ask for another autograph. I stepped out of the cab and stood before the double doors of the decaying mansion. I watched the minivan pull away and disappear through the gate. The last image I had of the vehicle was of the overweight woman in the front seat turning around and backhanding her eldest child.

The doors to the mansion were unlocked, so I let myself in. Once again, I found myself in the great parlor standing on the black and white checkered floor. I assumed the echo of the door slamming shut would be my only greeting to the great house, but it wasn't. Brian sat cross-legged in an antique chair that looked like the throne of a Nordic king.

"Greetings," he said.

I had completely forgotten about Brian, and meeting him there was quite an unpleasant surprise. I hadn't thought about the little rat since the melee at the junkyard. His forced smile sat upon his face like an overweight cat and his fingertips on one hand danced across the fingertips of the other, illuminated by the soft glow of his iPalm. He looked like a villain from a James Bond movie sitting in that ancient chair, and that made me hate him even that much more.

"Mr. Savage. I've been expecting you."

I told him I was there to see Klaryse.

"I know," he said. "Benny said you'd be dropping by."

His fingers continued to dance as the glow of his iPalm dimmed and faded.

"Is she here?" I finally asked.

"Oh, yes. She's here. And she really wants to see you."

"She does?"

The revelation gave me hope. My greatest fear was that she would refuse to see me. I thought if I just had the opportunity to explain myself I could make her understand we were both victims of the same plot.

"She's down in the basement," Brian said. "With some friends. I'll take you to her."

He rose from his throne and led me down the hall with the creepy pictures of the old dudes. He ushered me to the basement door with a grand sweep of his arm.

The lights were off downstairs, but I assumed they'd snap on automatically so I tiptoed down a few, but the darkness did not dissipate even after I had navigated halfway down.

"What's with the lights?" I asked. "Forget to pay the electric bill?"

I vaguely remembered telling the joke upon my first descent into the basement, but that day seemed like a lifetime ago. There were no snickers or giggles to greet the joke this time.

"Oh, umm, Klaryse likes to, uh, sit in the dark when she's depressed. Just head on down. I'll hit the lights as soon as you're down there."

The handrail on the stairs led me safely to the bottom, and I remembered enough of the layout that I was confident I wouldn't crash into anything. My foot landed on the carpet and I felt around with my hands for the back of the banana sofa.

"Klaryse?" I asked the darkness.

In answer, the lights flicked to life, but it wasn't Klaryse I found waiting for me. No, it was a dozen Walmart store security guards who immediately closed in around me and returned me to the darkness.

215

Chapter VI

My eyes fluttered open to find the darkness replaced with a blinding, white light. I sat up on the floor of a high-ceilinged windowless cell with walls of glittering porcelain. Overhead lamps flooded the cell with cold light, and there was a low, steady hum of air simultaneously being blown into and sucked out of the room. A low bench ran around the back wall, so I rose to take a seat. I stood on quivering flower stalks and had to lunge for the bench to avoid collapsing to the floor.

I was overcome by a groggy, dizzying sensation similar to the feeling one gets after waking up the night after taking too much cold medicine. I assumed I had been drugged and that I was somewhere within the Walmart complex. I felt the sensation of being deep underground, but, again, there was nothing to support that feeling except for intuition, which needed some work since I had walked straight into an obvious trap.

While I was contemplating how the hell I was going to escape, the cell door swung open seemingly on its own. Outside the cell was nothing but darkness. I considered testing my legs but figured there was nothing but trouble waiting for me in the dark. Fortunately, I didn't have to bother. Trouble came to me.

The sound of footsteps echoed in the void, and then in walked Brian, looking taller than he had before. He held his chin out and his hands cradled behind his back.

"Savage, good to see you alive and well," he said.

"Oh … Brian. Hi."

"You're probably wondering what you're doing here."

"No. I think I've got it pretty well figured out."

He didn't seem to hear me—or care. He paced back and forth in front of me, bouncing from one wall to another like a mechanical duck in a shooting gallery.

"I have some shocking information to share with you, Savage."

"Is it that you betrayed me to Walmart?"

"See, I haven't been totally honest with you," Brian continued. "All this time you've considered me an ally, but—and I know this will come as a shock—*I've been working with Walmart and President Savage all along!*"

"Yeah, I know."

"When you first arrived, it was I who tipped off the SS to your whereabouts."

"Obviously."

"And it was I who sent you walking into the trap at the dump!"

"Well, duh."

"And now it is I who sold you wholesale to Walmart!"

"No shit."

Brian paused and repositioned my limp body so I was sitting up straight and rested his hand on my shoulder. The weight of the hand made me slump further onto the bench.

"You must learn to not be so trusting, Johnny boy."

My first instinct was to shoot my hands out like a viper and wrap them around Brian's throat, but my body still felt full of lead, and, even if I did manage to drag my ass out of the cell, I had no idea where I was or how much security I'd have to escape. Plus, the whole plan reeked of effort, and, at that moment, I was content to sit and drool on myself.

Instead I asked, "And how about your sister? Was I a fool to trust her, too?"

Brian stood up straight, forced a crooked little half-smile, and then slapped me hard across the face. The blow staggered me, the hot sting biting into my cheekbone, but the second blow that followed knocked me to the floor.

"That's enough!" a voice erupted.

I glanced up to see Brian frozen in mid-swing. Footsteps from the void approached and soon Brian was joined by Tiberius Winston Ivanhoe Trump. The sweat on his orange forehead glistened under the bright lights of the cell. Brian sat me back up on the bench.

"Hello, Jonathan Savage," Trump said. "I told you this is where we'd meet again, and here we are."

"Yes, but you said we'd meet in the place where there is no darkness."

Trump snorted and waved his arms in a grand motion indicating that the room proved his statement true.

"But look." I closed my eyes tightly and then opened them. "See? Darkness. Do they still have lawsuits for false advertising?"

Trump's giant sweaty mitt swung like a mallet and clubbed me on the top of the head, piercing my tongue with my teeth and drawing blood. The taste of iron was the first real evidence I was still alive.

Brian produced a tiny bottle of hand sanitizer and sprayed the clear liquid onto Trump's hands, which the Walmart CEO vigorously rubbed together.

"Please, don't make me touch you again," he said. "You've spent so much time with those filthy losers in that disgusting Prole District I'm sure you're diseased. Filthy people. Really disgusting."

"You're free to send me back there anytime you like."

"Afraid I can't do that," Trump said. "See, you've proven to be a much more capable opponent than anyone could have predicted. You're quite the political strategerist."

"I'm really not ... and I'm pretty sure that's not even a word."

"Oh, don't sell yourself short, Jon. A sex scandal—genius! Really fantastic. When you first announced you were running, I wrote it off as nothing more than a publicity stunt, but I thought it was a tremendous opportunity to kick President Savage's ass out of the White House. Now, I see that you could actually win this thing."

"Please listen," I begged. "I had nothing to do with that sex scandal—I mean, besides taking part in the actual sex. I don't even want to win the election anymore! I just want to go home!"

Trump snorted. "You think you can fool me? You can't fool me. Tiberius Winston Ivanhoe Trump *invented* the sex scandal. By screwing a Walmart heiress, what you basically did was screw Walmart. And by screwing Walmart, you're screwing me—and I don't enjoy being screwed, Johnny boy."

"Then you must not be doing it right."

He bonked me on the head again, compacting my spine and sending tingling sensations shooting down my fingertips. Brian immediately hit Trump with the hand sanitizer again.

"Enough of these games! I have plans for you, Savage. As the old saying goes, 'If you can't beat 'em, force 'em to join you!'"

"I'm pretty sure that's *not* how that goes."

Trump wrapped his arm around Brian. "Brian here is going to be working exclusively for Walmart from here on out. He's finally come home." Brian wiped a tear from his eye. "He's going to be seeing to your … reeducation."

Trump patted me on the shoulder, and, after another squirt of sanitizer, turned to Brian and delivered directions to have me prepped for my *transformation*.

I didn't like the sound of any of it. The last time I had gone through a transformation was when I experienced puberty and that had been a complete mess.

"I'm looking forward to working with you, Jon," Trump said over his shoulder. Then he left me with Brian, who wore both halves of his smile now, which I assumed was not a good sign.

"What's going to happen to me?" I asked.

"You'll be transferred to another room for your transformation, but not just any room. The most dreaded room in this entire facility. A room where all your worst fears come true."

"Room 101?" I guessed.

"No! Room 102! Which is one *worse* than Room 101!"

He broke into an obnoxious cackle, which I'm sure he thought sounded evil and intimidating, but it certainly needed work. It went on too long, and his voice cracked throughout. It got annoying to the point I was glad when he finally stabbed me in the neck with a needle and returned me to the shadows.

***

I awoke in a room where there was no light (they certainly liked extremes here at the Walmart Corporation). I sat suspended in the darkness, strapped to some sort of metal chair. My arms and legs were held in place by what felt like leather straps. The way I sat, high and slightly reclined, reminded me of sitting in a dentist's chair. I tried to look around but found that my head, too, was trapped in some kind of vice so my motion was limited.

Brian's voice cut through the darkness. "Welcome to Room 102, Jonathan Savage!"

I could sense someone else moving in the darkness that wasn't Brian, someone scurrying from one side of me to the other. There was the metallic *clink* of metal touching metal and the sloshing of liquids. Then the stranger in the darkness started to hum some familiar jingle, which helped me follow his movements in the void.

"What's happening?"

"We're going to turn you from foe to friend," Brian answered. "We're going to teach you to love Walmart … whether you want to or not."

I laughed and it felt good to fill the darkness with my defiant laughter.

"Think it's impossible? You won't shortly."

The other person in the room drew close, breathing directly over me, and then I felt a hand covered in latex touch my face. I instinctively tried to raise my hand, but I was strapped to the chair and powerless to do anything.

A cold, metal object was clipped to my forehead on the right side, raising my eyelid and making it impossible for me to close my eye. A similar object was clipped to my forehead on the other side. I tested this one as well and after some rapid fluttering of my eye, something snapped and I was finally able to close my left eye again.

The person above me grunted in frustration, and I heard the person whisper to himself, "Goddamn cheap Walmart eye clamps—"

The metal object was removed and replaced with another, and, this time, I was unable to close either eye. I could feel my eyes drying almost immediately as I tried to shut my eyes from whatever horrors were to be inflicted upon me.

"You are to become Walmart's most fierce and loyal spokesman. Everyone learns to love Walmart sooner or later. How could you not with its vast selection and low, low prices?"

"Please! I just want to go home!"

"Oh, you are coming home. And Walmart will welcome you with open arms."

The lights suddenly flashed on, illuminating the room in all its hideous glory. I was strapped to a metal chair with dozens of wires and electrodes running into a machine that looked like a mix between a gas generator and a wood chipper. The three walls in my field of vision, the ceiling, and the floor appeared to be telescreens similar to the one in the Goldsteins' basement.

The worst sight, however, was the mysterious third party in the room.

The mystery man towered over me, wearing a lab coat covered in dark red stains and what appeared to be night vision goggles on his face. In his hand, he held a syringe equipped with the longest needle I had ever seen. He stepped toward me, brandishing the needle like a small sword.

"This is Dr. Brodsky," Brian said somewhere behind me. "He's going to give you something to help you across the friendship rainbow."

Dr. Brodsky circled around the chair until he, too, was somewhere out of view behind me with that giant needle.

"Please," I begged. "I don't need any help across the friendship rainbow. I love Walmart. I do."

"You may say that, but soon you'll mean it. See, we're going to remove your free will. By the time we're done with you, you'll have the appearance of a flesh and blood human being, but your brain will be nothing but cogs and gears designed to do Walmart's bidding like some sort of—oh I don't know—*wind-up grapefruit* or something."

The tip of the needle pierced the back of my skull and traveled downward into my spine. I could feel it chewing through my skin as it traveled deeper and deeper, ready to release its venom. A shot of pain tore through my spine and sent aftershocks coursing through my limbs, which eventually died in my fingers and toes. My vision blurred, faded, and when it returned, Brian and Dr. Brodsky stood in front of the chair.

"What did you do to me?"

"You'll see soon enough," Brian said. "Enjoy the show."

The lights clicked off, showering me in darkness again. A few seconds later, the sensation of being alone overwhelmed me. The telescreen directly in front of me lit up the room with a white standby screen. It counted down five … four … three … two … one …

The screen showed an African-American family barbecuing in the backyard—a father, mother, and two kids. The camera panned to their picnic table, highlighting several products while the family's plastic laughter played in the background.

"What is this?" I asked the darkness.

The telescreen to my left flickered to life and showed several products traveling down a conveyor belt to an automatic scanner. The words, "IF YOU CAN'T FIND IT HERE, YOU CAN'T FIND IT ANYWHERE…BECAUSE THERE'S NOWHERE ELSE TO SHOP!" rolled vertically down the screen.

The telescreen to my right flickered to life with an exterior shot of Walmart, complete with dancing mascot Jesus. The ceiling came to life with a Latino woman wearing a blue vest with a smiley face pin waving at the camera. The floor transformed into a first-person shot of someone traveling along the Walmart automatic walkway at high speeds, passing department after department after department.

While images and slogans bombarded me from all sides, I became aware of a feeling deep down in my gut that crept and crawled up my throat. It slowly traveled through my bloodstream until the feeling infiltrated every part of my body. It felt like I was going to be sick without the sensation of having to vomit. A wave of panic swept over me, but there was no way to escape it since I was strapped to the chair.

"WE'LL MATCH ANY PRICE BY ANY OF OUR COMPETITORS. HA! THERE ARE NO COMPETITORS!"

Sweat cascaded down my face and into my open mouth but immediately dried in the desert of my throat. I wanted desperately to throw up, to release the feeling of being sick, but release would not come.

A talking dog walked through Walmart pushing a shopping cart.

A yellow smiley face bounced around the store, lowering prices with each bounce.

Mascot Jesus drove off in a brand-spanking new Ford Pinto.

The sick feeling and thirst were unbearable, and all my pain seemed to be coming out of the telescreens. I could feel the pain coming from the screen behind me even though I couldn't see it. I tried to close my eyes but there was no escape from the bombardment of crappy Walmart commercials washing over me in torrents.

"Please, stop! Stop the crappy commercials! I'm going to be sick!"

I opened my mouth, my stomach muscles tightened, and I retched and heaved, but nothing flowed out of me, no relief came.

A Christmas scene. An Asian family unwrapped present after present under the tree. All the presents were wrapped in Walmart blue, dotted with yellow smileys.

UNWRAP THE FUN … AT WALMART!

"Please! I'll do anything! Just make the commercials stop!"

But they did not stop. They boxed me in, crept closer and closer, surrounded me, until, finally, a bright yellow smiling face engulfed me entirely.

Chapter VII

I dreamt I was back in my own time, sitting on the sofa inside the home I shared with my fake wife, Millie, watching myself being tortured on television. The entire living room seemed to be filled with a puke green haze. Klaryse entered the room glammed out in a designer dress and heels instead of her usual Walmart-issued togs. She wore pearls around her neck and wrists that accentuated her elegant neck and creamy white wrists. She sat next to me holding a giant bowl of popcorn.

We were not alone, though.

Crammed into the living room were a dozen camera crews staring, gawking, and ogling us with their periscope eyes. They drew closer, creating a human barricade around the sofa, and the closer they crept, the more the me on the screen seemed to suffer.

Knockknockknock.

I felt my non-corporeal self rise from the sofa, unable to ignore the call from the front door. The blockade of cameras opened like a gate to allow me passage. Klaryse reached out for me as if she didn't want me to leave, but I was too far out of her reach. I passed through the human gate and levitated to the door. It swung open on its own to reveal not a person but a building just a few feet from my home. It was so close only its brick exterior was visible, but, somehow, even with just this snapshot of the entire building, I knew it was the Walmart.

I continued my involuntary exodus, levitating over the strip of dead lawn that separated my home from the Walmart complex. The brick wall morphed into the entrance of the commercial palace, complete with inflatable Jesus mascot. He waved me toward the entrance, bouncing up and down and frantically waving his giant inflatable hands.

An unseen force continued to push me forward, for I could see the grass below me moving past, but I didn't seem to get any closer to the entrance of the building. Then the building morphed again, this time transforming from the Walmart complex into a towering blue church adorned with a giant yellow smiley face on the steeple where the bell should have swung.

Mascot Jesus morphed into the actual Jesus (at least my version of Jesus) complete with beard and flowing white robe. He continued to move in the same fashion as mascot Jesus, his body swinging and swaying rhythmically to some unheard song with the fluidity of someone dancing under water.

The space between me and the building evaporated and I found myself being dragged through the entrance of the church. As I passed the man I perceived to be Jesus, I heard someone whisper, "This is your new religion," although the words did not seem to come from Jesus, and his lips did not move.

The inside of the church was an exact replica of the lobby of the Mega-Walmart but instead of the giant hanging directories' usual labels, they were labeled with departments like *Gluttony*, *Sloth*, and *Greed*. The lobby was the site of a silent riot, citizens of the future in blue and red tunics punching, kicking, and clawing at one another without a sound being made.

As I floated further into the lobby, the two sides seemed to separate with the individuals in blue being pulled by an invisible hand to the left side of the lobby while the individuals in red were yanked to the right. Eventually, the entire mob separated like oil and water until there were two distinct sides.

In between the two mobs stood my other self, President Savage, waiting. The eyes of the mob focused on me, waiting for whatever it was I was supposed to do. Their cold, vacant stares made me more uncomfortable than the camera crews back in the house. No one smiled or frowned or even moved. They were machines waiting to be activated.

I stood face-to-face with President Savage, who had done some time traveling of his own and looked exactly like me now. He extended his hand, which now contained an iPalm screen. I glanced down at my own hand and realized that, I, too, was now equipped with an iPalm. His eyes were overcast in violet, and the reflection off his pupils showed that mine were, too.

We both raised our right hands simultaneously and exchanged a handshake that melted our skin together, forming a two-headed Savage hydra. A *thud* echoed in the soulless lobby, and when I looked away from the overcast eyes of my other self, everyone, blue and red alike, lay on the ground motionless, staring at me with doll's eyes.

I turned back to my twin to find not a mirror image but a face that was mine and, at the same time, not mine. A mustache began to sprout underneath my twin's nose, and his eyebrows grew thick and bushy. My mustachioed doppelganger applied pressure to our melted hands, sending shivers of pain coursing up my arm. I tried to pull away, but we were fused together. We were one. The pressure increased until I felt the bones in my hand snap, and then there was laughter echoing in the lobby but it was leaping off my own lips—

My eyes snapped open to find myself back in my original cell, sitting on the bench while Tiberius Winston Ivanhoe Trump and Brian Goldstein towered over me. My body felt numb. My limbs were heavy, but I found I could move them with some effort, and I could now turn my head freely. The two men were speaking but their voices were on mute.

A ringing sound like someone banging a spoon on sheet metal grew in volume and intensity in my skull until it finally crescendoed and faded, drifting down the knobs of my spine. Then the men's voices were audible again, the volume slowly rising from whispers.

Brian was saying, "—and he should be coming out of it any minute. Wait—Yes, I think he's back." He stepped forward and snapped his fingers at me the same way someone would snap at a dog to get its attention. "Hey! Hey! Savage! On your feet, boy."

My feet beneath me planted to the cell floor, and I felt myself slowly rising. I swayed uncertainly for a few seconds until I steadied and stood at attention. Brian ordered me forward into the center of the room, and, again, I complied. Brian drew in so close his hot breath rustled the whiskers under my nose (which usually took a few days to fill in), and circled around me, inspecting me like a lobster he was considering for dinner.

"Did the doohickey work?" Trump asked.

"Of course. Go ahead. Ask him anything."

Trump shoved Brian aside. His hand shot out and cradled my chin in his palm while his thumb jammed into my right cheek and his other four fingers into my left. He stared into my eyes and my open mouth as if he was trying to find a soul rattling around in my skull. He stepped back, and Brian immediately sprayed hand sanitizer into Trump's palms.

"Answer me a question, Savage," Trump said. "What do you think about Walmart?"

My answer was immediate and certain. "I love Walmart, Mr. Trump."

"Fantastic. And perhaps, Mr. Savage, you would be kind enough to share with me what it is you like so much about the Walmart Corporation."

"Gladly, sir. Walmart offers quality products at low prices and offers people the opportunity to save money and live better lives."

"Tremendous work. Tremendous. And would you be opposed, Mr. Savage, to representing the Walmart Corporation in the current election by joining forces with your former on-screen wife, Millicent? Perhaps as her running mate?"

"No objections, sir. Anything I can do to help promote a positive image of the Walmart Corporation."

Trump smiled and motioned as if he was going to slap Brian on the back but, in mid-swing, seemed to think better of it and simply returned the hand to his side.

"You've outdone yourself, Brian, my boy. Really top-notch work. Your father would be proud."

"Thank you, sir." Brian's face grew so flushed it seemed inevitable that cranberry juice would pour from his nostrils.

"You made the right decision turning this turd over to us instead of that loser president. We're going to take care of you, Brian. Believe me."

Trump ordered Brian to prep me for a press conference where I would announce my intention to drop out of the race and join Millicent as her running mate. Then he left us alone in my locked cell.

"Well, alone at last," Brian said to me, drawing in close again with his stinking breath. "I thought he would never leave. Let's take care of the pesky security cameras, too. That will really give us some privacy." His fingers danced across the screen on his iPalm. There was a loud *beep* and a *whir* behind the walls of the room. "There. Now, it's just you and me. Isn't that nice?"

"Yes. Very nice."

"You know, I have to thank you, Jon. Tiberius and I used to be pretty close, but we had a falling out after my family's finances forced me to seek opportunities elsewhere. I've done surveillance and reconditioning work for various entities, including your White House doppelganger. That orange troll never seemed to understand that a credit is a credit, even if it's not issued by Walmart. Your reeducation, however, has really brought us back together."

"You're very welcome."

"Now then, you and I have some personal business to attend to before your work for Mr. Trump begins. My sister has become collateral damage in your political scheming, and, as her big brother, it is my responsibility to protect her. Do you understand what I'm saying, Johnny?"

"I'm afraid not, sir."

"Then let me make it crystal clear: I'm ordering you to stay away from her. Do not contact her, do not agree to meet with her, do not message her. My sister is off-limits to you from here on out. Do you understand?"

"Get bent."

"That's what I wanted to—Wait. What?"

I don't know much about fighting. The only fisticuffs I've ever taken part in were in fifth grade after my gloating during a kickball game infuriated the biggest kid in class, Ozzy Alvarez, who proceeded to pull my shirt over my head and beat me unmercifully. I learned little from that beatdown since I was blinded by my own shirt and pounded into the ground within seconds. The singular bit of knowledge I do possess about throwing down is that men, in general, do not appreciate being kicked in the testicles.

That information seemed to hold relevance even decades in the future because when I shot my foot forward and connected solidly with the Goldstein family jewels, Brian dropped to the floor. I kicked him again for good measure. He uttered a tiny yelp, opened his mouth wide, and spewed vomit in a straight stream across the floor.

"You—" he half-whispered, half-coughed. "You're supposta—A zombie! How?"

I knew exactly what he was trying to say. He wanted to know why I wasn't a compliant brainwashed Walmart zombie.

"Please," I said. "Walmart's brainwash serum worked just as well as the rest of their product line."

The truth was that the sick feeling I felt at the beginning of the brainwash session quickly faded after a few minutes. I sat in the dentist chair watching crappy Walmart commercials for hours before I eventually fell asleep from sheer boredom.

My acting may not have been worthy of Sean Connery or Daniel Craig, but it was good enough to fool Brian.

My former captor attempted to struggle to his hands and knees, but I put an immediate stop to that by stomping on his hand, and then following that with a kick in his nose. His schnoz exploded like a grape being squashed, creating a bloody mustache above his upper lip.

I knelt next to Brian and slapped his face with the back of my knuckles to keep him from passing out.

"Stay with me, Brian. Where am I? What is this place?"

He lay wheezing on the floor before finally recapturing his breath. "You're … you're in the Tower of Walmart. It's where Trump keeps political prisoners."

"And how do I get out of here?"

"You can't—impossible. Too much security."

Almost on cue, the telescreen walls blinked red and a siren whined outside the cell. The words "SECURITY BREACH" blinked across the screens. Apparently someone else hadn't gotten the memo about the impossibility of breaching Walmart's security. The security message disappeared to show a security camera view of a narrow hallway labeled "Corridor C" in black stenciled block letters.

A thick cloud of smoke obstructed the view of the far end of the hallway, but there was a pile of store security agents strewn on the floor in the foreground. A fierce firefight raged in the corridor, the *pings* and *pows* of lasers echoing in the narrow hallway. Eventually the *pings* and *pows* ceased, and a solitary figure moved in the smoke. The figure drew closer to the foreground, and out of that foggy mist stepped the mustachioed assassin himself, John Wilkes Booth, holding a glowing cube in his hand.

I couldn't help but be impressed. The guy just did not quit!

I grabbed Brian by the collar of his tunic and shook the bastard awake. "Brian! Which corridor am I being held? Brian! Answer me!"

His eyes fluttered open. "OK, OK. Corridor F. You're in Corridor F."

I let the dead weight of his head slam back down onto the floor and raced to the door of the cell. I searched for some sort of keypad or retina display, but there didn't seem to be any kind of release for the door.

Another firefight erupted in Corridor D on the surrounding telescreens. The cube in Booth's hand formed some sort of shield around him and then exploded in a blast of light. All the store security agents fell to the floor and Booth marched on.

I raced back over to Brian and picked him up again by the shirt collar. "How the hell do I open the door?"

But there was no answer. Spit bubbled from his mouth and oozed down his chin. I shook him a few times, but that was more for my own self-satisfaction than anything else. Without the aid of my captor, though, one thing was clear: I was trapped.

Corridor E was the only obstacle standing between Booth and my cell. Resistance was fierce here, an obvious last stand effort, but Booth's cube seemed to be a device store security was not prepared for. This was no Walmart-issued firearm. This time, Booth turned the cube onto another side, and it leaked some sort of yellow gas that transformed Walmart's elite fighting corps into sleeping babes. He stepped over their bodies with the care of a kindergarten teacher during naptime.

He entered Corridor F, walked immediately to the third cell, and banged on the door with his fist. The metallic *clang* rattled the walls of the cell. I retreated to the far wall and collapsed onto the bench. My only option was to decide which telescreen to watch. It was the ultimate in reality television. Strangely enough, even though I knew Booth's goal was my demise, I found myself rooting for him. He was so damn determined. I felt completely detached from the action on the screen. I chalked that up to years of watching television. It's turned us into observers of our own lives.

Booth's luminous cube seemed to be some sort of Swiss army weapon. He flipped it on a different side and held it to the hinges of the cell door. The cube flared red and emitted a fiery orange glow that slowly transferred the color to the hinge. I watched the progress on the telescreen, wondering what the expression on my face would be when the hinges finally gave way and Booth stepped inside. Then I reminded myself I would never see it since Brian had shut off the camera in the cell.

The hinge turned from a bright orange to a cherry red and seemed to turn to putty and split in half. The entire door shifted, opening a sliver of triangle that offered a view into the corridor. On the screen, Booth peered into the opening of the cell.

I reminded myself I was a part of this drama and turned my attention from the screen to the cell door. Booth's beady eye peered through the opening like a cat staring into a bird cage. He tried to jam the cube through the opening, but it was too small to accommodate the weapon.

Back on the screen, Booth went back to work on the other hinge with the welding side of his cube. Again, I caught myself cheering him on. The tension was rising, and I had a hankering for a snack, maybe some popcorn or cashews.

Below the bench, Brian uttered a tiny moan.

"Shh," I told him. "I'm trying to watch."

On the screens, the final hinge was slowly transforming from solid metal to chewing gum. I closed my eyes and waited for the *clang* of the hinge giving way, which I assumed would be followed by the feeling of my soul escaping my body. Instead, I felt the bench beneath me begin to quake. Then the quake expanded to the wall behind me.

A crack rippled from the floor to the ceiling of the cell. I stepped over

Brian and stood in the center of the room, glancing from the wavering cell door to the growing crack in the far wall, wondering which horse to root for.

The cell door groaned, and it appeared as if the death Booth brought would be the first to cross the finish line, but the mysterious crack made a stunning comeback, ripping the entire wall away and revealing a hovercopter emblazoned with the presidential seal floating next to the building. A giant metal claw shot through the hole and wrapped its three prongs around my body. It yanked me out of the hole and reeled me in like a struggling catfish on a fishing line.

Being torn from the cell into the smog-covered sky was as traumatic as a newborn being ripped from the womb. I shielded my eyes from the natural light of the outside world, a world I hadn't been sure I would ever see again. My vision cleared just in time to throw one last glance back toward the building. Staring out from the hole in the building was John Wilkes Booth, stroking his mustache to an obscene degree.

One might think I'd feel a sense of relief at being rescued from Booth and the Tower of Walmart, but feeling relief would be a waste of emotion. I knew I was simply being rescued from the current life-and-death situation to be tossed into the next. Out of the frying pan and into the fire, and then from the fire into the sulfuric acid.

The claw dumped me into the cargo bay of the hovercopter, which immediately shot into the air, sending me tumbling onto the cold, metal floor. When I finally rolled to a stop, I glanced up and found myself surrounded by SS, who dumped a black sack over my head. I sighed heavily and embraced the darkness.

The sack was completely unnecessary, of course. I knew exactly where I was going.

Chapter VIII

The sack was removed from my head and there he—I—was, sitting behind the Resolute Desk in the Oval Office, which was completely trashed. The ping pong table was upended and broken glass lay scattered across the carpet, which appeared to be peppered with burn marks. The window through which I had exited my last visit had been boarded up but never repaired.

The look on President Savage's face made it clear who was responsible for the destruction. My hair tends to frizz out into dirty-blond cheese curls when I'm upset, and my doppelganger was rocking some serious snack doo. I prayed for a quick end to my misery, for my older self to take pity on me and end my involvement in all these shenanigans in the quickest and least painful way possible, but I knew I wouldn't be that lucky.

"Well, here we are again," President Savage said. He slowly rose from his seat and then mule-kicked it against the wall. "Past and present meet once again in the hallowed halls of the White House, a place where the future has been written by great men of the past for centuries."

"Got anything to eat?" I asked. "I'm starving."

They hadn't fed me very well during my last imprisonment and if I wasn't going to die, I figured the least my most recent captor could do was feed me.

President Savage pressed a button behind the desk and a lackey instantly entered with a Cherry Coke and a Snickers bar. I collapsed into a chair and inhaled my snack.

"Enjoy those," he said. "I know they're your favorite. Mine, too. They come from my personal supply. They don't make either of those products anymore. Now there's nothing but Walmart brand, and you can imagine how those taste."

I tried to say thanks, but, with my mouth full, it came out more like *dnkks*.

The president circled around the desk and took a seat on the corner of the massive slab of wood, towering over me as I continued to munch.

"You know, I have to give you credit. You've proven yourself to be a political savant beyond your years."

I licked the chocolate off my fingers and downed the rest of the Coke.

"Screwing Miss Goldstein and plastering it over the interwebs? Brilliant!"

"Yeah, that was due more to general horniness than political savvy."

"And then disappearing for a week afterwards? The screwing I could have thought of on my own, but your disappearing act was truly inspired. Always leave the people wanting more."

"I was kidnapped! Those Walmart goons locked me up and tried to brainwash me!"

The president chuckled. "Oh, that old bit. They tried the same thing with me at the beginning of my second term. It never works. You're just lucky the dumb bastards shut off the surveillance in your cell. That's how my techs found you. There are nearly a thousand cells in the Tower of Walmart. When surveillance was killed in one of the thousand, we knew we had you. See the latest polls?"

When I reminded him I'd been locked away in a cell for over a week, he flicked on the telescreen and changed it to the Walmart News Channel. A reporter was going over the latest polling numbers. Millie still held a slight advantage with 34% of the vote while my other self and I shared 33% each. Going into the final week of the election, only a single percentage point separated me from claiming the Oval Office for myself. Not bad for someone who hadn't done anything in the last week besides make a viral sex tape and watch 72 straight hours of Walmart commercials.

"You see?" my other self said. "You and I are mirror images of each other, even in the polls. Your political savvy is attracting just as much of the vote as my threats on their lives."

It was at that point I realized the president hadn't made a single threat since I arrived. Obviously, he had snatched me for a reason, but only mascot Jesus knew what it was.

President Savage abandoned his perch on the desk, chuckling as he did so, and circled around behind me. I kept waiting for the icy cold grip of my own hands to wrap around my neck, but, instead, they fell down hard on my shoulders. Usually I feel uncomfortable when people invade my personal space, but my other self's presence failed to trigger even a hint of anxiety.

"Jonathan, I brought you here to make you an offer."

He circled around the chair and stood in front of me, studying my eyes. He ordered me to stand. I obeyed the order. We stood toe-to-toe—same eyes, same lips, same jawline—as a single entity separated only by time and space.

"I want you to join me. I want you to run this country by my side. What I'm proposing is an alliance between past and present for the purpose of saving the future of the United States."

"So ... I'd be your vice-president?"

"No, no, no. What I'm suggesting is a partnership—equals. Twelve years ago this country voted Jonathan Milhous Savage into the office of the presidency, and you are the biological entity known as Jonathan Milhous Savage, so, *technically*, you have as much claim to the office as I do."

For some reason all I could picture was Darth Vader reaching out to Luke Skywalker near the central air shaft on Cloud City.

"Why would I agree to join you?" I asked. "You sent an assassin back in time to murder me, and then you tried to kill me yourself!"

"You're living in the past. It's time to focus on the here and now. You and I have the same goals. We both want to free the people from the death grip of Walmart. We just have different approaches."

"Different approaches? You're murdering your own citizens! Why would I agree to join forces with a homicidal maniac?"

"Because *you're* the homicidal maniac. Like I told you before, I'm just you a little further down the road. You're tainted by the optimism of youth. You still believe that people know what's best for them. Trust me, they don't. They're stupid and they either need to be converted or slaughtered. The only way to take Walmart down is to eliminate its customer base."

"Which is everyone!" I pointed out.

I tried to look away. I didn't want to share the same room with this monster, let alone the same DNA. But there was no denying we were one in the same. He was me and I was he. This genocidal megalomaniac was who I was destined to become.

President Savage seemed to read my mind—*his mind*—because he smiled and rubbed his hands together.

"Yes, you're starting to accept the truth. The only difference between the life I lived and the one you're currently living is Millie's presence and now that you've shed her like a layer of dead skin, there's nothing standing between you and your destiny. This office is where you'll end up eventually, so why not just cut out the middle of the story and jump right to the end?"

"Because maybe this isn't where I want to end up!" I yelled so loudly the president took a step back. "Maybe I don't want the responsibility or the power or the ping pong table! Maybe I just want to be Joe Nobody whose biggest responsibility is deciding which pizza place to order from on Friday night because, if I'm being honest here, I don't *want* to be president, or a reality television star or an anti-establishment rebel or a pushover husband! What I really want is to travel back to my own time, watch a Bond flick, and drink a beer!"

President Savage studied me, but this time he looked like someone studying the face of a stranger. Then a strange smile spread across his face, an unsettling smile that started as a twitch of his lower lip but eventually blossomed into a full-blown, Joker-style madman grin.

"Well why didn't you just say so?"

He jogged behind his desk and rummaged through his desk drawers. Eventually, he jogged back around and tossed me a blue mobile iPalm.

"What's this?"

"Your ticket home."

He helped me strap the iPalm on. It fit like a glove (minus the fingers) onto my left hand. From the base of the device hung what looked like an IV. Then I realized that was exactly what it was since the president jammed the needle-like projection into the big blue vein traveling up my wrist.

"It runs on your body's natural electrical impulses," he explained. "It's a presidential iPalm so it gives you unlimited access to the interwebs and all the country's cybersystems. It also gives you access to every single iPalm in the country. You can lock someone's screen, open their mic, cut off access to every iPalm in Kentucky if you want. It can also provide information on any U.S. citizen living or dead, unlock any digital lock, and check this out. It's even got a laser."

He demonstrated, aiming at a pencil on his desk and slicing it in half.

Zaaaap!

"Why the hell would I need a laser?" I asked.

"Why the hell does James Bond need all his fancy gadgets? He never knows until the exact moment when he realizes he has the perfect tool for the job. But forget about the laser for right now. Let me show you the true worth of this gift."

His fingers clumsily navigated through the iPalm's interface. He typed in our locker combination from middle school, and the screen faded to black. It took a few seconds before the screen blinked back on. When it did I found myself staring at a long line of numbers and letters, some sort of serial number, and a date at the bottom of the screen.

"What is all this?" I asked.

"It's what you asked for. One of the privileges of being president is I can grant instant time passports. How do you think I gained access to Booth?"

"Are you telling me—"

"You can be home in time for supper."

I should have just accepted the gift, but I felt the need to ask why.

"Why not?" President Savage answered. "If you're not going to join me, then the best thing I can do is get rid of you. You can't be much of a martyr for the opposition if you abandon the cause. All I ask in return for my fervent generosity is that you live as boring a life as possible to ensure your show never gets picked up for another season. Don't do anything even remotely entertaining, settle down with an ugly girl with a nice personality, and don't stand up for anything … ever! Do we have a deal?"

He extended his hand—my hand—in a gesture that, once consummated, would symbolize exactly what I desired all wrapped up in a pretty pink bow. Things could never go back to the way they were before I dove down the rabbit hole in that dentist's office, but I figured I could enjoy my mediocre existence of serving moderately appetizing meals and watching mind-numbing television as well as most people do. It sounded like the best deal I could hope for, but my hand remained at my side.

"What's your hesitation? I thought this is what you wanted."

"It is," I said. "I want to go back, but I guess it feels a bit like running away."

"And?"

"I guess I thought I might be able to do some good around here. I thought maybe I could make a difference without killing everyone."

President Savage laughed deep and hard, channeling his best Baron Samedi (my favorite Bond villain for those Bond noobs out there).

"Oh, what a young, naïve fool I once was. Do you think this country is just some spilt milk you can clean up with a few paper towels? This country's problems weren't created overnight. They were underway well before we were even born. Basically every decision this country has made since World War II has been wrong. The only solution now is complete annihilation. Only then, when there is nothing left to save, will it be possible for something better to be built over the ashes of what was once a great country. Some problems can't be fixed in four or eight years ... or even twelve."

"I don't believe we're that far gone."

The president nodded toward my hand. "Your pinky's twitching."

I looked down, and, sure enough, my pinky *was* twitching. I hated that he knew I was lying. I figured my hatred for him might speak volumes about my self-esteem.

"All right, so maybe you're right," I admitted, "but that doesn't mean I'm willing to abandon all the people who believed in me."

"Then you have a choice to make: stay or go. And don't dawdle because those pass codes will expire at the end of the day. At midnight, your chances of ever returning home turn into a big, fat pumpkin. If you're still hanging around in my timeline tomorrow, you're fair game."

President Savage left me sitting in his office—*my office*—to think things over. My head swam with the faces of everyone who depended on me in one way or another: Klaryse, Zimmerman, Spoonz, Granger, and the clueless faces of the billions of registered voters. They needed me, but the only thing I needed was finally strapped to my hand.

I had a way out.

Chapter IX

Benny dropped me off in front of the Walmart Hotel 9-43B, nicknamed "The Huxley Hotel." It had been some sort of Soma den back before blanket legalization. The Huxley Hotel was the new headquarters of The Morlock Party.

The Huxley Hotel wasn't my first stop after leaving the White House. After calling my reliable chauffeur, I had him truck me back to the Prole District, where I assumed I would find my advisors and the rest of my associates.

Instead, I found the Winnebago abandoned (now nothing more than a giant toilet on four wheels) and a mob of devoted followers ready to welcome me back with open arms. Some of the children even asked me to sign copies of my sex tape. I was eventually informed that my headquarters had been relocated earlier in the week to the Huxley Hotel after the Winnebago broke down and an influx of donations had poured in from Granger's resources.

The hotel was a dump, but I assumed that was the case for most of the hotels under the Walmart banner. The bar in the lobby was called Huxley's Hole, a wood-paneled dive bar populated with dimly lit booths and lopsided tables. The walls were lined with drug paraphernalia from early in the 21st Century: makeshift bongs made from milk cartons and toy trains, hundreds of lighters adorned with skulls and marijuana leafs, and several display cases of medical syringes. These items were considered so archaic they were safe to hang on the walls as novelties, much like a musket or powder pouch.

I found my political team (which had grown considerably since I had last seen it and now included several of the screaming girls from Klaryse's basement) filling out the booths and tables on the far half of the bar.

They were so busy no one even seemed to notice me enter. Then someone did. It must have been someone near the bar because that's the area that grew silent first. The silence spread throughout the room until it completely covered it like a wool sweater. Their eyes revealed a buffet of emotions from relief to hope to unadulterated joy.

The sad thing was that these people believed in me … for whatever reason. Maybe it was because I represented a time they considered to be more wholesome and prosperous or maybe it was because they felt like they knew me from all those years watching me on my reality show, or maybe they had just been that impressed by my sex tape (all right, it probably wasn't the sex tape). Whatever the reason, these people truly believed I could save them.

It saddened me that they had chosen their messiah so poorly.

Dr. Zimmerman emerged from the throngs of supporters wearing a half-cocked smile. He waddled over, wearing what looked like a brand new sweater vest (this one checkered red and brown), and leaned in close so that only I could hear him.

"You still you or are you a Walmart zombie?"

"Unfortunately, I'm still me."

That seemed to be all the assurance he needed. He made a grand sweeping gesture with his arm and thrust his hand in my face.

"Ladies and gentlemen, the next President of the United States!"

A roar erupted from the bar that hung thick in the rafters for a solid thirty seconds before eventually dying with a cry of, "Spoons!" I awkwardly raised my hand and offered a little half-wave in response, which elicited another roar from my supporters that lasted even longer. This time, the ovation inspired nothing but guilt.

Zimmerman must have seen that I wanted a word alone because he ordered everyone to return to work, which they eagerly did, moving about the bar between different makeshift stations sorting through digital buttons, digital signs, and making phone calls on their iPalms. The place looked like a beehive of activity with me as the slothful queen.

My sweater-vested mentor ushered me into a booth on the empty half of the bar. Zimmerman wasn't the reason for my visit, but I figured he could help me accomplish my actual objective.

"It's good to see you, lad," the old man said. "Don't take this the wrong way, but I was kind of hoping you might not turn up until tomorrow night's final debate. The numbers since you disappeared have been staggering. Taking yourself off the grid after your public sexual outing was brilliant."

"I was kidnapped."

"I know, I know. But it was still brilliant! I wish I had thought of it. I would have kidnapped you myself."

"I promise I'll disappear again shortly, but I need your help first. I need to find Klaryse. I know I'm the last person she'd want to see, but I just—I need to talk to her."

Zimmerman's face wrinkled like a raisin. He tilted his head, and his entire sweater vest seemed to puff up like an irritated blowfish.

"What? What's wrong?"

"This may surprise you," he said, "but—"

He stepped aside and motioned to the corner of the room, where Klaryse sat alone at a table for two, staring at me. Zimmerman's face unwrinkled into a mischievous old man grin.

"Sometimes, things just work out, eh?"

I didn't know what the hell he was talking about. For the last few years, *nothing* had worked out. I had suffered one kick to the groin after another in life and things only got worse when I stepped outside my own time period. Discovering Klaryse through nothing more than serendipity nearly brought me to tears.

According to Zimmermman, he had hunted Klaryse down after my disappearance to explain that I had nothing to do with our public sex outing and apologize for exposing her in our sexcapades. He offered her a position as part of my campaign team as a sign of good faith, assuming she would reject the offer. To his (and my) surprise, she accepted and had been helping to keep my bid for the presidency alive in my absence.

"I want to apologize to you, too," Zimmerman said. "What I did was the desperate act of a desperate man. It was a dirty move, and that's not the kind of campaign I want to run. If I want you to be a better candidate than your predecessor, then I need to run a more moral campaign. So I hope you can forgive me."

I had nearly forgotten that I was supposed to be pissed at Zimmerman with all the being kidnapped and brainwashed and everything. I gave him the lip service he was seeking because, really, forgiveness seemed pointless considering what I was planning to do. Since I would soon be bouncing out on him and my campaign, thus negating all the hard work he and everyone else had been busting their humps to produce, I figured we were about even.

Zimmerman ushered me over to the table and turned to leave, but I grabbed him by the sweater vest and stopped his retreat. His face wrinkled again, confused by my hesitation. I'm sure the old man assumed we'd have plenty of time to catch up, but the truth was we didn't. After all the old man had done for me, I owed him at least a few parting words.

"Hey," I said, unsure what I was going to say. "I just wanted to thank you—for everything you've done for me and, I guess most importantly, for believing in me. And even though I know you choosing me had more to do with my other self and my reality show, I'm still grateful.

No one's ever believed I was capable of—anything really. So, thanks."

It may not have been Shakespeare, but it would have to do. Zimmerman's wrinkles shifted as he blinked hard. His arms expanded, and he pressed his sweater vest against me in an all-encompassing bear hug. He held me there, cradling my head in his arms, and I lost myself in that hug, traversed through time, and it was the first time since I stumbled into that dentist's office that I felt safe.

Zimmerman finally released me from his sweaty sweater grip, and even I was surprised to see tears in his eyes. Those tears made my leaving that much harder.

When I finally took a seat across the table from Klaryse, neither of us said anything. We both smiled quietly, a small candle burning between us. The soft glow cast a shadow over her face that made the illuminated parts even more beautiful. Her beauty seemed more middle class sitting in a dive bar, the sweat of a day's work still fresh on her brow.

I had been so sure that finding her would be an arduous ordeal that I wasn't quite sure what I wanted to say besides begging and pleading her forgiveness. I started to speak, but she cut me off with a raised finger. She made a small motion with her head, indicating the bar behind me.

"We're not alone," she whispered.

I glanced over my shoulder and realized what she meant. Everyone in the bar was still making phone calls and programming digital campaign buttons, but they were only half paying attention to their task. The other half was focused on our table. I'd be lying if I said it didn't piss me off a little bit. What? Did they think we were going to tear our clothes off and go at it right there in the bar?

Klaryse danced her fingers across her iPalm and a blue light illuminated the screen. The light started as small as a pinprick but began to pulse, expanding like a balloon filling with helium. The light continued to grow until it created a small tent that encompassed me, Klaryse, and the entire table.

"Private chat room," she explained.

I glanced back over my shoulder, and, sure enough, everyone had turned their attention back to their tasks. They couldn't see us or hear us even though we could see them. I turned back to Klaryse, assuming that when I did I would say something. I didn't … mainly because she was aiming a laser can directly at my face.

"What the hell are you doing?"

"I'm here to kill you," she said. "After my brother's royal screw-up, Tiberius said this is the only way for our family to remain on the payroll. He said it was my duty as a Goldstein."

Her slender arm quaked, her knuckles whitened. I glanced around frantically, praying someone was watching, but then I remembered the private chat room. Yelling seemed pointless. I was going to be assassinated in the middle of a crowded room and not a single person was going to notice.

Then something happened I didn't expect. Klaryse set the can down on the table and slid it over to me.

"I decided that maybe it was time the Goldsteins stood for something more than a dollar sign."

I let out my breath and snatched the can off the table. Then I checked to see how bad the damage was in my underpants.

"Holy shit!" I said. "I thought you were going to kill me!"

"I'd be lying if I said I wasn't thinking about it," she said. "Consider that payback for the millions of people who now know what a Klaryse Goldstein orgasm sounds like."

"Yeah, I'm really sorry about the whole sex scandal thing—"

She waved off my apology like a troublesome mosquito. "I know you had nothing to do with it. Zim explained everything. Besides, it gave me a small taste of what your life's been like for the past few years. It's a little different when you're on the other side of the telescreen."

"Welcome to my nightmare."

"At least our little indiscretion rejuvenated your campaign. You might actually have a shot at winning this thing and you better considering I sacrificed my line of credit for you. I'd prefer not to be poor for nothing."

"Are you sure this is what you want?" I asked. "You're throwing away *everything*."

Her fingers moved toward her iPalm, but at the last minute, she stopped. She returned her hand to the top of the table and looked at me instead. "Do you remember the first day we met? Our drive through the Prole District? And the pretzels?"

"I remember the pretzels."

"I figure I've eaten a lot of pretzels in my life. More than my fair share. Me helping you win this campaign, helping get you elected? This is my bag of pretzels that I'm tossing out the window."

"Metaphors are great."

"They really are," she agreed. "Besides, I believe in you. You're totally going to win this thing!"

"Yeeeaaah, that's what I wanted to talk to you about," I said. I pulled my presidential iPalm out from under the table. "I'm going home."

I explained the president's offer. My news was not met with the enthusiasm I expected.

"Can you give that laser can back please?"

"I understand your frustration, but how could I possibly pass up his offer? I can get out of here with my life intact."

"But what about your campaign? Your promises? You were going to change things. Can you really just walk away without a second thought?"

"I can walk away without a *first* thought. If I don't leave now, and I lose the election, I'll be stranded here. I'll be as good as dead."

Klaryse leaned back in her chair, cradling her springy curls. She seemed to look past me, over my shoulder at the anthill of activity. When her eyes returned, they were daggers.

"This thing is bigger than you now. People have sacrificed everything because they believe in you. You once accused me of being a good person, and now I'm returning the favor. You could topple Walmart and the president and finally give us the future we deserve."

It scared me to hear how genuine she was. This young woman actually thought I was capable of solving any of these titanic problems.

"I never asked you to sacrifice anything for me," I said. "I'm just one man. I can't fix any of these problems. Besides, some problems are too big to be fixed in four or eight years. Or even twelve."

Her eyes studied me, burrowed deep under my skin. "Those sound like someone else's words."

I assured her they were mine, which was technically true.

"Really? One man can't make a difference? Why don't you tell that to Martin Luther King Jr. or George Washington or Jesus Christ!" Her iPalm chastised her with a loud *beep*. "The point is, a person who believes strongly enough in his convictions can change the course of history. Maybe it's time for *you* to believe in something, Jon."

"I do," I said. "I believe in self-preservation, and the only way to ensure my safety is to get the hell out of Dodge. I thought it meant something to be loved by millions, but I realize how meaningless that is now. All I need is one person's love and that's why I thought you might consider … going with me."

Her eyes softened, peering at me through glistening emeralds. There was a secret in those eyes struggling to the surface.

"Jon, I can't. Even if I wanted to, I can't."

"But why?"

She wouldn't answer. Whatever her secret was it was buried too deep for excavation with our limited time. I was working with a ticking clock, so I gave her one of her own.

"The burnout at the front desk offered me a room free of charge. I'm going to grab some much needed sleep and some room service.

Consider my offer. There's nothing here for you, Klaryse. I may not be able to offer you a life of luxury, but … I've got Netflix."

She laughed, although it was obvious she didn't want to.

"Are you at least going to tell Zim?" she asked.

I spotted the sweater-vested old man throwing out orders among the troops. He waddled from station to station, making sure everything was running smoothly.

"I thought maybe you could tell him," I said.

Klaryse shook her head, tears forming in the corner of her eyes. "I won't. I won't crush that dream for him. He believes in you more than anyone … because he has to. You're his chance for redemption. If you want to rip that man's heart out, you use your own hand." She stood with such force she almost knocked her chair over. "I hope you reconsider. Otherwise, this would be a pretty lame series finale, Johnny Savage."

She left me then, returning to the throng of supporters and advisors busy working on getting me elected to an office I technically already possessed. I watched those curls disappear into the crowd and knew it was for the last time.

Chapter X

The Huxley Hotel's rooms had all the charm of a mausoleum. There was a bed with white sheets and a beige comforter with no pattern facing a wall-encompassing telescreen, and instead of a carpet and wallpaper, the floor and walls were covered in a beige tile similar to the floor of an operating room. The room was being cleaned when I arrived. Instead of a maid, an elaborate sprinkler system filled the room with a smoky gas that smelled like roach repellent.

I couldn't have cared less at that point. I plopped down on the bed, expecting it to be wet from the cleaning solution, but it was completely dry (even though the sheets reeked of the mystery solution). I started to slip into the dark embrace of sleep when there was a knock at the door. I rolled off the bed and stumbled to the door, unlocking the bolt and throwing it open for Klaryse … only it wasn't Klaryse.

Millicent stepped inside as if I had invited her in. She walked to the bed and took a seat, crossing her legs and resting her folded hands on her lap, sitting up straight so her chest was on full display in an absolutely stunning one-strap red sequined dress that looked to be more in the fashion of our time—my time—than the future's bland offerings.

"Hello, hubby."

"How the hell did you know I was here?"

"Please, Jonathan. Privacy is as extinct as the dinosaurs."

She rose, almost levitated from the bed, and clicked over in her stiletto heels. She led me, her fingertips gently grazing the nape of my neck, back over to the bed. It was a familiar trek. She used to use the move to Sherpa me into the sack before we were married. Funny that those excursions became almost non-existent once she had that ring on her finger.

She motioned to the bed. "Come. Sit."

And I did.

"I came here to offer you a future more glorious than any you could possibly imagine."

"I'm sorry, honey dearest, but what is this about? I thought Trump wanted me dead after his little brain-washing venture didn't work out."

"Tiberius is under a lot of pressure from his puppeteers in Beijing to deliver the presidency. He's not thinking straight. History has shown that killing someone is the *worst* way to get rid of them. Look how the whole crucifixion thing turned out. No, I'm here to do what Tiberius and his brainwashing couldn't. I'm here to recruit you. I want you to stop all this silly nonsense and join me as my running mate. I want it to be your *choice*."

I almost wish I would have been drinking something at that moment so I could have done a spit take.

"Me? Join you?" I said, making a show of the absurdity of it all. "Why in Jesus' name would I make that mistake again?"

A *beep* echoed off the porcelain walls. I was unsure where it came from until I noticed Millie staring down at her iPalm. She had been reequipped.

She sashayed past me and around the bed. I told myself not to look, not to care what she was doing, but I looked. I saw exactly what she wanted me to see: the back of her. And, yes, the view was spectacular.

"You treated me worse than something you found stuck to the bottom of your favorite heels," I reminded her—and me. "I was *miserable* when I was with you."

"You're still stuck in the past, Jon. I'm talking about the future. Imagine being America's most powerful couple, fully funded by Walmart. All the luxury and prestige of being in charge without any of the responsibility."

"So this is a business proposal?"

She inched closer, resting her hand on my inside thigh. "I don't see any harm in mixing business with pleasure. As I recall, we had some pretty good times together once upon a time. You remember?"

And I did. We dated for eight months before we were married, and I remember those first few months being pretty good. In fact, they were perfect. It was the reason I married Millie in the first place. We would listen to The Smiths while we made out in the shitty apartment I owned before Millie and I got married. We visited Atlantic City and played skee ball on the Boardwalk until the arcades closed, and then walked out onto the beach, illuminated by the moon, and made love. Those first few months with Millie felt like a dream.

Millie must have seen the memories bouncing around in my noggin because she smiled and made a noise like the coo of a dove. She rose and bent over, making it quite clear she wasn't wearing underwear, and pressed her hand against one of the ceramic tiles. The wall hissed, and then several of the tiles slid out, projecting into the room, to reveal a container hidden in the wall. She reached into the container and pulled out a bottle of wine.

There was more to the room than met the eye.

Millie stood up straight and shot a glance at me over her shoulder, flinging her strawberry-blonde locks behind her. She pressed another tile and a tabletop protruded from the wall. Another touch of her fingertips produced two cushioned seats. Millie set the wine on the table and let her body lightly descend onto the cushion. She nodded to the other cushion.

"Come," she said. "Join me."

And I did.

Two more tiles slid away to reveal wine glasses, which Millie filled with wine and set on the table.

"I'm terrified to even think what Walmart wine might taste like," I confessed.

"Oh, it's not Walmart. This is something I brought from—home. Technically, it's illegal for civilians to carry goods from one time to another, but I've managed to smuggle a few items over the time border during my trips back and forth through the years."

I suddenly realized that all those trips to *see her mother* probably weren't what they seemed to be.

She sipped from her glass, her lips glistening with red wine. She lowered her glass and stared me down, daring me to do the same. I complied, raising the glass, but her stare was almost too intense, too hopeful. I lowered the glass back to the table, unsipped.

"Jon, I already told you I'm not interested in killing you. Now drink."

And I did. It wasn't half bad.

"How the hell did you get this bottle in my room?" I asked. It seemed like a fair question considering I didn't think anyone knew I was even there.

Millie shrugged, sending her perky tits bouncing. "Room service. I know a guy who works in the kitchen. We had a thing two years ago."

"We were still married two years ago!"

"You're not focusing on what's important. This is your opportunity to live the life you've always wanted as my husband and vice-president. I know you don't like making decisions and you prefer to stay uninvolved, and there's no better job for lack of decision-making and uninvolvement than the vice-presidency. Think of the possibilities."

And I did. I thought about being someone important, living in luxury, pretending to run the country at the side of my beautiful pseudo-wife without a care in the world except how to spend all our money. Basically,

I thought about being a member of England's royal family. But while I thought about the future with Millie, I couldn't help remembering our past.

Millie read the hesitation in my eyes. She dropped to her knees in front of me and nestled her head in my lap, increasing the difficulty of the decision-making process.

"Please, Johnny," she cooed. "Say you'll do it. Say yes. For me."

But I didn't.

"No."

Her head shot up out of my lap, her eyes blazing. "What did you say?"

"I told you no," I said. "No, no, no, no, nonononononononono. NO!"

She rose to her full height so fast she almost toppled over. I stood to meet her. With the height of her heels we stood eye-to-eye. She opened her mouth as if to say something, her coral lips parting, but then she snapped them shut again. Instead, she reared back with her right hand and shot her open palm toward my face. I intercepted it, clutching her wrist in my hand. My fingernails dug into her flawless porcelain skin.

"Stop!" she cried. "You're hurting me!"

"No. I'm putting an end to you hurting me."

I threw her back down onto the cushion.

She rubbed her cherry wrist and tried to shoot back up to her feet, but I immediately shoved her back down.

"Let me tell you something—" she said.

"No, let me tell *you* something! For years I allowed you to push me around, and that ends today! You told me what to do, what to think, how to feel, and I let you do it 'cause you were hot, but now I see you for the soulless bitch that you are. As far as I'm concerned when it comes to you and me, it's 'til death or time travel do us part. Now get in the kitchen and make me a chicken pot pie!"

She glanced around, wide-eyed, as if this were actually a possibility.

"But—there's no kitchen!"

"Then just shut up and listen."

All those years of living under Millie's thumb washed away in that moment, watching real fear reside for the first time behind her eyes. I saw her for what she really was. Without the aide of her Walmart overseers, she was nothing but a scared little girl.

"All this is mute anyway," I said.

"Moot."

"What?"

"It's *moot*. You said it was *mute*. You always say *mute* when you mean *moot*."

"Whatever! Listen. You can tell Trump and your Walmart cronies that they won't have to worry about my political aspirations anymore. I've got other plans." I showed her the presidential iPalm.

"You're going back?"

I nodded.

She fell to her knees again, but this time she wrapped herself around my leg like a terrified child during a thunderstorm.

"Oh, please, please, please take me with you!"

"Wait—What? You want to come back with me? What about Walmart?"

Her head shot up, whipping me in the face with her hair.

"Screw Walmart! You can't leave me here in this shithole! If I have to wear another puke green dress I'm going to … well, I'll *puke*! Plus, I'd finally be able to pursue my dream."

"Your dream?"

It suddenly struck me that I knew nothing about this woman in reality. All I knew about her was what she pretended to be. I had known this woman for years, and I knew nothing of her hopes, her dreams, her fears.

She stood and walked very dramatically to the far wall. She pressed her hand against the telescreen like it was the face of her lover.

"All I've ever wanted was to be a famous actress," she said. "I remember watching old sitcoms as a child and just wishing it was me on that telescreen, but scripted television was extinct by the time I started my career. I was stuck playing pretend in Walmart's cheap reality shows, and, sure, I've won two Wally's for my performance as your wife, but that's not *real* acting. If I traveled back I could pursue an *actual* acting career. I could be part of a production with a director and a script and other actors. Instead of playing the antagonist, *I* could be the star!"

There was a glimmer in her eyes I had never seen before. This was the real Millicent … uh … whatever the hell her real last name was. I was meeting my wife of three years for the first time.

Before I realized what was happening, she crawled into my lap, clamping me to the chair with her thighs. Her hair fell into my open mouth, choking me. I coughed and spit until I was finally able to dislodge her silky strands from my throat.

"Take me with you. You don't have to have anything to do with me. Or we can go back to playing house," she cooed. "Whatever you want. Like I told you before, I'm quite the little actress."

Beneath the canopy of blonde, Millie's lips found mine. Everything about that kiss was familiar: the lips, the tongue, the taste. But it wasn't the same. The curtain of deceit had lifted, and something tasted sour. I tried to pull back, pull away, but she dug her nails into the back of my neck and bit my lip. I finally managed to escape her embrace but not before leaving a large chunk of my lip behind.

"So what do you say, Johnny?" she asked. "Shall we screw on it?"

"I think that you have as much business in the past as I have in the future."

I shoved her off my lap and onto the floor. My fist pounded the ceramic tiles enough times that the table and seats retracted back into the walls, allowing me passage around the heap of my fallen wife. I marched around the bed and threw open the door.

"The truth is," I said, "I just don't see much of a future for us, Millie."

She flung her hair over her shoulder, swooshing it directly into my face.

"Whatever," she said. "You have a small penis anyway."

And my wife marched out of my life.

Chapter XI

Benny's cab passed through the SS checkpoints and stopped in front of the deserted Time Port. Maybe it was the smoke filling the back of the cab, but I felt like I was trapped in a sort of malaise that kept my hand in my lap instead of reaching for the door handle. The timer on the presidential iPalm still had 43 minutes left before my window of opportunity closed forever.

Klaryse never showed up at the room back at the Huxley. I eventually slunk down to Huxley's Hole and searched for her there. I couldn't find her, and since I was terrified of running into Zim and suffering an outbreak of conscience, I skedaddled out of there, leaving all the dramatic farewells to play out in my dreams.

Benny must have felt my hesitation through the haze because he killed his roach and stuck his head through the smoke into the backseat.

"What's wrong wit you, boss? I thought dis is where you wanted to go."

"It is. It's just—"

There was no good way to end the sentence. I was minutes from escaping this nightmare, and I felt like I was returning home after a week at summer camp.

"Why you want me bring you ere, anyway?" Benny asked. "You ain't leaving us, is you?"

"I'm afraid I is, Benny."

"But what 'bout t'morrow's big debate? The election just be 'nother week away."

"I won't be there. For the debate or the election. I'm afraid this is g'bye, Benny."

Benny's face crumbled. It disappeared back into the smoke but then reappeared a few seconds later looking less compact but equally as anxious.

"But who 'ol Benny supposta vote fer? Benny ain't gonna vote fer no Walmart crony or no tyrannical monster like yo other self."

"You were going to vote for me?"

"'Course. Why you think I'm givin' ya all dese free rides? Not bad havin' the president owe you a few, eh?"

Benny's support should have inspired a spark of pride, but it didn't. It made me feel rotten. I guess it was one thing to hear faceless members of the mob chanting your name, but it was different when it was some poor as dirt cabbie hitching his future to your back.

"Is a real shame," Benny said, retreating back into the smoke. "Thought things might up 'n change 'round 'ere. Had 'nough of them crooks in Washington. Ah well. Guess everyone belongs where they belong."

I parted ways with Benny, stepped out of the cab and watched the van packed full of screaming kids drive off, weaving between abandoned vehicles until it finally turned a corner and sped out of sight.

The SS had cleared the building under the guise of a terrorist threat by the Historical Preservation Society to ensure my departure would go uninterrupted and unnoticed. I found the building locked and deserted. As promised, my presidential iPalm granted me access.

The last time I had been in the lobby I had been too busy running for my life to take it all in properly. Walmarts lined both sides of the lobby, and, unlike most train and airport lobbies, there wasn't a single bench or place to sit down. I figured the thought process must be that a lack of benches would force people into the stores. It frightened me that I was starting to think like Tiberius Winston Ivanhoe Trump and the rest of his cronies.

I was so busy admiring the spider's web of commercialism that I didn't notice the figure looming over me until it was too late. I knew when I turned, Booth would be there pointing some can or cube or fork at my head and this time there would be no escape. I spun quickly to at least get one last glance at that thick mustache before buying the farm, but it wasn't Booth who had joined me. No, it was a young SS guard decked out in his shiny helmet and uniform. He was short and a little chubby and looked like he would be more comfortable in a cubicle than under a bucket helmet.

"Abend," he said. "English?"

I nodded.

"Good evening, President—er—Mr. Savage. My name is Agent Max Walker. I'm an SS technician. I've been sent here—by you—to assist with your transportation needs."

President Savage mentioned he'd be sending someone to help with my departure. Obviously, I couldn't send myself back in time since time travel was a bit more complicated than working a toaster oven (which I also struggled with).

Agent Walker led me through the deserted lobby, goose-stepping beside me in annoying fashion.

"Do you really have to do that?" I asked.

"I'm supposed to, but I guess I don't *have* to."

He stopped the goose-stepping and stepped into stride beside me. He seemed to relax a little, which made me less nervous. I didn't totally trust that this whole ordeal was on the up-and-up, but Agent Walker didn't seem like much of an assassin if that was his purpose. In fact, if anything, he seemed rather tame for an SS man.

"You been working for the president long?"

"No, sir. I actually come from the private sector. Used to work right here as a time travel technician for Walmart, but I developed some health issues. The government is the only entity that offers health benefits so I switched careers a few years ago. I just recently got the call for the SS. As you can imagine, the turnover rate for the president's private security force is pretty high. Don't get me wrong, the benefits are great, but they do have the highest rate of suicide of any occupation in the country."

"I'm a tough man to work for," I joked.

Agent Walker marched me through the security area and into the hallway leading to the time terminals. At the end of the hallway, he ushered me into a time terminal that was much larger than the one I had arrived in. Walker identified it as the VIP terminal. It was equipped similarly to the other terminals. There was the featureless terminal with a leaf blower and fire extinguisher. The major difference was that the walls were adorned with pictures of some sort of sports team, but, instead of pads, they were decked out in what appeared to be bulletproof vests and body armor. Each member of the team carried a weapon that ranged from melee weapons like spiked clubs and spears to projectile weapons like crossbows and lasers.

"What's with the death squad?" I asked.

"Oh, that's Team Evolution. This is the terminal Walmart's television studio uses for *History's Greatest Warrior*. You've never seen it?"

I admitted I had not. Attempting to become the most powerful man in the country left little time for leisure viewing.

"It's a great show, Mr. Savage. My favorite actually. See, there's these ex-military guys, Team Evolution, who travel back in time and fight history's greatest warriors. Like last week, they went back and fought the Spartans, and before that they fought Genghis Khan's forces. It's pretty wild."

It's amazing how, no matter how long man exists on this Earth, human beings will always be entertained by violence and death.

"The fights aren't exactly fair," Agent Walker confessed. "Team Evolution always wins. They've got better equipment and weapons and with personal force fields, they never suffer a single casualty, but that's not the interesting part anyway. The interesting part is watching how the opposing forces lose."

"I don't follow."

Agent Walker struggled to explain. "It's, uh, it's like watching a bunch of ants fight off a wasp invasion. You know the ants are going down but they lose with ... style. You should have seen these Spartans trying to defend Sparta from what they thought was a hostile invasion of the gods. They stood and fought to the last man. They knew they had no chance of winning, but they fought because that's all there was to do—fight. You havta admire that kind of balls, y'know?"

But I didn't.

When I didn't say anything, Agent Walker drifted over to the time console and did his thing until the doorway lit up and the aqua blob appeared in the door frame. As the blob continued to pulsate and grow, I thought about everything that had happened since being shat out into the future: Walmart's totalitarian control and the enslavement of the general population. I'd be traveling back to a time where all those things were inevitable. I'd have to stand by and watch the future unfurl like a bad rerun. And in the current timeline in which I stood, Walmart's domination had been slowed by my tyrannical alter ego. What would the future look like without me in the White House slowing their progress?

A cold wind snapped me back into the room. The aqua blob quaked and pulsed in the doorway, reaching out to me, calling me into its embrace.

"Everything's all set for you," Agent Walker said. "Kind of a shame, though."

"Why's that?"

"Well, I know this doesn't matter none now, but you had my vote, Mr.

Savage. I really thought you could change things 'round here. Can't blame you for leaving, though. This place is beyond saving."

"Is it?" I asked.

The question really wasn't for Agent Walker. I stared into the aqua gelatin, knowing that surrendering to its embrace meant accepting the terrible vision that America 2076 had to offer.

"Time to go, Mr. Savage," Agent Walker said. "It's now or never."

And he was right.

Chapter XII

The next morning, Zimmerman, Spoonz, Granger, and Mustafa let themselves into my room at the Huxley Hotel. They seemed confused when they found it empty. Klaryse trailed after the rest, entering in a dejected haze. She made a beeline for the bed and plopped herself down while the others continued to bounce from wall to wall in a desperate attempt to discover me in some nook or cranny.

"I don't understand," Zimmerman said. "He should be here."

"Maybe he's at the continental breakfast," Granger offered.

"Spoons," Spoonz said.

"Only if the continental breakfast was made fifty years ago," Klaryse said under her breath but loud enough for everyone else in the room to hear.

Zimmerman and everyone else slowly migrated to the bed.

"Do you know something I don't, my dear?" Zimmerman asked.

"Well," Klaryse began with a heavy sigh. "I was hoping he'd be here, but, since he's not, I'm afraid I know exactly where he is. He's—"

"Taking a dump," I said, exiting the bathroom.

Klaryse shot to her feet, staring at me as if I was some sort of specter from her past. The other men parted to pave a path from the bed to where I stood in the doorway of the bathroom trying to air dry my hands (the hotel bathroom came equipped with no towels).

She stood in front of me, her eyes glassy and her shoulders trembling, apparently trying to decipher whether or not I was real. She sort of slid forward, tumbling into my arms. Her lips rose from my chest and found my mouth, kissing me so deeply I could feel the other men blush from across the room.

"That's, uh, quite the good morning," Granger said.

Klaryse shoved me against the wall, cutting our connection at the lips. "You're here,"

"Where else would I be?"

Of course we both knew where else I could be and should have been. Instead, I had chosen to lose with style.

Klaryse leaned in close and whispered, "You may regret your change of heart very shortly."

Which, of course, I knew would be the case. Doing the right thing always has a tendency to bite one in the backside.

Klaryse retreated back into the room and joined the rest of my political advisors. I stood before them like a firing squad, waiting for the first shot. Zimmerman stepped forward. He didn't even offer the courtesy of a blindfold.

"We got real problems, Johnny boy. President Savage and Walmart are playing some serious hardball. You see the headlines this morning?"

Klaryse walked me through the process of bringing up her preferred news dispenser, The Walmart Weekly 13-E, on my presidential iPalm, which I still had even though now it was just a souvenir of a missed opportunity. I had to X out a dozen Walmart ads ranging from shoelaces to therapy sessions before the headline finally flashed across the screen.

President Issues Executive Order Making iVoting Mandatory.

The video that followed the headline (apparently no one read anymore) explained that all votes for presidential candidates would now be sent to voting centers via iPalms. What was left of Congress (controlled by Walmart-backed lackeys) offered no resistance to President Savage's latest executive order/dictator decree.

It was clear that the president knew himself too well. This was an insurance policy in case I refused to accept his offer to escape (which I did). Like they say, you can fool everyone except yourself.

"Do you know what this means?" Zimmerman asked.

"That Congress is just as ineffective and spineless as they were back in my time?"

"What it means is they've made it impossible for the majority of your supporters to cast their votes. The Proles are your voting base and their voices have been silenced. There hasn't been this blatant of an attack on the lower class since land ownership was a requirement to vote."

He was right, of course. Most of the denizens of The District didn't have a lot and one of the many things they didn't have were iPalms. With the new law passed, my chances of claiming victory were zilch.

"Can they do that?" I asked.

"They did it," Zimmerman said. "This is class warfare at its most vile."

"What can we do about it?"

Silence had never been so terrifying.

Here I was finally ready to fight, and my advisors were ready to wave the white flag.

"Spoons?" Spoonz offered, glancing at Zimmerman out of the side of his eye.

"Absolutely not," Zimmerman said. "I won't stoop to such reprehensible actions."

"Spooo-OONS!"

I asked what Spoonz was saying, but Zimmerman dismissed it.

"Don't worry about it. After the debacle with the video of you and Miss Goldstein, I no longer wish to travel down that reprehensible road. No, if we're going to win this election, we're going to do it with dignity."

"That's wonderful in theory," Granger said, "but our financial backers could care less about dignity. They want a victory. Promises have been made."

"I'm not here to bow to my financial backers," I said. "I promised my supporters a victory, and that's what I'm going to give them. By any means necessary. Surrender is not an option."

"A tainted victory may be as damaging as defeat," Zimmerman said. "We played that game once before, you and I, and the end result was a tyrant in the White House."

"Yes," Granger interjected, "but it was a victory nonetheless. What does it matter if we play nice if the end result leaves that same tyrant in the White House? Or a Walmart puppet?"

"Because you can't defeat evil with more evil," Zimmerman explained. "If we're going to do this, then let's do it right. We still have the debate tonight to try to get the damn thing repealed. If we can get enough public outrage—"

"There's no time! The election is in less than a week. Congress could drag their feet for months. Something drastic must be done!"

"SPOOooonz," Spoonz agreed.

I expected the conversation to break down into chaos, for profanity-laced diatribes and personal attacks to zing across the room like so many slings and arrows, but it never came to that. In fact, the silence returned but this wasn't the silence of indecision. All eyes turned to me. Something strange had happened. Maybe they noticed the difference in me. Or maybe they were just that desperate. They actually saw me as some kind of leader. The decision was mine.

"What do you think, Mr. Savage?" Klaryse asked.

And then it was decision time. My gut told me that Granger was right in this instance, but I couldn't betray Zimmerman again, not after what I had tried to do the night before.

"I think," I said, "that if we're the good guys, as we claim to be, then we have to be the good guys."

The answer was not what Granger or Mustafa wanted to hear. They stormed past me and threw the door open, marching out of the room. A smile washed over Zimmerman's face, and he patted me on the shoulder with his big bear paw.

"Thattaboy," he said. He motioned to Klaryse, who added a kiss on the cheek for positive reinforcement. "We have a speech to write, and your girl Klaryse here is going to get a petition up and running on the interwebs to get that bill overturned. You rest up for this evening. We need you fresh, ma'boy."

Zim and Klaryse left, returning back to the command center in Huxley's Hole. I hadn't slept all night so the idea of a nap was extremely appealing. I turned toward the bed but found that I was not alone. Spoonz still stood in the room, staring at me, his spoon hanging at his side like the proverbial elephant in the room. His lower lip hung open as if he wanted to say something (which I assumed would be "spoons"), but he just smacked his lips once—twice—thrice—and then sauntered toward the door, maintaining eye contact as he walked past.

When he finally reached the door, though, instead of exiting, he slammed it shut and locked it. He turned slowly toward me, his spoon pointed at me in an accusatory gesture.

"You soddin' cunt," he said.

Hearing actual words spill out of his chapped lips was as shocking as hearing a squirrel deliver The Gettysburg Address. Instead of the dumb, hollow voice he usually used to utter his catchphrase, the voice now contained a hint of a cockney accent with a lisp. Or maybe it was a Jersey accent. It was hard to tell.

"Did you just … say something?"

"Yeah," Spoonz said. "I called ya a soddin' cunt, you gloopy bratchny. Spoons!"

"I thought you couldn't talk. Zim told me that whole backstory about you and the texting obsession and you cutting your hand off. It was very elaborate."

"Well that's all soddin' true, but course I can govereet, ya knob. I just neva found the need to do it, is all, with how adept I was with textin'. Why wouldn't I be able to govoreet?"

"*Literally* all you've said to me for the entire time I've been here is *spoons*."

"I'm just not one for chatta, my little droogie, but I govoreet plenty when I got somethin' to govoreet. There's a reason there ain't no honest moodges in politics. You know why there ain't no honest moodges in politics?"

"Why ain't there?"

"Because they neva soddin' win, that's why! Da guilt o' puttin' your tyrant self on the throne got that veck Zimmerman all messed up in the gulliver. He ain't thinkin' straight, droogie. Politics is a cut-throat game, yes it is, and you gotta be willin' to shiv some gorlos if you plan on winnin', oh my droogie."

"So … what I *think* you're saying is that we're going to lose if we play it Zimmerman's way?"

"I'm govoreetin' that you already lost, Johnny Savage. They ain't never gonna let ya win their game. That's why you's got to change the rules. Spoons!"

As strange as it was to hear anything from this man's lips that wasn't a common dining utensil, I had to admit his arguments were sound. I didn't want to side with this deformed enigma, but I knew he was right. As important as it was to play by the rules, the victory was really the only thing that mattered.

By any means necessary.

"You's gonna have to play a bit on the badiwad side of things. After you win you can play things on the up and up. 'Til then, everything's fair game."

"What exactly do you have in mind?"

And just by asking, I had already consented.

Spoons produced a small device that looked like an old flash drive from his pocket. He explained the device contained a plague computer virus.

"I been developin' this 'ere bugga since we got our rookers on the Bye-Bye Bug," he explained. "Same thing, only this bugga is designed specifically for iPalms. It's what we call an 'end of days' virus. See, we upload the veshch into the iPalm network and poof! Your troubles are gone, oh my brother. You won't have to worry about that soddin' iPalm voting law no more because *no one* will be able to use one!"

"So what? It'll corrupt the iPalms of everyone in the country?"

"Not just corrupt 'em but shut them buggas down real horrorshow. Anyone on the network will get a kick right to the yarbles. Take weeks to get the veshch back up and running, and by then you, oh my brother, will already be the soddin' president!"

Use technology to kill technology. I love plans that involve irony.

If the virus could do what Spoonz claimed, it would certainly put a kink in Walmart and the president's plan to exclude my supporters from voting. The problem was that this certainly went against Zimmerman's desire to win the election fair and square. But if I wasn't willing to sink as low as the president or Walmart, what chance did I have? Still—

"Wait—Why ask me to participate at all?" I asked. "Why not just download the virus yourself?"

Spoonz looked away and itched the back of his head with his spoon. Clearly this was the part of the plan he didn't want to reveal.

"I'm an ace hacker, but even I can't get behind the soddin' iPalm network firewall." He pointed his spoon at my presidential iPalm. "But you can, oh my brother."

I glanced down at the presidential iPalm, a parting gift from my other self and also, ironically, the possible tool of his undoing. According to the president, the presidential iPalm gave me access to everything, including a backstage pass behind the entire network's security. Strapped to my wrist was an instrument of digital apocalypse. With that iPalm and Spoonz's virus, I could spread a cyber plague that would sweep through the digital world with all the horrors of the Black Plague.

In a way, destroying their precious iPalm network would set them free, free of their dependency on technology and their world of instant gratification. If nothing else, there would be a lot less bumping into each other.

Suddenly, my arm felt strong—not physically strong but powerful. I knew it was wrong but the idea that I could take something so valuable away from so many people excited me. It was the kind of power God must feel. I thought about what I would do (not me but the *other* me), and I knew he wouldn't allow something as insignificant as morality to stand between him and victory.

"What's it gonna be then, eh?" Spoonz asked. "Zim always says that an army of lions led by a deer'll never be an army of lions and you gots a lot of lions down there in that pub roaring for ya, droog. So is you a soddin' lion or ain't you?"

I realized that President Savage was indeed a lion, and I was not. He was willing to make the sacrifices that would make a normal man's stomach turn in disgust, and, to beat him, I'd have to do the same. I would have to become him.

Against my better judgment and Zimmerman's recommendation, I agreed to the proposal of a man who, minutes earlier, I wasn't even aware could speak coherent English (not that that matter was entirely settled). The technological delinquent wasted no time in jumping into action. I held out my iPalm while the fingers of his good hand danced across the liquid screen. There was venom in the malicious grace of the man's movements.

I watched his face while he worked. It was clear he both loved and despised his God-given ability—or maybe God didn't exist in the cyber world. Maybe that was what we were doing. Maybe we were helping to usher God back into the world by returning some eyes to the heavens instead of buried in a screen.

It only took Spoonz a few minutes to do whatever the hell he was doing. A kind of deathbed smile crept across his face as he stepped away from the iPalm, his fingers red and quivering. He held out the flash drive at full arm's length as if it was an actual virus contagious to us both. I took it, the sense of power expanding as I held it, and slid the device into the port on my portable iPalm. I hadn't had the device for long, but I could see the attraction. There was something to be said about literally having all that information in the palm of one's hand. I even flirted with the possibility of having my own installed until I remembered that Spoonz and I were in the process of destroying the entire iPalm network.

The word "Execute" blinked red on the liquid screen. The word seemed appropriate for the digital Holocaust we—*I*—was about to unleash on the world. I looked up at Spoonz, expecting him to be basking in the glow of his long-awaited victory. But, instead, I found his back pressed against the wall and wearing a look that was either restrained fear or constipation (probably fear). I realized that this was most likely a bittersweet moment for him, the equivalent of an alcoholic at the announcement of prohibition.

"Would you like to do the honors?" I asked, praying for him to say yes.

But Spoonz waved me off with a grand sweeping motion of his spoon, which he seemed surprised to find at the end of his arm. "No, by Bog. If it's to be done, oh my brother, it's to be done by yer rooker, not mine."

My finger hung like an anvil over that liquid screen, waiting to splash down and deliver the final blow to the iPalm network. I glanced back up at Spoonz looking for some sign of encouragement, but he had his spoon in his mouth now, his teeth clicking against the cold metal. When I glanced back at the screen, my index finger lay soaking in the liquid.

The blow had already been delivered.

"Spoooooooons," Spoonz whispered.

I expected some kind of doom's day siren or air horn to herald the end of the iPalm era, but there was only a soft beep from the device and the word execute had been replaced by a countdown.

"What's this?" I asked, referring to the numbers.

"It's a ticking clock, droogie. It's a device used to add drama to a story, usually as a cheap way to spice up the climax."

"You couldn't have it just execute right away?"

"But this is real horrorshow dramatic. It's a ninja virus," Spoonz explained. "It'll spread through the entire soddin' network, hiding, waitin' for the perfect moment to strike, and when that countdown ends—"

He ran the spoon across his throat.

Of course nothing could be easy. The numbers on the screen continued to count down and for the first time the mobile iPalm felt cumbersome strapped to my wrist.

Twelve hours. That would place zero hour in the middle of tonight's debate.

Talk about real horrorshow drama.

I pictured what my older self's face would look like when he learned what I'd done, how I had countered his checkmate with one of my own. I knew, even though it ruined his attempt to ruin me, in a sick way he'd be proud of me.

One step closer to walking in his shoes.

Chapter XIII

The final debate of the 2076 presidential election was set to take place in historic Madison Square Garden in New York City ... or at least what I used to know as Madison Square Garden. Now it was the Walmart Events Center #39B4. The entire stadium had been renovated since I had last stepped foot there for a Knicks game nearly a century earlier.

Needless to say, the arena was standing room early, but, unfortunately for the economically-challenged citizens of the Prole District, tickets for the final debate were kind of steep (Walmart was making a killing at the ticket booth) so this was a hostile crowd full of iPalm-possessing elitists who were fully behind either Walmart or President Savage.

Just one more obstacle to overcome.

I sat in what I assumed was some sort tiny janitor's locker room with my election team buzzing around taking care of last minute preparations and checking the latest polls, which were still holding me even with the president and at a one-point deficit to Millie despite news of the iPalm voting law. I assumed Millie and President Savage were enjoying the luxuries of the home and visitors' locker rooms as they prepared for our final showdown.

The atmosphere in the room could best be described as somber. It was like a funeral where the corpse was still walking around and everyone was waiting for it to realize it was dead so they could stuff it in the ground and return to someone's house to eat cheese squares and ring bologna.

Little did they know this corpse still had some life in him. Most of the talking heads predicted I wouldn't even bother showing up for the debate. Not only was I going to show up, but, rather than be on the defensive about the iPalm voting law, I was coming out swinging. It was the last thing Millie or the president would expect.

While I sat on a crud-encrusted bench in the janitor's locker room, Zimmerman approached and placed a big bear paw on my shoulder. It was an act of consolation.

"You wanna review your talking points?" he asked.

"Nah. I'm good."

Zimmerman seemed confused but wandered off with a shrug. Spoonz shot me a knowing glance and raised his spoon to his lips. I worried about what Zimmerman would say when the iPalm plague struck. I knew he was intent on winning the election fair and square, but a victory was impossible without evening the odds a bit. I knew he might be a bit perturbed, but I was sure I could make him understand. Victory cures all maladies.

Granger popped his head into the room to inform us that the start of the debate was being delayed by ten minutes. Walmart wanted to force a few more commercial breaks upon its massive telescreen audience. I didn't think much of the announcement until Spoonz whacked me in the side of the head with his spoon.

"Ow! Whaddaya do that for?"

He grabbed my hand and danced his fingers across the liquid screen on my mobile iPalm. He tapped the screen with his spoon. It was the countdown to the execution of the cyber plague. The countdown was down to less than twelve minutes.

I understood why Spoonz was so upset, but there was little we could do about it. He had planned the virus to spread during the heart of the debate for maximum drama. The delay would mean the virus would spread as the debate was just starting, but I wasn't sure what he wanted me to do about it.

I shooed Spoonz away to clear my head. Klaryse's arrival offered at least a momentary distraction. She asked if I was ready, and I assured her I was. She, too, wore a look of consolation, but I knew it wasn't for the election she assumed I had already lost. No, it was for the opportunity to return home that I had spurned. I'm sure she felt responsible, but, hell, I made the decision and all was not lost until the election ended without my butt in a chair in the Oval Office (which I wouldn't even have to redecorate).

"You know," she said, "whatever happens out there tonight, I want you to know that you've made a positive difference in this world whether you realize it or not."

"I'm not sure that's true."

"No, it is true. Maybe you can't save the country or the world, but you helped save me from myself. And for that, I am grateful."

It was the nicest thing anyone has ever said to me. I'm sure there's a saying about how if you change one person's life, you change the world, but I certainly couldn't think of it. I wanted to kiss her, to feel her lips against mine, but for some reason I didn't. I just sat there staring at her like an idiot until the moment had passed.

"Well," she said, doing her best to transition out of the awkwardness, "good luck out there. I'll be cheering you on from the front row."

She moved to run her iPalm-equipped hand down the side of my face, thought better of it, and then used her real hand instead. The warm skin pressed against my cheek, and the feeling her touch elicited could best be described as the following: it felt human.

She left me then, and I wanted nothing more than to follow her and escape the future, the past, and the present and just allow Klaryse to be my world. Unfortunately, the arrival of my advisors put those dreams to rest.

"Your lovely wife will be making her entrance shortly," Zim explained. "You'll be introduced second, and President Savage will enter last. I expect the iPalm voting executive order to be brought up early so be ready. I suggest—"

"Zim, I've got it," I assured him. "You've prepared me well. Before we go out can we just, I don't know, relax and enjoy each other's company or something?"

He smiled his big, jolly smile and chuckled. "That's the nicest way anyone's ever told me to shut the hell up. You have turned into one hell of a politician, lad. Let's keep you loose, though."

He circled around behind me and placed his hands on my shoulders, kneading the muscles in my upper back. While the old man was occupied, I stole a glance at the countdown, which was approaching five minutes. Spoonz and I shared another secret smile in preparation for the blow that was now only minutes away, but, in the middle of that smile spawned by deceit and subterfuge, the seeds of our lie sprouted its horrible fruit.

"What's this?" Zimmerman asked.

He stopped kneading my shoulders. I could feel his eyes burrow into the back of my neck.

"What is it?"

Zimmerman instructed me to hold still. I could feel his clumsy fingers pulling and tugging at something. His fingernails dug into the skin of my neck. He must have been successful because the pain suddenly disappeared and I heard him say, "Oh my." Granger disappeared behind me and uttered an, "Oh," of his own.

There were some veiled whispers, followed by some kind of conference between Zimmerman and Granger. I tried to turn around but Zimmerman kept me in place with a bear paw placed firmly on the back of my neck.

"Is someone going to tell me what the hell is going on?"

My only answer was a heavy sigh from somewhere behind me. Zimmerman circled back around with his hand clenched into a fist.

"Listen," he said. "I know you've got plenty on your plate already, but, after discussing the situation with Mr. Granger, we both agree withholding this information prior to the debate would be more detrimental than beneficial so …"

His fingers unfurled like the petals of a dying plant. In his hand, he held something I had seen before: a tiny metal circle no bigger than the tip of a pen. It was the Bye-Bye Bug. I immediately glanced over at Mustafa, who wore his usual stone-cold glare, his arms crossed over his chest, but the stoic man shook his head immediately.

"Nope," is all he said in denial of the unspoken accusation.

The discovery was upsetting and certainly a mystery, but it didn't become an emergency until Spoons pushed his way through the group, picked up the bug, and dumped it into his spoon.

"Oh, fuck me!" he screamed, recognizing what it was.

The coherent speech caught everyone off-guard (except for me since I had heard it before). Zimmerman's face fat jiggled, his chin quivered, and he took a step back.

"Spoonz, my lad. You're *speaking*—"

"Quiet, you 'ol cunt!" He latched onto my tie and dragged me to my feet. "How long 'ave you had this veshch attached to you? When did ya git tagged?!"

The panic in his voice hinted that the answer was important.

"I have no idea," I told him. "I didn't even know I had it on me."

He rapped me repeatedly on the head with his spoon. "Think, you soddin' nazz! Did you have this bugga on ya when you downloaded the virus?"

"What's it matter? I'm not traveling back into the past. No harm, right?"

"No 'arm?" Spoonz rapped me several more times on my noggin. "You gloopy cocksucka! If you downloaded the virus with this 'tached to ya then not only did you download my virus onto the 'etwork but also the bio plague in this 'ere bugga! And if the two mixed, what we git den is a deadly bio plague that can spread to anyone with a soddin' iPalm!"

"You mean that instead of just disabling the iPalm, it'll actually *kill* people?"

"'Xactly! Now think damnit! When did ya git tagged?"

My memory raced through the last couple of days, but as my brain raced, it suddenly offered the very simple answer.

Millie.

Her late night visit to my room at the Huxley. Her fingers digging into my neck. Despite her lengthy monologue about wanting to travel back to seek fame and fortune, Millie had no intention of coming with me. Walmart had decided to cancel my show … permanently.

As pissed as I was at Millie for attempting to kill me and everyone else in my time period, one thing became abundantly clear: The bitch could act!

"Last night," I said. "Millie put it on me last night."

"Bloody 'ell," Spoonz whispered. "We just unleashed the soddin' apocalypse!"

And as troubling as this news was, I didn't picture mass graves full of iPalm owners. No, I just pictured one corpse with springy, strawberry-blonde curls and the most elegant neck I'd ever seen on a woman.

I sprang to my feet with a handful of Spoonz's tunic in my hands. "Stop it! Stop the countdown!"

"I can't! I didn't include no soddin' failsafe!"

I glanced down at my iPalm. Less than four minutes until I wiped out a large portion of the country's population, which wasn't going to win me many votes.

My loafers hit the concrete running as my pulse pounded in my neck, counting each precious second that separated the world now from what it would be after the clock struck zero. The arteries of the stadium were clogged with debate organizers and campaign advisors and members of the press. I slammed through them all like a human angioplasty.

The hallways emptied into the staging area. I sprinted past the event coordinators and ran onto the stage. Millie was already out there, her introduction music playing as she waved her hands—one of them a giant target for the coming plague—to the massive crowd that filled the former Garden.

Not many of the technophiles noticed my arrival behind their violet veils that were simultaneously showing up-to-the-minute polls and user comments live as the debate progressed. Eventually, Millie's cheers turned into jeers for me—not that that would matter much in a few seconds.

Millie shook her head and sashayed over to my microphone to no doubt say something witty and rude, but I didn't give her the opportunity. I pie-faced her, a move that drew audible gasps from the crowd, and screamed Klaryse's name into the microphone. Me screaming the name of my lover into the microphone only enraged the crowd more. They surged forward, their voices rising in a single disapproving roar. But that hate-filled roar was suddenly choked off by another sound.

A high-pitched screech filled the entire arena like a microphone being brought too close to a speaker. Then a woman screamed. What happened next could only be described as the Angel of Death's version of crowd surfing. The phenomena started on the far-left side of the arena and rippled through the crowd like a tsunami gathering strength. It appeared as if the crowd was performing the wave, but, instead of entire sections of the audience rising to their feet simultaneously, entire sections of the crowd crumbled to the floor with a dense *thud*—dead. Their eyes were vacant behind their violet curtains.

It would only be a few seconds before the entire crowd was wiped out as the plague infected the iPalm network, and then spread from person to person outside the arena and across the country—from sea to shining sea. My mind became extremely focused as time slowed and the crowd members began tumbling to the floor.

Then I spotted her in the front row. Klaryse stood on her tiptoes, her elegant neck stretched, trying to catch a glimpse of the thudding noise bearing down on her. Finding her was only half the battle, and it was really the only half I had planned for. The second half was the difficult part, but, in that moment of clarity, the solution presented itself.

Two words: James Bond.

I jumped off the stage and landed next to Klaryse in the front row. She looked at me and smiled a sad kind of smile, as if she knew this was goodbye. The rolling thunder of death was right on top of us now. Out of the corner of my eye I could see crowd members just a few rows over collapsing to the cold concrete.

Klaryse's eyes met mine.

"Do you trust me?"

She nodded.

I held out my hand and she extended her iPalm. I raised my presidential iPalm into the air, activated the laser, and sliced Klaryse's hand clean off at the wrist. Then, in almost the same motion, I tore the mobile iPalm from my own hand. The IV tore a strip of skin from my wrist, spraying my face with a streak of warm blood. Klaryse's eyes thanked me in the moment before they rolled into the back of her head. She collapsed to the floor in perfect synchronization with everyone else in her section.

The wave continued to roll on until it completely cleared the arena. The silence that followed was even more gut-wrenching than the rolling thunder that had preceded it. The bodies lay piled on top of one another like firewood. There were a few moans and groans from the crowd and a few stray cries, but, other than that, I was in the largest mausoleum in the world.

A faint voice mumbled my name. I rolled back on the stage and found Millie curled around the base of the podium, her face gray but still wheezing through her coral lips.

It occurred to me that I had just as much opportunity to save Millie—my wife—as I had to save Klaryse, but the thought hadn't even crossed my mind.

Millie raised a perfectly manicured index finger and motioned for me to kneel. She whispered, "Are the cameras still rolling?"

I glanced around. No one was left standing, not even the telescreen crews there to broadcast the debate.

"Yes," I lied. "The camera's moving in for a close-up. This is your big scene."

She pulled me closer, and I cradled her head in the crook of my arm. The light in her eyes was fading fast. It was in that moment I realized we were both still wearing our wedding rings. She squinted hard, sending tears cascading down her cheeks.

"Look," she said. "Real tears. Not every actress can pull off real tears."

I nodded my approval. "That's why you're a star."

Then she sort of half-laughed, half-coughed, and forced a smile. "It wasn't all fake, Johnny, not all of it." Then she forced a few coughs, her eyes squinting, searching for the camera. Then they sprung open, and she coughed for real. "There are no cameras, are there?"

I thought about lying again but figured I'd extend to her the courtesy so few had extended to me and offer some goddamn honesty.

"No," I said. "But you're still pulling off one hell of a death scene."

"You bastard," she whispered.

Then she flipped me off and died.

It was the smoothest divorce in the annals of recorded history.

As I returned to my feet, every ounce of me screamed to avoid staring out at the crowd, a plea which I immediately ignored. I walked to the edge of the stage and looked out upon the sea of registered voters who would, in all likelihood, not be casting their vote for me on Election Day. Most of the moans and groans and death rattles had stopped. Now it was just me and the silence. A hundred thousand flesh and blood human beings had been transformed in seconds into department store mannequins. Outside the walls of the Walmart Events Center, the entire country was now full of mannequins, betrayed by their digital demigod.

Of course, America had been turned into a department store long before I showed up. Now it had the mannequins to match.

A slow and solitary clap shattered the silence of the mass grave. I turned and there he—I—was. President Savage sauntered across the stage wearing a Cheshire cat grin, directing his applause not at the slaughtered audience but at me. He joined me at the edge of the stage, and together we surveyed the ocean of corpses.

"Bravo," the president said. "Jon, you have truly surpassed even my wildest expectations."

"Don't—"

"No, no, no. Now don't be modest. Even I had no idea we were capable of such monstrosity. You've put me and my population control mandates to shame. Over 150 million iPalm users—dead. You've put Hitler to shame."

I glanced down at Klaryse, who lay as motionless as the rest of the crowd. I prayed she wasn't conscious to hear my other self's rant, which, unfortunately, was entirely true.

"This wasn't how it was supposed to be," I tried to explain. "It wasn't supposed to *kill* anybody. I only wanted to destroy their machines."

"And you've done it. You've destroyed 150 million machines. Each and every single one of them was a consumption machine. They voluntarily sacrificed their humanity for the right to *need* and to *want* and to *have*. As far as I'm concerned, you've saved more people than Jesus Christ." Even with the utterance of that trademarked deity, not a single beep rose up from the ocean of iPalms. "You've found the only known cure for mass stupidity. Bravo."

He motioned toward the crowd. I surveyed the sacks of meat and tried to find some semblance of humanity etched on their gray faces or in their violet-shaded doll eyes but found none. The worst part was that I didn't totally disagree with myself.

Walmart couldn't be entirely to blame. One corporation can't sell an entire country's soul. Every American owns a piece, but if the majority is willing to sell that piece off, then all that's left is a hollow shell. All good has to do in order for evil to triumph is nothing, and American citizens had spent decades sitting on the sidelines while evil had the run of the field.

I retreated to the safety of my podium and my other self did the same. With Millie still wrapped around hers, it looked like the most macabre debate in the history of politics.

"What now?" I asked.

"Now, we rebuild this sorry sack of a country—together. Walmart's entire customer base just disappeared, and Beijing will want nothing to do with us now that it can no longer profit from our exploitation. The only people left are the disenfranchised and the poor, so they'll be easy to control. We can reshape this country as we see fit. I'm sure we can settle on a shared vision. I suggest instead of a country that measures its worth in dollar signs, we create a country that measures its worth in ideals and morality and stresses ideas such as charity and brotherhood instead of greed and materialism."

The president's vision sounded just as grandiose and unachievable as every other politician I had ever heard. In truth, all politicians are liars … whether they realize it or not.

"What's it gonna be then?" the president asked. "You wanna help me build a utopia?"

I didn't get the chance to answer. A great cry of "Sic Semper Tyrannis!"

rose up from offstage and President Savage and I both turned in a single motion—two mirror images of one another—to find the mustachioed assassin, John Wilkes Booth, exploding out from behind the curtain wielding a .44 caliber Deringer pistol. Apparently, he was fed up with the future's unreliable weaponry and had decided to go with a reliable classic.

Booth stood equal distance between me and the president, pointing the Deringer at the side of my head. His mustache twitched, and out of the corner of his beady eye he spotted President Savage. His mustache twitched again, and the Deringer moved to the space between us, faltered, and then found its way back to my head. Then his mustache twitched again, and he turned and fired—

The bullet entered the president's head just above the right temple. One more body hit the floor, motionless. Booth's eyes returned to me. We shared a long stare-down before he eventually backpedaled toward the edge of the stage.

"Sic Semper Tyrannis!"

He jumped awkwardly off the stage and landed hard on his leg. He limped off and disappeared out a side exit.

President Savage was still alive when I knelt down to check on him, although that seemed to be only temporary. He made a few gurgling noises and looked up and seemed generally pleased to see me.

"I thought for a second I was hovering over myself," he said, "but it's just you."

We both smiled simultaneously.

He seemed to be searching for the right final words. When he couldn't think of any, he said, "Looks like I hired the right guy for the job."

"The man is good at what he does."

We both waited for him to die, but he didn't, which seemed to give my future self time to reconsider his final words. I knew exactly what he was thinking, since I was thinking the same thing. He wanted to say just the right words at the end, to leave the world with something poignant and meaningful, but what was there to say?

The light in his eyes dimmed, and his eyes fluttered. The look of consternation on his bloody face was replaced by a grotesque smile.

"Useless …" he mumbled. "Useless …"

He died with that word on his lips.

I saw my reflection in the president's lifeless eyes. The streak of blood from my presidential iPalm had landed in the exact same place President Savage wore his scar so that we truly appeared to be mirror images of one another.

And with that, I became the fifth president in the country's history to die at the hands of an assassin, the second at the hands of John Wilkes Booth. I continued to stare into my own dead eyes, knowing that this was my future. I was to die at the hands of a 19th Century assassin shortly after committing the worst genocide known to mankind.

Something to look forward to.

At least next time I'd be better prepared with some quality last words.

I stood and surveyed the carnage—one dead president, one dead wife, a mutilated love interest, and an arena of dead Americans. And that was only *inside* the stadium. What the hell was going to happen next was totally unclear. The only thing that was certain was that the president's vision of a utopia died with him.

Chapter XIV

I won the election in a landslide. It certainly helped that my opponents were dead. Most people didn't want to vote for me after word got out (probably from that rat, Granger, and his lackey, Mustafa) that I was responsible for spreading the iPalm virus and wiping out a large majority of the population, but, since I was the only show in town, they didn't really have much of a choice.

Most viewed my ascension to the presidency as the equivalent of Hitler being elected president of Israel. It was impossible to determine exactly how many people I killed because most of the people who dealt with statistics like that were dead, and no one could do math very well without the assistance of an iPalm. Most people concluded it was a lot and that I was an evil bastard.

People just kind of dismissed the iPalm voting law after the plague spread and cast their votes on whatever scraps they could find: bits of cardboard or fast food wrappers or burned my name into wood. It was quite a hassle since pens, pencils, and paper were as obsolete as typewriters. The total number of votes was the lowest in American history, although the percentage of people who voted was pretty much on par with most presidential elections.

I was sworn in on the steps of the Capitol by the only remaining member of Congress, some guy named Bueford Tannen. The guy was about a million years old and the only member of Congress not equipped with an iPalm. My inauguration was attended by almost two dozen people, most of them members of my campaign team. My inaugural address consisted of a single word:

Sorry.

I had always planned for my first act as president to be several presidential mandates that would put an end to Walmart's monopoly on the American economy, but that turned out to be unnecessary since Walmart declared bankruptcy three days before the election. It's difficult to stay in business when all your customers are dead.

Most of the blame for Walmart's collapse was dumped into the lap of Walmart's American C.E.O., Tiberius Winston Ivanhoe Trump. It's unclear exactly how he came to exit his tower office through his second favorite window, but whether he jumped or had some help from his friends in Beijing, the end result was the same.

Splat.

The only plus side to Walmart's demise was that the citizens of The Prole District and all the other poor districts across the country would be able to survive for years picking the corpse of the fallen Walmart beast.

I don't think it's an understatement to say that I was the most hated man in America following the iPalm Plague. The general feeling was that if I was left alive long enough, I would find a way to finish off the rest of the planet's population.

Surprisingly, there wasn't a single attempt on my life (not that it wouldn't have been justified). I certainly gave everyone every opportunity to pull a Booth, but I guess people were too exhausted by all the death brought on by the plague to want to add another corpse to the pile.

It was the honorable Bueford Tannen who finally figured out a way to get rid of me in the most bureaucratic way possible. He declared me an illegal time immigrant (which I was), and Congress voted unanimously to deport me back to my own time. Only a single vote was cast but that vote was unanimous. I could have easily vetoed the one-man Congress, but I figured it was the most humane out I was going to get. Besides, I certainly wasn't cut out for the whole presidential thing.

My week-long presidency was marred by the largest population decrease in United States history, a shattered economy, a 100% unemployment rate, and, although no formal approval poll was taken, several people I passed on the street expressed their opinion that, "I sucked," which I assumed represented the general opinion of the remaining population.

Essentially what I had done, on our country's tricentennial birthday year, was press the reset button and send the country right back to where it started: as a sparsely populated country full of uneducated poor folks. I figured that easily rocketed me to the top of the list of worst presidents of all time.

You're welcome, Herbert Hoover.

A week after being elected to what was once considered the most powerful position on Earth, I found myself back in a terminal at the Time Port prepared to abandon the ship I had essentially sunk. The only people who thought enough about me to appear for my departure were Zim and Klaryse. Spoonz had gone missing after the plague struck. He hadn't handled being an accomplice to genocide very well. He was presumed dead ... or at least very, very sad.

He was there in spirit, however, since Klaryse was sporting a brand new artificial hand with a spoon attachment. It was the best the doctors in the Prole District could come up with, and, since they were now the leading physicians in the country, that was as good as she was going to get.

Since I was president, gaining access to the passport codes was no longer an issue. Most of my former self's files were kept in an honest-to-God filing cabinet so all the country's most important files would live on after I was gone. Apparently, my predecessor had seen the inherent danger in keeping all of America's secrets inside a computer network.

Of course, there was the sticky question of what to do about the presidency after I left. I didn't want to leave the question up in the air, so I decided to resurrect an outdated custom and choose a vice-president.

The choice seemed obvious.

Vice-President Zimmerman and I managed to hunt down an old time port tech in The District who was willing to help us get the portal up and running for nothing more than a bottle of scotch.

In his words: "Anyting to git rid of that dirty rotten murderin' bastard."

While the aqua blob grew and clung to the edges of the time portal, I said my goodbyes.

Zimmerman was first. The big polar bear and I stood face-to-sweater vest. We hadn't spoken much since the Walmart Events Center incident except to make plans for my departure. He had accepted my suggestion he fill the VP position as the only logical solution. Besides that, what else was there to say?

"I'm sorry for everything," I said. "I should have listened to you. You can't defeat evil with more evil."

There was a long pause as Zimmerman digested my apology. His bulldog cheeks rose up and down a few times like a cat smelling a dead fish and then he finally shrugged.

"Who is to say what is right and wrong? You tried something—yes, it murdered millions of people, but at least you did *something*. There are far too many people willing to stand by and do nothing in the face of injustice. Had you done nothing, you probably would have lost the election fair and square and nothing would have changed. Still, I think it will be a long time before I endorse another Savage, young or old, for public office."

He smiled, and his big bear paw found its way onto my shoulder. In that moment, I knew that this man would not remember me as the monster history would describe, and that made history's opinion seem rather insignificant.

"I guess I should let you get to work, Mr. President," I said. "You're going to be a busy man over the next four years. God, where will you even start?"

"We'll start at the beginning. In a way, you've given us the greatest gift a country can receive: a chance to start over. Maybe we'll start by building a mirror factory so we can all take a long look at ourselves and remind ourselves what it was we allowed ourselves to become."

"Hmm. Interesting choice," I said. "I would have gone with a pharmacy."

The tech chimed in and informed us that the portal was prepared for departure. Then he spit on the ground and left. He clearly had no intention of seeing The Tyrant 2.0 off.

"Actually, I know exactly what I'm going to do first," Zim said. "I'm going to demolish these damn Time Ports. How the hell can a society move forward if it's got one foot stuck in the past? I think it's time we start thinking about the future. I suggest you do the same."

I asked him what he meant. After the misadventures I'd had, the future was the *last* thing I wanted to think about.

"I mean that this doesn't necessarily have to be your future. Remember that there are an infinite amount of possibilities and roads a timeline can take. Just by being here, you've already changed yours. I guess what I'm trying to say is be the change you want to see in the world."

Those were the last words he said to me. There was no long, drawn-out goodbye or tearful hug, which would have only made our parting that much harder. Besides, there was no guarantee this was goodbye.

We could always meet again—in the future.

Behind me, the time portal pulsed and reached out with its aqua tendrils. My feet inched closer so that the tendrils just brushed against my chest. Every ounce of me screamed to take one more step forward, to let the tendrils wrap around my body and send me hurtling back through time and space.

But Klaryse's hand on my shoulder drew me back. I turned, and our eyes locked. We stood in the glow of the time portal, a warm, steamy heat pressing against my back.

"You weren't going to leave without saying goodbye, were you?" she asked.

"It might have been easier."

She raised her left arm to run her hand down the side of my face, but, instead, paused when she realized she was about to press a cold spoon against my cheek. She smiled and traded the spoon for her intact hand instead. The warmth of that hand drew me away from the time portal.

"This spoon is going to take some getting used to."

"At least you'll always be ready to eat cereal."

She forced a smile. "I can't thank you enough for what you did for me. If it's a choice between a missing hand and being another corpse, I'll gladly take the spoon. Besides, with Walmart's stock bottoming out, I haven't a credit to my name. I'm broke, which I guess is par for the course."

"Come with me," I blurted out. "There's nothing here for you now, and, hell, the doctors of my time can probably fix you up better than any of the docs here. We could build a life together where there's still some hope for the future."

She laughed a sad kind of laugh. "That's what I've been trying to tell you, Jon. I'm already there."

"What?"

She blushed. Whatever she had to tell me was difficult for her. "I'm older than I look. Who do you think loves historical reality shows the most? It's us old timers who remember what it was like to live back then. It's the nostalgia factor."

"Wait—are you telling me—"

She nodded. "Brian and I were embarrassingly rich once upon a time, remember? We were some of the first people ever to receive Fountain Surgery. Seemed like a good idea at the time. Staying young forever. Who wouldn't want that? If only I had known then what I know now."

This revelation, of course, explained a lot. It explained why the Goldstein mansion was in such disrepair, and why their fortune was dwindling, and why they didn't have any heirs. They had been riding the Goldstein gravy train for decades. Klaryse wasn't some crazy fan girl but an eccentric old biddy wearing a younger woman's body.

"The reason I can't go back with you," she continued, "is that I'm already there. And the first thing I want you to do when you get back home is find me. Find me, Jon, and remember that love cannot be bound by the limitations of time. Love doesn't wear chains ... but I will."

And with that suggestive comment, she shoved me back into the time portal. I felt the liquid blob wrapping itself around me, carrying me back through time and space, back to where I belonged.

Back home.

Epilogue

The time portal spit me back onto the floor of the dentist's office covered in French onion soup debris just seconds after I had left. To anyone else, I hadn't been gone for more than a few seconds, but, for me, it might as well have been a lifetime. The leaf blower in the corner was no longer a mystery. I used it to blow the glop off me and gain a sense of non-ickiness.

The leaf blower worked on the first try.

Outside, the world was beautiful. The Capital lay chained and docile miles away, trees swayed in the summer breeze, and the sun shone down through an ocean of blue. The only pimple on the face of the world was the Walmart looming in the distance with its giant asphalt desert packed full of automobiles.

There was no time to worry about that, though. I was late to accept an invitation to meet a beautiful woman. Actually, I was early—fifty years early. I jumped into my catering van, which now seemed as luxurious as a Ferrari, and drove off toward the Goldstein Mansion.

There were certainly some nerves that needed to be calmed during the trek to accept Klaryse's invitation. After all, the present-day Klaryse knew nothing about it. In fact, she had no idea who the hell I was. Present-day Klaryse had never seen my historical reality show, had never spent that wonderful night with me in the Winnebago, or owed me gratitude for saving her from a deadly cyber-plague.

Of course, she also had no idea I was responsible for killing millions. Oh, and she still had two hands … which would be nice.

All I could do was hope that that spark between us—whatever the hell it was—would traverse the great expanse of time and rekindle upon our second first meeting. Like Klaryse said, "Love cannot be bound by the limits of time."

I just prayed she was right.

***

The Goldstein Mansion stood isolated by sprawling forests on three sides. The city still had not spilled over onto its doorstep. This earlier version of the mansion was much more impressive than the dump it would become. Rust had not yet claimed the outside gate, and the building itself stood in pristine condition. The front gate was open, so I drove in along the cobblestone drive, lined with poplar trees on both sides.

A Latino housekeeper answered the door, peering through a crack in the door at me suspiciously. I told her I was there to see Klaryse.

"Miss Klaryse? You wanna see her?"

"Yes. Very much so."

She seemed confused. Her thick eyebrows lowered over her eyes like two curtains being pulled over windows. The door started to close, and I thought for a moment she might shut it in my face, but she stopped and thrust her head out the small gap.

"What you want with Miss Klaryse?"

"It's a personal matter. Please. I really must speak with her."

The housekeeper mumbled something in Spanish, and the curtains hanging over her eyes raised and lowered several more times.

"She's downstairs watching her shows," she finally said. "Go to the backyard. I send her."

"Gracias," I said.

The gratitude spoken in her native tongue only seemed to annoy the housekeeper, who slammed the door in my face. It didn't faze me, though. In a few moments, I'd be with Klaryse again.

I circled around the front of the house to the side of the mansion, reciting my rehearsed speech as I marched to the backyard. I had this whole spiel about love and destiny, and I thought I might even throw in her line about love not being bound by time. I figured the words would register with her since they were her own.

I know it sounds like cheating, but I was trying to convince someone I had never met that we were soul mates. I needed all the help I could get. My rehearsal was going flawlessly until I reached the back corner of the house and something rustling in the bushes made me lose my place. I stood still, waiting for the noise to repeat itself, but, when it didn't, I continued on my way.

I followed a stone walkway through a colorful garden of red peony, yellow gladiolus, purple clematis, and orange milkweed. Butterflies fluttered past me as I traversed the walkway to a three-tiered fountain adorned with a cherub pissing from the top tier. I couldn't imagine a more perfect setting for a second first meeting. I waited for almost ten minutes for Klaryse to appear. I checked the time every two minutes on my watch (since I no longer had my phone and had no intention of owning one ever again).

Finally, I heard footsteps on the stone walkway. When the owner of the footsteps finally emerged from the garden walkway, I was disappointed to find the footsteps didn't belong to Klaryse. No, it was a girl of about ten with strawberry-blonde curls. She wore a trendy-looking yellow sundress with a chain-link belt draped around her thin waist.

The girl stared into her phone as she walked and almost marched right into the fountain. She side-stepped it at the last minute and paused in front of me. When she finally looked up and I saw the girl's eyes, I realized that Klaryse's age wasn't the only secret she kept from me.

Klaryse had a daughter.

"Hey," the girl said before returning her eyes to her phone.

"Hi there," I answered. "I think there's been some confusion. I'm actually here to see your mother. I can see the resemblance, though. You have your mother's eyes."

The compliment seemed to make the girl uncomfortable. She rolled her eyes and danced her fingers furiously over her phone.

"Is your mother home? I'm an old friend of hers … that she hasn't met yet. It's complicated. Is she here?"

The girl nodded without looking up from her phone. "Yup. We were watching a Kardashians marathon. That's what took me so long to get out here. I wanted to wait until the end of the episode." She held her phone out to show me a picture of her and a woman with strawberry-blonde hair. "I don't have my mom's eyes. My eyes are pretty. She has muddy eyes like my brother."

I looked more closely at the picture. The woman standing next to her had her hair color but not the Slinky-like curls of the little girl. She had the svelte body and the hard face of a socialite, a woman who would look good on a wealthy man's arm at a dinner party without discouraging the affairs he was certain to have. One thing was immediately clear, though.

The girl's mother was *not* Klaryse.

"What's your name?" I asked the girl.

"Klaryse Goldstein. That's who you said you wanted to see, right? That's what Maria said, but she can barely understand English. You're probably one of my mother's boyfriends, aren't you? I swear, Maria is useless. I keep telling Poppa we should just fire all the servants. Who needs them?"

Then I saw it. She was thin as a stick, and her nose was covered in freckles, but the eyes gave her away. No one else could possess eyes as piercing and vibrant. This young girl was not Klaryse's daughter. This *was* Klaryse.

I glanced at the chain link belt wrapped around Klaryse's waist and remembered her final comment to me about wearing chains and immediately felt dirty all over.

"How old are you, Klaryse?" I asked.

"Ten and a half."

The age difference was certainly a dilemma. Love may not be bound by time, but the law certainly was. I glanced up, looking for some assistance from God-only-knows who, but the only person I spotted was the housekeeper watching my interaction with Klaryse from the second-floor veranda.

"Listen to me, Klaryse. Can you put your phone away for a second?" She didn't right away. She kept fiddling with her phone, but, eventually, she managed to tear her eyes from the screen. She looked at me and smiled, and, in that smile, I saw her—my Klaryse. "Listen, do you have someplace you keep things, things you don't want anyone else to find?"

"Sure. My big brother is *always* watching me and messing with my stuff."

"Then this is what I want you to do," I said. I handed her one of my business cards from my catering business. "I want you to keep this card someplace safe, but you're going to have to keep it there for a long time, until you're about twenty—No, until you're twenty-one, all right? Then we can go out for a drink. On your twenty-first birthday, I want you to call this number, okay? This is important. Can you do that for me?"

"Why?" Klaryse asked. It wasn't a question of suspicion, though. It was one of intrigue. I could tell from the sparkle in her eyes.

"Because I want to test a theory of someone who loves me."

She studied me with her emerald eyes, a strange little half-smile slowly appearing on her cute prepubescent face. She looked at the card again, fiddled with her phone, and then handed the card back to me, which nearly knocked the wind right out of me.

"You're not going to keep it?"

"Don't need it," she explained. "I added you to my contacts and created a reminder to call 'Cute Mystery Man' on my twenty-first birthday. Even if I don't remember, my phone will."

No wonder people decided to sew the damn things into their hands. Who needs to remember when you've got a machine to do it for you?

I wasn't sure how to end the conversation. I didn't want to tell her too much. Fate would have as much to do with whether we ended up together than anything else.

It was Klaryse, though, who broke the silence.

"I like you," she blurted out. "I don't know why but I do. Am I supposed to know you?"

It was a tough question to answer.

I settled for, "Not yet. But you will … in the future."

I rustled the curly Slinkies on top of her head—something I knew she would never let me do as an adult—and sent her back into the house to finish her Kardashians marathon. I didn't know if she would still be attracted to me without the reality show, which would never happen in this timeline, but I was willing to find out.

I returned the same way I had come. I was intent on walking straight to the van and driving home to figure out how I was going to keep myself occupied for the next decade, but, when the same bush that had rustled previously rustled again, I reached in and dragged Brian out of the shrubbery, kicking and screaming.

He was a runt for a twelve year old and looked awkward like most boys do right before puberty kicks in, with teeth that were too big for his mouth and noodle-thin arms. It didn't make me hate the bastard any less. I grabbed the phone out of his hand and saw that the little shit was recording me.

"Oh, Brian," I said. "How unpleasant to see you again."

It didn't matter that the bastard's transgressions against me hadn't occurred yet. That fact garnered no sympathy from me since I knew what the kid was capable of and the asshole he would eventually become.

"Lemme go!" Brian cried in a whiny, high-pitched voice.

"Oh, Brian, working for Big Brother already, huh?" I tossed the phone into the dirt and crushed it beneath my foot. The screen cracked with a satisfying *crunch*.

"Hey! What's your problem! I don't even have a brother!"

"Not yet. But you will someday. My suggestion is you find a way not to grow up to be a giant douche."

Then I threw the kid on the ground and kicked dirt in his face.

I know it seems cruel, kicking dirt in the face of a kid like that, but after you've slaughtered a large percentage of America's population, it seems pretty insignificant.

***

The drive home was rough. The question *Now what?* kept repeating in my head over and over again. I'd have to figure out how to explain the disappearance of my wife (hopefully there was no polygraph because, technically, I *had* murdered her), and with Booth shooting up my last catering gig I couldn't imagine that being very good for business. I had ten-and-a-half years to occupy and not a single clue what to do with the next ten minutes.

I was so preoccupied with my pity party that I completely forgot about the protest outside the site of the new Mega Walmart and drove straight into the traffic jam—again. The van inched forward as angry drivers honked and cursed at the shaggy protesters with their sandwich boards and posters with Walmart's giant smiley face X'd out.

I was nearly past the protest site when the kid with the chubby bulldog cheeks and the chinstrap beard jumped in front of the van and screamed, "End the corporatocracy!" again.

"I heard you the first time," I said.

Chinstrap squinted at me through the windshield. "Oh, it's you again. The guy who was playing with himself earlier. Still not willing to get off the sidelines?"

I was about to verbally tear the kid a new one when I looked at him more closely.

The puffy bulldog cheeks.

The early attempt at a beard.

The silly, naïve optimism.

Chinstrap must have mistaken my realization for interest because he pressed his face against the window and yelled, "Walmart must be stopped. If we don't stop them—"

"Soon, everything will be Walmart," I finished for him. "And they'll spread all over this great country like a plague until Walmart dominates the economy, politics, and religion."

"Exactly!" So, what's it gonna be then, lad?"

I cut the engine and stepped out onto the road. The guy in the car behind me honked wildly, but the honk just blended into the breeze after a few seconds. Chinstrap joined me in the street.

"Whaddaya think you're doing?"

"I'm doing something about it," I answered. "Who's in charge here?"

"Well, I mean I organized the thing but no one's really in charge. This movement belongs to all of us."

"That's stupid," I said. "An army of lions led by a deer will never be an army of lions."

"Hmm. That's good. I may have to steal that."

"You're welcome to it. It's already yours. Although, I'm pretty sure you stole it from Napoleon. Hey, did you ever consider wearing a sweater vest?"

Young Zimmerman thought about it for a few seconds. "That might actually be a good look for me, I mean, when I get a bit older."

Then, to my surprise as much as everyone else's, I started shouting orders. I ordered all the protesters to form a human chain across the other side of the road, the lane the van wasn't blocking.

"Link arms. Don't budge an inch. I don't want another car passing this stretch of road. The only way we're going to get these people to listen is to inconvenience them."

Even more surprisingly, the ragged hippies obeyed the orders immediately. They linked arms and formed a hemp-scented chain of human beings, blocking any further traffic from passing. I grabbed an anti-Walmart sign and climbed onto the roof of the van, thrusting the sign high into the air while the angry honks and curses rained down upon me.

Young Zimmerman stood below me. He seemed comfortable in his newfound subordinate role. By his own account, he was never much of a lion.

"Maybe we should try to recruit more troops," he shouted up at me.

But I knew it was unnecessary. What young Zimmerman had yet to discover is that the consent of the majority is rarely necessary to steer the world in the right direction. Really, it only takes one individual to save the world ... or destroy it.

Anything is better than sitting on the sidelines.

Acknowledgements

The first person I have to thank is President Donald J. Trump (We share the same initials!). Without his ridiculousness, none of this would be possible. Thanks for being you, Donny!

The other people I need to thank may not have served in any political office, but they played a significant role making this book a reality, and they have much better hair than the president. I'd like to thank Nina Solomon and Taylor Polites for reading early drafts of the novel and providing invaluable feedback during my time in Wilkes University's MFA Creative Writing program. Ashley Siebels is my cover artist who created a cover totally different (and so much better) than the one I had originally envisioned. She did amazing work. My editor, Tim Marquitz, also deserves some credit for his work on the novel and fixing all those commas. Stupid commas. A special thank you also goes out to all my beta readers. I also need to thank my former partner-in-crime, Josh Zimmerman, for giving me the idea of a tech rage self-help group. I promised I would name a character after him in the book, and, even though it didn't make any sense thematically to do so, I am a man of my word.

Finally, I'd like to thank my wife, Cindy, and our children, Owen and Denna. Cindy has been my first reader for over ten years now, but I am most grateful for her providing me with a reason to escape my fantasy worlds and return to reality. And Owen and Denna are always more than willing to provide me with a welcome distraction when I just don't feel like writing. You are my favorite distractions.

Thank you to all the Troxellites worldwide. Drink the Kool-aide.

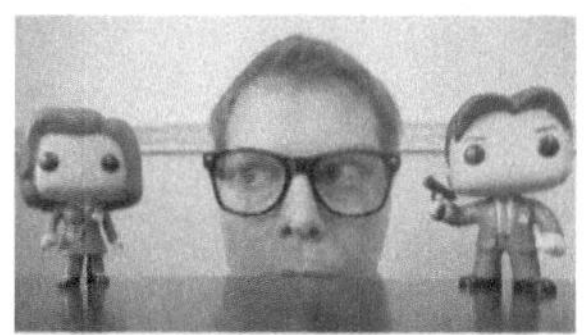

About the Author

Douglas James Troxell lives and writes in Macungie, Pennsylvania. He was born with six fingers on each hand, and his life has remained consistently interesting ever since. He writes humorous science-fiction, funny fantasy, and Troxellian comedies (a genre he made up inspired by the work of Kurt Vonnegut and Joseph Heller).

Trumptopia: The United States of Walmart is his first published novel. Follow along with his writing shenanigans at douglasjamestroxell.com or sign up for his newsletter and receive instant access to his exclusive short story, Donald Trump vs. The Aliens.

You can connect with me on:

- https://douglasjamestroxell.com
- https://twitter.com/douglastroxell
- https://www.facebook.com/douglasjamestroxell

Subscribe to my newsletter:

- https://www.subscribepage.com/douglasjamestroxell